THINGS IN THE NIGHT

THINGS IN THE NIGHT

MATI UNT

TRANSLATION AND AFTERWORD
BY ERIC DICKENS

DALKEY ARCHIVE PRESS
NORMAL · LONDON

Originally published in Estonian as *Öös on asju* by Eesti Raamat, 1990
Copyright © 1990 by Mati Unt
English Translation copyright © 2006 by Eric Dickens
Afterword copyright © 2006 by Eric Dickens

Library of Congress Cataloging-in-Publication Data:

Unt, Mati, 1944-2005
  [Öös on asju. English]
  Things in the night / Mati Unt ; translated by Eric Dickens.
    p. cm. — (Eastern European literature series)
  Originally published: Tallinn : Eesti Raamat, 1990.
  ISBN 1-56478-388-X (pbk. : alk. paper)
  I. Dickens, Eric. II. Title. III. Series.

PH666.31.N75O6713 2006
894'.54532—dc22

                                                    2005049212

Special thanks to the Estonian Literature Information Centre and
Traducta for supporting the translation of this novel.

Partially funded by a grant from the Illinois Arts Council, a state agency.

Dalkey Archive Press is a nonprofit organization located at
Milner Library (Illinois State University) and distributed in the UK
by Turnaround Publisher Services Ltd. (London).

www.dalkeyarchive.com

Printed on permanent/durable acid-free paper and bound in the
United States of America.

star, darkness, and lamp,
cloud, illusion, dewdrop,
lightning, dream, bubbles in the water.

—*The Diamond Sutra*

THINGS IN THE NIGHT

My Dear, I feel I owe you an explanation.

First, I have to admit that I have always been interested in electricity. For the most part I've kept my passion a secret, but have not always been able to avoid temptation, so one or two of my plans have leaked out to the general public.

Some ten years ago or so, I felt that I had to restrict myself by some kind of vow, which may sound rather intriguing, and so I began issuing IOUs. I announced that I was writing a book on electricity. Of course, people wanted to know immediately what kind of book I had in mind. I said: One in the most general sense of the word. I was met with sympathetic stares, the kind you get if you say you are going to write a novel about Life, which is too broad a concept, or white mice, which is too narrow. I wasn't taken seriously, and people were right, of course, because I didn't have any idea what I really wanted either. Sometimes I suspected that I'd become pretentious, or having grown fed up with long novels about marriage, that I was simply lazy. Who writes about electricity, anyway? You might as well tell people: I'm going to write about a flowing river.

I cannot conceal the fact that one of Francis Ponge's compositions appeals to me, one that was commissioned by some electric company. With Professor Ivask's help, I managed to find it in a bilingual collection:

> *De l'électricité, telle qu'actuellement a la sensibilité de l'homme elle se prepose, aucune grande chose dans l'ordre poétique, après tout, n'est sortie non plus. Ce retard, chez les architectes comme les poètes, ne tiendrait-il pas aux mêmes causes? Les architectes comme les poetes, sont des artistes. En tant que tels, ils voient les choses dans 'l'éternité plus que dans le temporel. Pratiquement, ils se défient de la mode. Je parle des meilleurs d'entre eux.*

(With electricity, as it is now available to man, a truly great thing has yet to be achieved, at least so far as poetry is concerned. Couldn't this lag among architects and poets be due to the same cause? Architects, like poets, are artists. As such, they see things in eternity more than in the temporal. In practical terms, they defy fashion. I speak of the best of them.)

I tried not to resort immediately to abstractions, tried not to make that *grande chose dans l'ordre poétique*. I wanted to start with memories, entirely personal ones. For instance, that around 1958, when I was alone in Aunt Ida's apartment where, on the wall, next to a copy of a Kuindzhi painting, or rather, between the painting and the window, there hung a table lamp. Yes, that's what I mean, a table lamp, except for the fact that it was hanging on the wall. It had a metal frame and what I understood to be decoration, at any rate some kind of bas-relief or veining. I remember that the shade had been burned from its original yellow to brown as if too strong a bulb had been put in the lamp. So there I was, standing at the window—I clearly remember the thick net curtains, which almost entirely obscured the view of Teguri Street (trees and a fence—or only trees—and other things, of course). What I was thinking, what led me to do what I did, is something I do not know. I perhaps had some boyish thoughts in my head, I was after all a boy at the time, and viewed life through optimistic eyes, at least I think so, though I don't remember exactly, but at that age there isn't much choice of torments, I mean to say you can choose between them, but the choice isn't difficult to make, mostly because of a lack of painful experiences. In a word, whether I was in a situation where I did the choosing or not, I tried to take the lamp down from the wall. It was daytime, that I'm pretty sure of, and I believe that the lamp wasn't switched on. I presumably wanted to take a closer look at it, or perhaps something had rolled under the sofa. At any rate, the electricity suddenly caused my hand to seize the lamp stand tightly. I don't remember any more, except, of course, my surprise. I didn't regain consciousness until the lamp had fallen on the sofa, though I remained standing where I was. I had clearly got my hand loose somehow, or maybe the current was cut. But what would have happened otherwise?

That is only one small instance of my encounters with electricity, and not even the most important one, because I had totally forgotten it and only remembered when I began to put together my personal memories of electricity. Especially the personal ones, was what I was thinking, as I had begun to suspect a good while earlier that electrical energy can have a great effect on the human organism and the subconscious.

Sometimes I would sit in the room and try to identify the effect of electrical waves. There had to be such waves all around me because I was surrounded by cables that ran in conduits through the walls, hung above me, and wound their way across the floor. It was difficult to listen to the radio in the bedroom. There was significant interference on the mid-range of the band. What else could cause this but electrical waves?

Waves all around me? What could be more intriguing? Was this a hidden enemy or friend?

I can't forget that I grew up at a time when science was both made mysterious and anthropomorphized. I remember various book titles: *Taming Water*! *Mobilizing the Forest*! *Machines Proceed to the Field of Victory*! There had to be one about waves. *Unseen Waves*! *Electricity as Epic Hero*!

I wanted to do some research. Where should I begin? I remember that Jay Gatsby used to learn the principles of electricity between 7:15 and 8:15 in the morning. Before these, exercises with dumbbells; afterwards, work. Quite. I had to start investigating, as I thought at the time, not confine myself to pathos (Whitman: *I sing the body electric*).

We are clearly dealing with enormous power. Richard Feynman offers this unworldly example in one of his lectures. Let us assume that we are standing next to one another as we are doing right now, at arms' length. If your body or mine suddenly were to gain *one* percent more electrons than protons, an electrical charge would be set up between us that could move a mass the size of the Earth. That also shows, by the way, how finely tuned matter is.

But I am getting off the point. Better for me to talk about my own experiments.

I didn't initially investigate electric eels or Saint Elmo's Fire. What interested me was the direct influence of electricity on the human organism. For some strange reason there were few substantial facts to be found on this topic. Still, they were vivid and intriguing though, so it didn't matter if they didn't offer much by way of explanation.

For instance, the waves of a telegraph broadcast can be sped up by solidifying a number of colloids. During thunderstorms, milk goes bad more quickly. When there are sunspots, the number of white corpuscles in the blood drops and they become flaky. In his time, Professor Chizhevski considered putting screens round hospital wards, or placing them underground. The relationship between solar activity and processes on Earth is a well-known fact and was discovered by that same professor. For example: earthquakes, mental illness, magnetic storms, epidemics, social upheavals, crime, the alternation between liberals and conservatives, marriages . . .

I moved on from general processes to concrete statistics. Some will remain with me till the day I die. For instance, the fact that the most active wavelength biologically is 200 megahertz, i.e., about one-and-a-half meters, because it is said you can regard human beings as aerials, and that there is a significant relationship between the height of a person and his wavelength.

With regard to the electrical potential between a person's head and his chest, this is at its greatest when the moon is full. For that reason, one famous surgeon claimed that the most sensible time to perform operations was during moonless nights, leaving those with moonlight for lovemaking. He had in mind the difficulties blood would have clotting during the full moon.

I once met a scientist who claimed that within a 100-kilometer radius of a TV antenna, the radiation emitted is as great as that from an explosion on the sun.

When golden hamsters' nests are surrounded by a weak electromagnetic field, the hamsters leave the nest within seventy-two hours, but ones with young leave within twenty-four hours. In the English Midlands, someone once discovered a 40% rise in cases of suicide for people living near high-tension cables.

It is said that electromagnetic waves are less harmful to people with brown eyes and dark hair. These characteristics are termed dominant and I share them to an extent: my hair is dark, but my eyes are not brown. Or are they? You're right, they change color. By the way, another dominant characteristic is premature baldness, which hasn't affected me because my youth is now over, and so only what is termed late baldness can get me. But my father really was prematurely bald . . .

In a word, the material accumulated with frightening speed, so what did it matter that it took a lot of effort?

For instance, at around two in the morning in Florence near the statue of David while listening to the roaring of protest songs, I caught myself thinking of Professor Piccard who had done experiments in this city demonstrating that electromagnetic waves affect an organism mostly in relation to the water it contains.

Have you heard that when water becomes ice the resulting crystals align themselves along the line of the Earth's electromagnetic field? We are made up of seventy percent water! No wonder we too react. Pigs are unusually sensitive to electro-magnetic fields, especially when pregnant, or "during gestation," as a zoologist would put it.

We know that when a fish doesn't know in which direction it's pointing it tends to move in the direction of the magnetic meridian.

A magnetic field causes headaches and insomnia, which alcohol in turn can exacerbate.

Magnetized water was used in the Middle Ages as an aphrodisiac.

People used to think that magnetic pull is stronger in the day than at night.

When you put a magnet near jewels, its force diminishes and returns only when the magnet is smeared with the blood of a goat. Not to mention magnetic bracelets that are supposed to protect the wearer against high blood pressure!

High-tension electricity causes hyperemia in chickens and causes the lobes of the brain to shrink. In human beings, hypersensitivity or listlessness have been noted, or a tingling of the skin, sweating, a reduced memory, a drop in work efficiency, and in rabbits thermoregulation is reduced and blood pressure rises.

A magnetic field shortens the lives of rats, while using a dowser's rod you can find lodes or bodies of underground water.

During a magnetic storm the number of small insects on the wind increases by some 50%. The *Drosophila* fly suffers a thirteenfold increase in lethal recessive changes under the influence of an electromagnetic field. You can see the mutations with the naked eye: deformed eyes, blistered wings, a yellow body color. Seventy-three percent of heart attacks occur during magnetic storms.

But there are also good sides to the picture: it is hoped that we'll soon be able to sort seed cells by means of a weak electric current; the male spermatozoa tend towards the positive pole, the female ones towards the negative one. Don't forget that the surface of the earth is negatively charged while the upper layers of the atmosphere are positive, and that between them flows a 1,500 ampere current.

I did indeed begin to grow tired of this, but had not forgotten the electrical current in all the subdivisions of the brain. I looked into the subjects of electric chairs, electrophoresis, electrocardiograms, and electric torture. Nor did I forget the experiments conducted by Olds and Delgado, especially the enthusiasm of the latter for the reduction and channeling of violence by applying electrodes to the human brain.

I moved imperceptibly down to a microscopic level, to that of membranes, neurons, and ions. I investigated the stability of calcium and sodium. I immersed myself in the problems of proteins and semi-conductors. I already knew that nucleic acids act on crystal formation. For a short while I even busied myself with nucleoside triphosphates and their role in the conductivity of energy.

But this only served to highlight my incompetence.

One night I asked myself the question: what is life?

I was amazed that ontological problems had been foreign to me until then.

I had no doubts about electricity. I had been on the right road, but ended up in the woods. I lost the summit of the mountain shining red in the evening sun. Facts crushed me underfoot and I began to grow paralyzed.

I had to retreat.

Look down the other end of the telescope.

I clutched at the notion of "fields." That looked more promising. It was a lapidary thought, the best possible for me. Not emptiness, just an open space! A space, but where any point can be activated, and so you can do what you like.

Qi condenses.

So I thought. What was I guilty of? I genuinely believed it. Of course, I had come across many condensed things in my life. Previous states remained a mystery to me. Nor had complete things evaporated before my eyes up to now. But you never can be sure. Where can I, for instance, get to know what happened to my grandfather? I'm not going to dig him up from his final resting place just on the strength of vague assumptions. But some do really do this, such as the heroes of Stephen King novels, which were very popular.

Those ghosts of our time first appeared in my thoughts when I gave up on microbiology and began to work on fields. It would of course have been safer to do research into nucleic acids. But I didn't understand them. They required groundwork that I had not done and which it was now too late to acquire. I knew that fields (at my level) were too easy a solution. At least it seemed so to my deeper understanding. But wasn't I, above all, a poet? A field is a poetic metaphor. Or from the *Chandogya Upanishad*: space is joy and joy is space. Unfortunately, you can apply universal principles to almost anything, as even without thinking in larger terms, without feeling any responsibility, I felt an element of ownership. I was secretly quite satisfied with the field because I knew that it wasn't a cul-de-sac. Black and white holes loomed over me from afar, the secret of God himself and all that sort of thing. But I came no nearer to the mirages, however much I tried.

Luckily, nothing showed outwardly. I acquired enough flesh to no longer feel hungry, enough blood to quench my thirst, thanks to the skin of my back I was not entirely naked, and my bones served as fuel to warm the room with. I even managed to put up some new shelves in the kitchen without worrying myself silly whether *qi* was concentrated in those shelves or not.

Then again—I was arriving at the final stage of my research into electricity and wasn't taking the slightest bit of notice of the world around me. For that reason, I can speak with some aloofness. The reason is, in fact, that I began to understand the fruitlessness of my endeavors, at least for me.

Perhaps the fact that they were second-hand experiences wasn't the most important thing. I myself didn't actually conduct one single experiment, didn't take one measurement. But nowadays you don't have to take part in such empirical matters.

The main thing was to get food for thought! But I just couldn't get any. The data wasn't linked even to a coherent philosophy of electricity, or if it was, only in an amateur sort of way that you couldn't do much with.

For instance, I could have subscribed with conviction to Lyall Watson's thought: *we are electric creatures, living in an electromagnetic environment that may well have shaped our origins and continues to determine the direction of our evolution,* but for me this sentence lacked anything personal. It concerned "us" and touched upon matters that did not depend on "our" will. Nor was I so infantile as to want to know what my *origins* were and which *direction* we are moving in.

True, I once wanted to know those and other things that lay beyond me, and were in fact unknowable. And I am lying now when I say that they no longer interest me in the slightest.

I feel that a small chip has been inserted in my brain that wants to know everything. It is located somewhere near the crown of my head and comes, of course, from the Devil. Everybody has one, but luckily in the case of most people the chip doesn't actually work.

Nor does it work very well in me. When I grew disappointed with one of the fields I was studying, I managed to survive without getting particularly depressed. In fact it didn't really matter what I'd been doing that year. Why get disillusioned? The main thing was not to have to face reality the whole time, eye to eye. And my research into electricity gave me enough subtle experiences and silent inklings for me to keep them to myself and not share them with anyone. Looking at it that way, it feels as if those years weren't at all wasted. At least I expanded my reading into a narrow, chosen field. Not everyone can become a specialist, so who cares that there was no reason for doing so? I know that I only failed to read one important book: David Tansley's *Radionics and the Subtle Anatomy of Man* (Bradford, Devon, 1972). Never mind. During that time I was sending requests and complaints all over the world: I want to know everything about electricity! If they didn't send me the Tansley book, then readers, it's their own fault, and I think to myself: read it and be satisfied.

Then one day it became clear to me that I *had* at last to start writing my novel—otherwise it would be difficult to look people in the eye.

Various ideas came to mind, among them to write it in dialogue form, where it remains unclear who is who—that is to say, the reader shouldn't know who is me and who somebody else.

The thought inspired me, and so I immediately started on the first chapter of the novel.

The dialogue flowed quite smoothly, and I willed myself now into the role of one character, now into the other, and this theatrical game amused me a good deal at first, in an egotistical way, of course—for what else can such amusement be?

–So it all happened in 1979?

–Yes, I believe so.

–Where shall we begin?

–You know the methodology, choose for yourself.

–This isn't an interrogation, everything'll remain between the two of us, so you suggest something.

–So, let's begin with the explosives.

–OK.

–What can you tell me about the explosives?

–The explosives weighed more than I could have imagined.

–And how much had you thought they would weigh?

–Why do you ask?

–I'll be more direct: with what are you comparing the weight of your explosives? Previous explosives? A box of chocolates? Silver, gold, lead?

–I'm not comparing it to anything, but as you can imagine, I had to avoid main roads, wade through marshes and waterlogged meadows, avoid . . .

–Settlements and villages?

–Quite. Settlements and villages, and I had about five kilometers to go, when the sun began to set.

–Where, if I may ask?

–It began to set behind the trees, otherwise it wouldn't have been able to rise again, it had no choice, it had been decided that way. You haven't asked by whom.

–No. I'm not going to. But what did you see?

–I saw an old shed for storing hay standing at the edge of the woods. This is where I'll stay, this is where I'll stay for my last night, I decided with some relief. I walked round the shed. Last year's hay, and how could it be otherwise? My eye automatically registered the violet upper leaves of the cow-wheat, the half-open door, the flight of a bee, something else, and even more than usual, but I'm sorry I don't remember what. I simply sat down in the lee of the shed. It may have already grown dark. You can think better in the dark, if you've got anything to think about. Endless light is tiring. The spotlight of the sun rips through the darkness of your outer space, everything's visible, you're a clown on stage. You may have shaved your beard, your fly may be pulled up, which is of course natural enough, but you don't want to have rules imposed on you the whole time. At night you can relax and roll up into a ball.

–And you did?

–Be quiet, let me do the talking, don't keep interrupting. Before relaxing I did of course listen. It had been windy that day, now the wind had dropped. You could hear noises that were hard to identity. There was a village beyond the woods. What else was there? A summer's evening in a village—who hasn't experienced that during our century? A lot of green, all kinds of soothing shades, the last haven for mankind. The milk pail, now empty, upside-down on the bench, rings when you shout into it, smells of sour milk. The tea leaves you can put on cuts, if the wound isn't too deep. The clouds that edge very slowly over the village, a bit like the minute hand of a watch, and are moving there above the village and here too, clouds that some cat or cock is observing, most likely a cock who has grown tired of guarding and organizing the hens, and who has, so to speak, over-organized his hens but can't be bothered to exchange crows with other cocks, and all he can now find the energy to do is follow the clouds, although any passerby would think this father bird is surveying the sky, full of suspicion that some goshawk may be about to pounce. Such a bird as a cock, whether he's looking at the sky or at his hens, he has brought an understanding of life after death to my consciousness, something I thought about even before reading Moody's or Grof's books.

–Whose books, do you say?

–Grof's, Grof's I repeat. It was, in fact, enough merely to watch a headless cock flying around the yard. All my life I have liked hens more than cocks, perhaps because of cocks' boundless pride, which maybe arouses a sense of rivalry in me. On the other hand, the nighttime dialogue of cocks is always expressive, even if you're not an expert, though I have never been able to observe a cock leaving after crowing, nor, for that matter, their return. But though we can't imagine devils leaving our room, they could be doing so in another part of the world. When a cock crows, you're taken back to the movies of the fifties, and a village dance is going to follow, you're coming through the dewy grass and you hear the cock crow and you can imagine that some tyrant, war criminal, or simply some philosopher astray in this world has met his end, thus leaving the road open to progress or at least to the temporary improvement of things. A cock can know things that remain remote to us. Perhaps he's suggesting that some African tyrant should resign. Other cocks pass on the message, even amplify it with their unanimous approval. I was thinking that such wise cocks also no doubt live in this village beyond the woods, and I remember also wondering whether crowing cocks weren't observing me that night, me who had arrived at a decision that would not meet with popular approval, in fact that wouldn't be approved of by anyone.

–How far did you still have to go?

–Five kilometers.

–Are you sure?

–Of course I'm sure. But I decided to kill time.

–Sorry? What did you say?

–Kill time. I decided to spend the night in the shed, and I would have gone to sleep right away if the sun had set faster.

–OK, going to sleep, fine, but who was supporting you?

–No one was. No one interfered, I wanted to make my mark on reality swiftly without anyone interrupting me. Alone.

–Like one hand clapping?

–Exactly. A cry in the wilderness, but they are free to choose whether to reply or not.

–But didn't you have the strange feeling that you had stepped outside of the law?

–Naturally I did. But this was only my own private feeling, because others hadn't noticed anything. I'd been walking along roads and riding on buses for some time by then, but no one knew that near to them a man was moving and breathing who had decided to spit on everything that was holy for Western civilization. Maybe my fingertips trembled slightly, that would have betrayed something, but nobody noticed. An ordinary person, walking past the people he encounters, just another ordinary person. I may have already passed thousands like that today! Not one of them knows the truth. Only I know it. I've weighed all the options. I've made my decision.

–*Had* made your decision. Let's talk in the past tense. You were lying down—where was it you were lying?

–I was lying in the glow of the setting sun and it was slowly rounding the shed. I stretched for as long and as broadly as I could, it's not impossible that I moaned with delight as I dug myself into the moss.

–Delight?

–Precisely. I was lying in the grass, strong as an ox, a Finno–Ugric man, with blue eyes, a taste for women and vodka, I was that "I," or somebody else, but anyway I was lying, stretched out in all directions as much as I could and saying to myself: that's enough of literature, it's not man's work, and I swore for quite some time, swore pretty quietly because if I were going to succeed it wouldn't be a good idea to yell through the primeval forest at Impivaara, I swore and I gave a good fart and said: fuck, life's what appeals to us today, life is joy! Anyway, never mind how I was lying there or whether I was, but at that time I felt that my efforts with regard to the creation of pure art or an analysis of our nation's problems had become laughable. Trying not to please anyone, trying to be alone, I had ended up isolating myself. I didn't even like myself anymore. It wasn't a question of whether I was a writer or not. The thing was that I needed, as a human being, to perform an immediate deed, an immediate act of self-destruction.

–Suicide?

–I don't know, something like that. I thought that when I left the arena I would at least do so with a bang. Or at least make a fool of myself, such a great fool of myself, such a fool that people would snicker for a hundred years to come, point and say: look, that's where he came from, that arctic hysteric, the man who wanted to blow up machines here in Northern Europe, wanted to become a new Luddite, a new Herostratus; naïve, but justified in his actions; crazy, but interesting; banal, but a man of his time; a human being, but an animal nevertheless.

–And then you went to sleep?

–That's right. I'd walked a long way and didn't notice myself dropping off.

–This was still in 1979, when you fell asleep?

–Yes, 1979, I fell asleep on my back in the grass on firm ground, on soil, humus, whatever, which I didn't like doing, because I didn't like anything except my honor.

–What happened while you were asleep? Were your dreams conventional ones?

–Well, of course, for Christ's sake, what should they have been? Don't forget I'm only human. As for what was happening all around me, that too isn't hard to imagine, perhaps a wandering dog reached the edge of the woods, and sniffed the air mournfully, but didn't start barking. Some quite indifferent birds flew overhead, swallows or crows, what do I care what species they were? At any rate it was dark when I awoke. I no doubt mentioned that I'm not going to describe my dreams? Sorry. But my wrists had gone numb. There was a breeze now in the bushes, the wind never falls asleep or wakes along with me. After that I sat up. The world and I were as if newly born. My former thoughts didn't quite fit anymore, but I hadn't had any new ones. I struck a match and looked: half-past eleven.

–The time?

–Yes the time, it really was half-past eleven. I had no desire to go into the dark shed, although that would have seemed the natural thing to do. But there could have been snakes in there and maybe some human being had forgotten to leave the shed, or someone had left him there. God knows. I regretted having decided to spend the night there. I knew that sleep diminishes your strength and your will. I forced myself to be critical.

–Which means?

–I began to wonder for a moment whether my ambitions were out of all proportion with what I was going to do. If I wanted to draw attention to global catastrophes, then was it enough with this sailcloth bag and a power station by the river surrounded by nettles, built sometime after the war by young people as a purely political symbol and now abandoned and of minimal local importance? Did the Liikola power station really have anything to do with Satan, i.e., with electricity? Of course it did, its very name said so. Should it be destroyed? Yes, once it had been chosen. But why that particular one? To avoid casualties. There was maybe only one watchman at Liikola who would have to be talked into going to pee in the woods, or go and listen to the birdsong, or go off to phone someone, so he would be spared, while the power station itself would collapse and rumor would spread throughout the land that in the backwoods an act of terrorism had been committed that had been aimed at the imperialist nature of electricity, a sign that our relationship with technology would no longer be a peaceful one.

–But you said that this obscure power station was also a political symbol after the war. Perhaps people would get the wrong idea, would think you were protesting against the authorities, so the greater pathos of your act would be lost, you would be regarded as just another dissident, and it would all end up in the dustbin of history.

–Yes, that risk was present, but I hadn't steered clear of all political ramifications. The name of the power station was well-known since my childhood. I had never been there myself. You have to understand, I was going to meet my fate, but at the same time it was like an excursion. Like a trip to the desert or the steppe. I even had sandwiches with me, I'd only forgotten to bring the lemonade. And in fact I hadn't paid too much attention to the consequences of my deed. Hadn't taken account of how highly the little plume of smoke rising between patches of forest in south-eastern Estonia would be regarded in Norway or Angola. I was, of course, sure that there were others like me. But above all I wanted to escape from the feeling of being a cornered animal. It was as if I wanted to blow up heaven. To blow everything open with a big bang, everything, with a bang, the disgusting inevitability, with a bang, because it could no longer hold together, my life was no longer possible to live. I awoke in disgust every morning, and so one day I said to myself: that's it! On your way to Liikola, onto the lawless road, the road to absurdity, the main thing being that I can manage to forget the rules of society, international coopera-tion, altruism, and everything the slightest bit normal. And now I was standing there at the door of the shed and could smell the soft (though it could well have been rough) hay warmed by the day and I feared that I would go mad, and turned round. No, today I will put an end to it and that'll be it! The main thing is to prevent reason from entering my mind, not to allow morality to win. Today Liikola will be burnt to the ground and I'll be pun-ished, tomorrow British nuclear power stations will be consumed by the flames, Silesian coal mines will cave in, presidents will drive their cars into ambushes, banks will collapse, and maybe a million years later when the grass grows again there will be no trace of us left, thank God, as if we had never existed—and perhaps we never have.

I had to begin somewhere!

Someone had to do it, one person had to be the outsider, someone had to light the fuse, to be the corrupter, the madman.

–Why you?

–I felt that the chain would break with me. I would break and no one would notice me, I would fall into the grass and the dung, but the bull would break loose from his chain and storm into the farmyard to gore blue-eyed children. How he has escaped from his meadow, no one knows. But he is here and is showing me his IOUs.

–What did you do then?

–I looked again at my watch and it now said a quarter to twelve as I had imagined it would. Then I looked at the burnt-out match between my fingers. Now or never, that parasitic idea was coursing through my brain. I had nothing more to lose. If I threw a match into the hay this shed would burn down too, the people in the neighborhood would become agitated and fearful, wondering if something were afoot. An old shed, no one would miss it, not even the old hay.

–But the woods behind the shed?

–Are you trying to be funny? I wasn't going to let myself get provoked. I threw the match on the ground and stamped on it. Then I groped my way to finding my rucksack and put it on carefully. It would have been stupid if the end had come in the wrong place and too soon. And then I started walking, walking, walking

. . . I could only feel through my soles that I was walking along a path towards the main road with the lattice of tree branches above my head, almost touching it. I glanced back a couple of times, suddenly, without expecting to do so myself, it was a habit from childhood, because I had in my time managed to fear the dark . . . yes, but why? Did somebody order it or suggest it? Why am I afraid of the dark, not just on that occasion, but maybe even now? Nictophobia, but where does it come from? Perhaps I'm not afraid of the dark. But in that case, why bother looking behind me? Perhaps I'm guilty of something, perhaps of blindness? For that reason, I'm trying to convince myself there are no will o' the wisps or dogs.

–Had I already written to you, then?

–You had. I sent you a postcard, in which I said that I didn't know how to relate to the world, whether to hate it or love it, and I also made it clear that I wanted to do something that would affect everything. It was a letter written with feeling, but your reply was very admonishing and theoretical.

–I don't know if it was admonishing and theoretical, but I tried as best I could to knock some sense into your head. You still have the letter?

–Yes, here it is.

–Read it out to me, I want to remember what's in it.

–"You are obsessed with your own version of the Zeitgeist, people tend to hide behind problems when they do not have the courage to look into themselves. You can only depend on yourself. There is no point in spreading yourself too thin; no point in dealing with issues that people cannot change. Please allow me to draw your attention to Kierkegaard's point of view. K. did not care for large public events because every crowd is in itself an untruth. The only way out is isolation, aloofness. Only the individual is a reality and only the individual is true. Maybe the process of isolation in an individual is one of the most important matters that exists. Is not the whole point of this world for people to separate and become individuals? You, in turn, speak of having the feeling, maybe based on pathological considerations, that you are nonetheless part of this world and have the strange feeling that you are responsible for something. Listen, my friend, only the individual can have a personal sense of responsibility, only the thoughts of an individual can be genuine, if you really are seeking something genuine. Stay on your own as much as you can. The more you can decide for yourself, the more perfect you will become. Because in that case there will be no absolute authority over you, neither friends nor public opinion will exist for you, and you will not have to be friendly in bars. K. says that being alone is an art, which can cost the artist his life. Because the individual is not only passive, just the opposite, he announces his loneliness quite actively. The real individual interests himself in society as a sociological phenomenon. Only the individual can take an interest in this. Bliss is only for solitary individuals. One truly exists only if he inhabits a painful loneliness. Note: painful. In that way, it is easier to deal with problems. For instance, the problems of youth, content and form, the four colors. Busy yourself with nothing but these, and be happy. But try to reach the ultimate in subjectivity, think only of yourself and shun things in general, which don't exist, at least not for us."

–Is that so reproachful? I was just full of myself. And full enough of the spirit of Kierkegaard, though to be honest he was beyond me. And that's all.

–In fact, the letter had the opposite effect. I wouldn't have put a rucksack on my back just to solve some sociological problem. My personal existence dictated the solutions you yourself had suggested.

–Paranoid ones, self-destructive ones, desperate ones. Was your plan desperate?

–It was what it was, but at any rate it lacked a constructive base. And nobody would have understood it.

–Didn't you have any friends?

–Not really, and in extreme situations certainly not. You must understand it was a personal act, painful and utterly subjective.

–It was a deed. A purely criminal deed.

–A deed? The plan itself would have been enough, who knows?

–You would have been able to experience all this in your imagination?

–Yes, I could have, but it was too late by then, because it was after midnight as I walked along in the direction of Liikola.

REALITY

In reality, I did go for a walk, alone and at night too. I'll give you one example to prove that I don't always think things out beforehand.

I have tried without success to find out who my uncle was and how he died.

My own memories of him are very scattered and vague.

As a child, I eavesdropped on conversations my parents were having, during which an uncle who died young was frequently mentioned. He was the subject of the conversation, true enough, but what kind of subject? Or perhaps it just seems in retrospect that he was being talked about. Maybe they were talking about someone else.

As far as I got to know, he died at the age of eighteen from tuberculosis.

Before doing so, he adopted a new name and began to write poetry.

It is possible that Uncle was insane. At least it felt convenient for some time to believe this. In the 1960s, it was a heartening thought that Uncle had been schizophrenic, his mind overexcited by tuberculosis.

When it comes down to it, ailments generate one another. That's what they do, when it comes down to it.

Uncle adopted the name Juhan Liiv.

This sounds pretty convincing, since Juhan Liiv is our most famous classical poet and he was definitely insane, at least towards the end of his life. He was as poor as a church mouse and thought at times that he was the King of Poland. He belonged to that class of poets whose memory every nation feels it ought to preserve. They keep their pangs of conscience alive.

For nations traditionally starve their poets to death, especially their first ones. The Finns have their Aleksis Kivi. He too was insane and died a pauper.

Anyway, during the sixties, I entertained the notion that my uncle had also been a poet like that.

I remembered that in the drawer of the kitchen table I had seen a brown exercise book with poems by my uncle who had died young.

Now, coming to the farm again I started looking for the workbook, but it was no longer there. There was no trace of my uncle left in the house.

I reminded my father that he had had a brother who changed his name, wrote poetry and died young of consumption.

Father remembered that he had had a brother, but nothing about changing names and writing poetry.

He even told me something else instead.

There was a paradox here because madness had recently become trendy. In town it was already known that a madman was more truly human than a normal person. A large proportion of the population believed that madhouses were symbols of a totalitarian society. Dr. Laing's ideas were supported ever more widely, ideas that said that one should help people to become mad because society was moving in a transcendental direction and such people would come back with worthwhile experiences.

Against this background it was surprising that my father was ashamed of his brother the poet.

But maybe he wasn't ashamed, maybe he had genuinely forgotten.

Do you really not remember a thick workbook full of poems? was what I asked, as insistently as I could.

Father did not remember.

Or maybe your brother never existed?

What d'you mean, of course my brother existed!

So anyway, the poet had vanished into thin air. I will never know whether there is creative madness in my genes, or whether I've had to think this all up in order to exalt myself, starting with the first generation!

My city friends had family trees in which insane relatives popped up. Creative madness too, of course.

In the countryside, amid mud and manure, amid all that which people flee to the city from, under a cloudy sky, in an alder copse, I thought up denigrating expressions about my uncle, ones that proved to be true.

I said: Fuck yourself, Uncle! Who changes his name to Juhan Liiv? The first famous name you think of! Repeating the life of a famous national lunatic is an act lacking in imagination! I can picture the clumsy poems with their spelling mistakes. I told myself that I was glad there weren't any. They had to vanish. They would have been a disappointment to me! All the more so because my uncle, at the age of eighteen, would have been too immature, even if he had later cultivated creative madness. He had died too young.

Afterwards, it was too late. My father died and I was no longer able to ask him and he now didn't need to lie to me any longer. Or tell me the truth.

The more popular that madness became in Europe, the more indifferent I became towards it. I demonstratively remained seated when 1,100 people stood up and applauded in a large opera theater, applauded the idea that madhouses should be burnt down.

But strange though it may seem, Uncle did come to mind now and again.

Especially when I was sitting before a blank sheet of paper, my head full of a total lack of inspiration. Then I would think that Uncle had not feared blank sheets. Quite the opposite—from his pen would have flowed critically unacclaimed but spontaneous lines of verse. He would have been creative by quantity. And an educated editor would, later on, have been able to make a selection.

Uncle wouldn't have been ashamed of writing a poem about fir trees or birches or pines. Nor about any tree or bird, for that matter. Nothing would have stopped him. Sometimes I would see in my mind's eye how Uncle's thoughts overtook his pen and how he pressed the nib, spraying ink, into the yellowing paper.

I myself knew I had an imaginary uncle.

And yet just at that time, and later, details were added to the picture of my uncle. Despite all the skepticism!

That's right, a picture of him! I found a picture of him in the attic, him at the age of thirteen. At first I regarded it as an important discovery. I thought that by way of that picture, I would be able to attain spiritual union with my uncle. But to my disappointment, the picture remained silent. Uncle was still too young in it. If he went mad later on, there was no sign of it here. In front of me I saw a very ordinary person.

And in the end I was forced to accept that the picture had no doubt been heavily retouched. If uncle was mad, then the photographer had disguised the fact. In those days, people were hostile to the mad.

My father retained that attitude until his dying day.

And yet: people talked about such things during my childhood! The only explanation is that I was thought to be so stupid that I wouldn't understand what was being talked about.

Clearly I didn't.

A couple of years passed.

A couple of minor clues from those years emerged without my prompting: a school report from the second form with above-average grades, one New Year's card from before the war, a forgotten side-branch of the family tree.

And then a real revelation!

His letter, in the attic, in the drawer of an old chest of drawers, under the right-hand eaves as seen from the stairs.

Dear Liisa!

Do you remember that I said to you at the last party that I wanted to eat you up?

I had another action in mind, one that would have been very difficult to express to a young lady in any other way, for where would I, a simple man from the country, be able to find the right words, ones that would be acceptable to an educated young lady? The jokes of a country lad are pretty crude, but even they may contain a grain of truth, if a dear ear wishes to hear them.

Doesn't the poet say:

'Tis a mistake to say to you
I thought that all was mine:
I drank up all the vodka,
Then ate up the girl after.
I send my greetings to You.

Are You coming to the party on Saturday?

Greetings from Juhan
July 12, 1918

Well this was another new thought, at least. Juhan Liiv did, according to official estimations, write his poem around 1910. How did that affect my uncle? Was he quoting? Or . . . ?

No one to answer my question.

Traveling from Tallinn to my father's house in the country is a very trying business, but owing to circumstances I'm forced to make the journey quite often. It's not easy catching the morning express. You have to get up at four in the morning, get to the station by 6:20, then travel till nine, arrive in the small town, wait an hour, set off with the bus at ten, travel for a further three-quarters of an hour, and walk the last two kilometers. For that reason, I have tried other means of transport.

In August or September I tried traveling to the small town on the train after lunch. It was delayed, and I arrived at seven in the evening. I soon realized that getting any further would be unlikely, but I still took the risk of getting on a bus that left half an hour later and which would take me to a crossroads about ten or twenty kilometers away—maybe I'd be able to travel on from there! I didn't have much of a choice. There were no taxis running, presumably the evening timetable was being followed—only two taxis for the whole small town and they would have to operate within a radius of fifty kilometers. So I took the bus to the crossroads and got off there.

My suspicions were well-founded. The last bus to my father's home from the crossroads had already left. It had come by half an hour before.

It had been raining the whole day, but was clearing up from the west, though only enough for me to see the cold, red sunset.

Before me I had the prospect of a fifteen-kilometer walk.

Nothing to be done. The autumn night was approaching and so I set off, and the more I walked, the darker it got, though it never got completely dark and the fog began to rise from the low ground. No cars passed in my direction, there was nowhere to phone from. One car did come in the opposite direction but that was no use and after that I saw no one.

A couple of kilometers further on, there was the graveyard near the road where my father and, as I understood, my much-discussed uncle lay buried, though I had never found a gravestone for him there.

I do not discount the possibility that they have a joint grave, Uncle being effaced when Father was buried above him. But maybe not.

At any rate, the fog was wafting low across the road and the lindens were sighing.

There was still a faint glow in the treetops, under the trees it was completely dark.

In the gloom, I could make out few white crosses.

A cold wind was blowing and the fog swirled.

I quickened my step: as the road rose up the hill the air grew warmer.

But the fog was so thick that I could not see much at all.

Then I heard the sound of a car engine in the fog.

The car was driving without lights.

I raised my hand and the car came to a halt some twenty meters away. I ran up to it and looked in the window. At the steering wheel sat a man with a beard who I didn't know. I said I wanted to get to village N. and he told me to get in.

He switched on the headlights and they penetrated the milky fog.

We said nothing the whole way.

He was going somewhere about a kilometer from my father's home. I got out there and it was now completely dark. He asked whether he couldn't drive me to the door, but I politely refused and walked the remaining distance in a quarter of an hour. Once home I went up into the attic and switched on the light. As I was undressing, I looked Uncle's picture straight in the eye.

Uncle looked normal.

I put out the light and Uncle vanished in the darkness.

(. . .)

That's all there is to say about him for now.

It shows that reality exists. Not like Liikola, which sometimes does and sometimes doesn't, depending on one's mood.

We will return to Liikola and ask questions about it and answer them right away.

–You wanted to change the world for the better?

–No! I knew that that was beyond me. I wanted to demonstrate my dissatisfaction, and do so by launching a protest against technology. Sometimes when I was standing in buses, among hundreds of people, and they were all breathing and smelling and jerked their limbs about, people who were sometimes fat, sometimes thin, but mostly hairy, and they sometimes opened their mouths and showed their reddish mucous membranes and made contented noises, even belched, so I gladly imagined them dead, but the rational side of things didn't escape me either, I knew that technology, which is based on electricity for the most part, has enabled such rank proliferation, spreading like cancer, and sometimes I even thought that my act of terror would set off a nobler, perhaps even revolutionary process . . . Many of them smelled, and their eyes were so empty, so self-assured, that I couldn't help imagining how they would gobble up forests and, when the forests are gone, gobble up the stumps, the orchards, the parks, gobble up everything they came across, always so demanding, so important, so egotistical . . . And I have heard and read that there are people who say that under no circumstances, for no money in the world, must you sink into pessimism. Let's be happy no matter how many of us there are! Firstly, I cannot understand why we must be happy, secondly, why for that particular reason? Is it nice to give the opportunity, over the next twenty years, for another 2,000,000,000 people to enter life? Let's not sink into pessimism, even when the mass of human flesh fills the whole solar system. I've spoken about this with many different sorts of people. People generally agree that there are too many children, but always other people's, such as those that belong to Chinese or Indians. People from small nations always get very angry at what I have to say. Exactly. There are so few of them and they're supposed to keep on increasing in number! But how many nations are there, how many languages? I realize of course that smaller nations suffer the most. But their salvation doesn't lie in wanting to be as numerous as possible, creating a mass. They won't succeed in any case. I have been told that my rage stems from the fact that thousands of immigrants arrive in Tallinn every year, people who only consume, but do nothing for the benefit of the country they have arrived in. This was, of course, quite true, and I also knew that the population of Tallinn has reached half a million, while Mexico City has thirty million inhabitants, São Paulo, twenty-five million. And I found out that the six billion people living on this Earth in the year 2000 needed as many resources as sixty billion would have in 1900! Since the rise of *Homo sapiens*, there have been some seventy billion people living on the globe. So the present-day population of Earth constitutes about six percent of that, and they use more resources than all their ancestors put together! But I had gone too far, was at full speed by now. In fact it wasn't the statistics that bothered me, just the physical proximity of people. They breathed in my face and made me sick. I've already had this idea . . .

–Try to calm down. There's only the two of us here. I'm sitting opposite you, with a table in between. I'm not going to get any closer, honest, I'm really not. Look around you, the room is completely empty. Do you want me to lock the door? OK. Now the door is locked. Take a slow, deep breath. I understand you. It always ends up like this. You're no exception. Lots of people feel like you do. It's natural. I too am a hominophobe. Everyone is. Can't do anything about it. But you can relieve the problem. Talking about it helps. Carry on.

–Optimistically?

–I'm happy to listen to you.

–I can speak about anything at all. A plain full of people is billowing towards me. Men are marching towards the sun in formation like one huge golden spear. The endless sands of human life are rushing over my gnarled hands. Joseph has procreated here in the burned and slashed woodland for millions of years. Hundreds of ordinary folks coming home laughing. Shall I carry on?

–Continue.

–Millions of brothers kissing me feverishly on the lips.

–But just think then that they are your brothers and that they have the same thoughts, the same desires. Think about how they see you.

–With greed. They have empty stomachs.

–Overcome that obstacle at once, address them as brothers!

–I can't.

–Say "brother" to me, then.

–Don't be a fool.

–Brother! Just say it straight out . . .

–Are you trying to frighten me?

–And why not? We have means enough of doing so . . .

–Brother.

–With such bile?

–Brother! OK, I'll go over to the window and say to the thousands who have assembled out there in the yard for some reason: oh my dear people, how much I am with you, let us go out and dance and sing, let us express our basic desires, they can be hetero- or homosexual ones or fetishism or pragmatism, or whatever you want. Sisters and brothers, are you aware that Arthur Koestler has already said . . .

–If you're linking Koestler to anything sexual, then it rather undermines your argument.

–It's all as it is, it doesn't count. Koestler, linked to sex or not, said that the spoken word is the weapon humans use in their death urge; without the words there would be neither poetry nor war; that we are Lilliputians who are squabbling over at which end to crack open an egg; that a Saint Bernhard doesn't need an interpreter to speak to a poodle, but that Americans and Uigurs or Russians and Bororos do, because our languages separate us. So what if there are communications satellites moving up there in space when what they link up is something we can't understand? And people can easily get to the Moon, but the road to West Berlin is shut. Well, we must understand, I would say to my pale-faced brothers, hi there Danes, hi Albanians, let's ignore the threat of alcoholism, let's sit together here on the stairs and drink a bottle of vodka; if the police come by, we'll pop it into our pocket and pretend nothing is going on. Our aspirations aren't that different really: we all need a quiet sky above our heads, lots of happy children and a satisfying job. We will give our flesh to the hungry, our blood to the thirsty, our skins to the naked, our bones to burn so that the cold have something to warm themselves by. Let us love others more than ourselves. Furthermore, it turns out that Estonians and Bororos and Russians and Uigurs need to believe in a tomorrow, in intensive but not extensive development, sometimes a bit of cultural entertainment, maybe culture itself to spice things up, but this last-mentioned ought sooner be brought to all mankind, to every home, within reach of our homes, reach our homes because at home, in addition to as living space, we need this too, wherever this home might be, whatever the local religion, like sand on the shore, amen. Yes, and they need simple joys too.

–In itself, that's quite a powerful passage, but now let's talk a bit more about you. We have reason to believe that you're a pacifist.

–Well, sort of.

–Nevertheless, were you prepared to have to kill someone?

–Who d'you mean?

–You.

–What are you taking about?

–Killing someone. Well, if circumstances had dictated it.

–When?

–On your way to Liikola, would you have been prepared to kill someone?

–Why kill anyone?

–In the hatred generated for a moment by disgust, agitation, a state of shock, a momentary blunder?

–How should I know?

–What's this nonsense? You either know or you don't!

–I don't know.

–That sounds puerile to me.

–Let it sound puerile. What interested me at the time was the fact that I'd just that spring reread Dostoyevsky's *Notes From Underground*. This time I could find no point of contact with the work. However hard I tried, I still found the protagonist unlikable. But at the same time, he influenced me by induction. Induced in me the wish to sink to his level and give everyone a slap in the face, even the person who is taking notes. There was something attractive in his contempt of humanity, but what right did he have to value himself so highly?

–He didn't.

–What d'you mean?

–He didn't. He didn't!

–Who are you to say that?

–And who are you?

–Sorry that I'm getting all worked up. Self-criticism may be good, but self-discipline is good as well. He went abroad with Suslov. Was always in Suslov's room, said he had to close the window, smiled oddly, went out again, came back, said he would kiss his feet, but didn't, then went away. What did he want? To love? To kill? Turgenev once said that Dostoyevsky had confessed his crimes to him. People don't really believe that. Dostoyevsky is supposed to have said in the end to Turgenev: how deeply I despise myself! And after a pause: but I despise you even more. André Gide has said that if we measure, for instance, Dickens against Dostoyevsky on the scale of values, then the former should be measured in terms of good and evil, the latter in terms of pride.

–Isn't that what Suslov said about Dostoyevsky: *on pervõi ubil vo mne veru*—he is the first person who killed faith in me?

–*Ubil?* I don't want to kill anyone!

–Let's get to the point: not even on that occasion?

–Well, I could say that I wouldn't let myself be killed for nothing. Especially by those who have nothing to do with the cause.

–You're always going on about other people. But what about you yourself?

–It's comic to talk about killing when every second there are people all over the globe dying a violent death. What I wanted was very little: that my deed would not be confused with the deeds of others. That it would stand out a little from its backdrop, even if only in my own eyes.

–Easy to deceive yourself, is it?

–Some say that everything is self-deception.

–See such words for what they are.

–Honestly, you shouldn't allow yourself to be put off by well-known defense mechanisms. At times you need to throw yourself bravely into the embrace of psycho-pathological phenomena. Mitscherlich says that a paranoid perception of reality, locating the enemy outside oneself, brings a person relief, for now at last he knows what he wants. Previously, the torments and fears were internalized and incomprehensible even to himself; now they are out in the open, visible, localized, concretized, if you like. Isn't that a good thing? But I myself was thinking: I loathe the world, what does the mass of human flesh amount to, I despise existence, I don't know why, so now I am shouting out, clearly and straightforwardly: I know what I want, I'm not some dickhead or druggie, I want to destroy the power plant, I want to rot in prison, I want people to take my rights away from me. Don't interfere, let me say it quickly now. Don't forget it was night. A summer's night in Northern Europe. I don't remember the birdsong, I'll admit that. It would be nice to think that the birds had fallen silent in expectation, in a word, that nature was silent on account of me, could smell the decadence and degeneration in the air. I continued on my way, oblivious of both the world and the mild July night. Near a roadside farm the dog, loved by its owners no doubt, started barking and I leapt over the ditch and ended up behind some bushes, I waited until the dog went quiet. Then I got back on the road again. Those dogs, those bloodsuckers from my childhood days, those sadistic house owners who would let loose their dogs and then peep out from behind the curtains to see what the dog was doing to a small schoolboy! Guard dogs, mongrel sheepdogs! What would the dog have done had a nationalist bandit approached from the scrub or a dogmatic KGB deporter from the road? And now afterwards nothing has changed, I am like a child. The farmers let the dogs loose and go to sleep in peace. They think that night belongs to rapists. But mild sunsets, helpless lovers, world improvers?

–Did you not expect any reward, of whatever kind? From some institution abroad, because of some principle, some cluster of ideals? From your own mind? I can understand that you were not aiming for privilege or gain. I even understand the fact that you wanted sacrifices, or to sacrifice yourself, but I do not understand for whom. If you make a sacrifice, they want something from you. *Do ut des*, I give so that you might give, an old adage concerning gifts. Perhaps you wanted pain and torment, in other words, punishment?

–I would of course have accepted punishment, either from lynch mobs or from the courts. But I didn't want the gravity of the courts. I was prepared to play the fool in order to draw attention to particular tendencies, for instance the pollution of society, an electromagnetic field . . . I was in my own way an emotional clown. I was at the foot of the hill with a half-kilometer rise ahead of me that gave the impression that a barely visible ribbon of road led to the heavens; actually it disappeared behind the hill. But the hill and the heavens merged into one dark mass. I stood down there in the darkness. I raised my hand and looked at it to convince myself of its solidity, that my flesh had not dissolved. Yes, the skin on my hand could be seen in the dusk. I moved my fingers and began going up the hill.

–Up?

–Up.

–Honestly?

–Wait, let me think. In fact you don't really understand in the dark whether you're going uphill or downhill. All you know is that you're not staying level.

–Falling is the same as taking to the air?

–More or less. I have, of course, little experience of this. I can drag the odd memory to the surface, for instance, when they blew up the ruins of the Vanemuine Theater in Tartu. As you remember, the first professional Estonian theater was established there in 1870, the building was finally built at the beginning of twentieth century and bombed to rubble towards the end of World War II. The ruins loomed for many years over the city and I remember them from my schooldays. Then one day in the early 1960s they blew them up to build a new road. I was somewhere in the lower part of the town at the time. I didn't hear the rumble or the explosion. The ruins collapsed all of a sudden in a thick cloud of smoke that floated down the hillside. A large, soundless, billowing cloud just kept on coming and I of course ran away. Later, it could be seen that instead of the ruins there was now a large heap of stones. I was a bystander to that explosion. Actually, I had myself tried to produce explosions right from my childhood days. For instance, I happened to hear that a mixture of sugar and saltpeter would explode. I prepared such a mixture, but the boy next door ate it. He thought I was bluffing and that it was pure sugar. In the years after the war, people did, of course, suffer from undernourishment. That explosion never happened. Later on, I managed to produce small explosions. Once when I had the flu, I amused myself by collecting the sulfur from the heads of matchsticks, put it all in a test tube and poured eau-de-Cologne over it. When I pushed a burning match into the tube, a flame shot right up to the ceiling. It whistled and hissed at the same time like the crack of a whip. Later I saw how people caught fish with dynamite. I think I remember the pillar of water too. And on one occasion, Russian filmmakers caused a scandal in the Old Town in Tallinn when they blew up a car belonging to a German officer. The windows of the nearby secondary school shattered, the car rose high into the air and landed in a park some hundreds of meters away.

–But what about Clouzot's film, *La Salaire de la Peur*, from 1953! A couple of years later it had already arrived in Estonia, although the Soviet Union very rarely bought foreign films. That film was about nitroglycerine and how it was transported. When a couple of drops fell onto a rock, there was an explosion. But there were hundreds of canisters of this dangerous substance all packed in the backs of large trucks, and the mountain roads in South America are so full of potholes. The film was set in some outlying district in Venezuela, and the bridges were about to collapse and an avalanche was on its way.

–Exactly, and the French, who were tired and in an existential mood, penniless and having lost all hope of ever returning home, took on this enviable task. They died, one after the other. People's fates don't change their minds.

–They call that sort of thing a *film noir*, a black film. In fact, one managed to survive.

–Yes, Yves Montand. But he was so overjoyed he crashed his little car and died. But there was a ray of hope nevertheless. I unfortunately don't remember what it was.

–Did you also think about that film there on the road?

–But of course. Was it easy for me to get hold of the dynamite? Luckily, sabotage is not very widespread in our society, only spies in novels practice it, so no one suspected that I had horrible, outlandish plans. No one imagined that I would be a danger to society; they simply took me for a fisherman. Look at it this way. The sort of thing I was planning was something no one could invent. That sort of thing occurs only to a lunatic. Has to think the whole thing through in his lair for years, as I did, by the way. Anyway, then the bushes at the side of the road began to rustle and I thought it must be the dogs that are always on your tail in order to bite you. Strindberg had a terrible fear of them. Karl Bachler thinks that Strindberg's base urges were personified in dogs, urges he felt to be on his heels and which did not like him. Well, what else? The corncrake of course, even that was present, uttering its cry—croaking, that is. But every step was taking me closer. For the last time I saw the sky, which I could see so dimly, for the last time I noticed a layer of mud covering the ditch, for the last time would I regard myself as an Estonian along with all the others who bear that label. I was like the maiden being sacrificed to the dragon. What's wrong with the metaphor? If I garnish myself with words it is, after all, only on my own serving dish. Perhaps I still want to tell about the mosquitoes whose proboscises were hovering above me in the sky, those soft, but nonetheless hornlike needles, observant, their legs stretched out or crooked under their bellies, the mosquitoes I mean, who look indifferently at how the end approaches, a tiny torch on various nights . . .

–I hear that you never reached Liikola that night. You mentioned that a kilometer before the power station, when you thought you saw clear lights in the distance, from a hated and distant village house, the helpless power station, its lit-up windows, that suddenly you changed your mind.

–I didn't say that I'd "changed my mind." I would not have used that combination of words to describe that situation. I didn't think of doing so then, nor am I thinking of doing so now. It was something else, but I can't put a name to it. It's too personal a matter. Perhaps I do know, but I don't want to talk about it. It's too private. It was too strange. Who would it interest? Better to put it like this: was it logical that the power station was not blown up? You all thought so before! Because, think, think with a sober mind, think this: *think* in your case is the right verb, think or do what you yourselves want—if I had followed through with my plans, would I be here now? Would leaving the plan unfulfilled have suited the idea that you have of me, would it have corresponded to my image? You see what I mean, don't ask anymore.

–You have, of course, the right to remain silent.

–Yes, unfortunately that's the case.

–OK. What did you do then?

–What did I do, what did I do? I threw the bag into a stream, there was a hell of a splash, then all went quiet, yes, and a few bubbles rose to the surface. I remember feeling that the world was overexposed. Or like a stage set. One or the other. Or something in between. What could I have done, you tell me. I could have bent down and felt the grass, but it burned, I could have wet my fingers with spit and tested the wind, but who knows, who knows and who will do it and who will look?

–You.

–Me?

–Of course. It's all the same to me whether you have been lying or telling the truth. We're old friends and I don't want to interfere in this matter in a professional capacity. Let's say it's all over and done with. But that's not the point, it's a question of accountability. In my opinion you have the same responsibility whether you do something or just think about doing it. In other words: moral responsibility. And in principle you ought to admit your guilt, because I know you, we all know you as a decent human being. You're no terrorist. That nocturnal walk to Liikola went, in fact, against your own personal codex. It doesn't matter what system of values you have in you, I'm absolutely sure of that. You see, I'm not making any judgment about your deed. No need to. Your point of departure was an implicit attitude in itself.

–I would maybe do the same today.

–You're lying. That is a sham attitude. Just as you left off then, you're not going to start now.

–And so you're going to leave me with the pangs of conscience you yourself have invented?

–Yes, of course, assuming you really have them, which I very much doubt.

–You don't think so? Listen here . . .

The playful maiden is all-present.
She loves you. She hates you . . .
The dakini is playful.
—Trungpa Rinpoche

At that point, I stopped writing the novel halfway, initially because I couldn't think of any good reason to have forced me (or
him) to abandon his plans. At times I felt that he (or I) had had
some kind of vision, a revelation or a warning. But what sort? I
didn't know, and neither did he.

The other reason for leaving the novel unfinished is more
complicated. I will nevertheless try to explain as best I can:

The thought that I could even conceive of writing about an
anarchist in the first place disturbed me.

I began to wonder whether I myself didn't maybe have destructive tendencies lurking inside me. The idea of blowing up
the power station at Liikola could, when it comes down to it, only
occur to someone whose societal ties have loosened or unraveled
completely. True, I have thought at times that the world requires
personal commitment from me. But imagine, why just me? Such
thoughts have been sporadic ones, nothing to do with my principles about them. I have certainly walked myself through the
landscape he (or I) moved in. From time to time I walked to my

old mother's house using that route, with a smoked sausage, a pack of butter, and a bagel in my bag (but never a bomb).

But all the same: hadn't I been writing about myself, hadn't the incense of violence been wafting up out of my subconscious?

Did the fate of the world really just enter my head out of the blue?

Something had to be done.

No, I have to get married quickly, I've had enough of this endless bachelor existence, is what I said to myself, whatever has happened or will happen. I forced myself to attend family gatherings and dances, compelled myself to go to the burlesque theater. I tried to get the ecological crisis out of my head but was afraid that some vague urge to act could pop up again regardless. I was more or less sure that I was sane. The only *idée fixe* that could torment me was a neurotic urge to go mad, *die Flucht in die Krankheit*. It didn't pay to play around with such things. I knew that abstract concepts should be replaced by very concrete actions.

I liked women, but no one in particular was so interesting that she could sweep away my parasitic thoughts once and for all. One was too tall, the next too short, but apart from physical parameters, the mind also interested me or, as has been asked before: *habet mulier animam?*

For an entire white summer's night an interesting married woman sat on my knee, but that experience taught me nothing.

I chatted about literature with a curvaceous secondary-school girl, but we couldn't find any point of contact.

I went to an upscale bar where there were nice young women but

I got too drunk during the evening, and would have got beaten up by some mafioso types if friends who happened to be there hadn't gotten me into their car and driven me home quickly.

I looked with one eye out of the train carriage window at a woman wearing a red pom-pom hat who was seeing someone off, but the train left before our eyes met.

I wrote to an old girlfriend from secondary school but the letter was returned with "addressee unknown" stamped on it.

A couple of weeks later I ended up at a party that was being held in a suburban house. I hardly knew anybody there and they didn't arouse any interest in me. I wandered about from room to room, went out into the garden and strolled under the yellowing apple trees and looked down into the drained swimming pool, just for something to do. People talked to me, but not with any real enthusiasm. Evening was approaching and I understood that I was in the wrong place and that there wasn't much I could expect from the party. The rest were no doubt in the right place; at least they were having fun, some were even running around the house shrieking, chasing one another, just for fun. I gathered some of the fallen apples and ate them, carefully spitting out the wormy parts. I was thinking that this was one spot on Earth, just one spot, one very small spot, one house and garden with a dozen or so people who had gathered there and were happy, but I was not, nor would I be anywhere else, and that I was being unfair to my fellow human beings. How were they to blame if I couldn't respect the rules of socializing? Why wasn't I drinking vodka like the rest? Did I think I was superior to the others? That wasn't right! But however much I tried not to smile ironically at the bragging of the people around me, it didn't change the situation one bit. Fearing that I would get on people's nerves, I went inside to look for the phone. I didn't dare to ask, but found one by following the cable that ran up near the ceiling. There was a writing desk in a small room and there stood the desired piece of equipment. There was someone else in the room, but I didn't look around, just focused on the phone and went to sit down in a nearby armchair. I started dialing the number for a taxi but suddenly felt a sharp pain in my leg. I looked down and saw a tallish woman who had just sunk her teeth into it. Her face was turned away from me, only a large tress of flowing dark hair met my gaze. What can you say in such situations? I waited to see what would happen. I didn't have to wait long before the woman raised her head and said she wanted me. I nodded and listened for the dial tone, then the voice at the taxi station switchboard. I ordered a taxi and told the woman I was leaving. I nodded again. The woman was no doubt a little tipsy, but it didn't seem natural for her. I got the impression that she rarely got drunk, maybe sometimes with girlfriends, always in the company of others. Otherwise, she seemed a decent sort of person.

When we got into the taxi, it was completely dark. The woman had been keeping quiet the whole time and looking at me with loving eyes. She didn't she say a word in the taxi either.

That made me glad.

I felt her principally as a biological being, and I'd been needing something like this a lot that autumn, because I had, at all costs, to free myself of trying to better the world and devote myself instead to concrete human problems.

As I had suspected, she didn't have any problems or complexes.

She was in favor of surrendering as soon as we'd entered my apartment.

Could I try to define her sexuality in some way?

Yes, I could and if I was not very much mistaken, I would say that her sexuality was natural and full of vitality.

In the green moonlight she stripped immediately, completely and quite unasked, but showed no feeling whatsoever. There was nothing more for me to do than make advances. Could I expect being rejected? Was not taking off her clothes a sign in itself? To my mind it was, but perhaps I'm a primitive sort of man. Did I order her to strip, there in my room, in my presence? No, I didn't. She was trying to tell me something. She then smacked me on the ear. I stepped back. She approached me. I expected another blow, but it didn't come. She only breathed heavily and strangely. I put my arm around her waist. She moaned and pushed me gently away. I got the impression that she was fighting with me. This was ludicrous because I had not intended any violence. I stood motionless, my arms hanging at my sides. Stop it, she moaned, don't touch me, you mustn't. I was on the point of asking: what mustn't I do? But I have to admit that the situation was so piquant that it affected me, just as did the still half-bare twigs of the trees against the moonlight that occasionally scraped against the windowpane when there was a slight gust of wind. After a pause she leaned against me. Out of obstinacy I did nothing. Waiting in vain for an explosion on my part, she grew weary of her own passivity.

The following, alternating states of affairs swept her along completely, something that from time to time caused an pleasant thrill to arise within me. I have always, in every situation and whatever role I am playing, tried to maintain a certain aloofness. Because of this, my behavior is maybe somehow less masculine, but certainly all the more filled with pathos. I have never been able to go along with the manifestations of organic life, with death and sperm, to the point of oblivion; rock concerts and marathon runs arouse skepticism in me and, of course, I don't like battery-farming and slaughterhouses either.

Nevertheless such an experience was very welcome at the time.

Now look, I said to myself, she's now in an orgiastic, even orgasmic, state and who has helped her to get into it? You yourself, who only recently were calling into question the likelihood of human relations ever being effective, and were despising everyone who was close to the soil, to oil, to life! Look how she's rolling her eyes and murmuring, how she is showing her motherhood, womanhood, and all that kind of thing; look how her eyes are turning inside out, how she is crying out: come on, more! and think now, you little intellectual, what you're like: enough of this ephemerality, this woman is joining you again to material life, something you had begun to drift away from!

I felt that a weight had fallen from my shoulders. I think it was all that had felt superfluous at the time.

She lay on her back and snored quite loudly. At that moment I was quite pleased with myself. I really knew now that my life up to then had been nothing but paranoia, and that now I had arrived, as men tend to say.

In the morning the woman, whose name turned out to be Susie, said that she'd once watched someone giving birth, and how she was filled with contentment. The same feeling she had when watching crocodiles making love at the zoo, or chickens being slaughtered at a battery-farm. I asked whether she didn't perhaps have an orgasm when she saw snowdrops pushing up through the soil in the spring, but she didn't utter a word. Instead, she asked:

"Don't you want to give me a baby?"

Not only giving, but a baby too!

This was an ominous sign, as if some sunny day, one glimpsed the tail fin of a shark for a moment in the waters of the bay.

Like lightning, a sentence from Kafka sprang to mind: "Women, or to be more specific, wives, are representatives of life with whom you sometimes have to come to terms."

I had hoped to become an internal exile on Earth, in this cosmos, but the dachshunds of life had managed to sniff me out.

What I in fact wished was that the reduction of the human race could start with me. I have one clear, bright blue childhood dream still intact in my memory. I have always imagined with pleasure a world with a population of around one million people. Let's say about two hundred thousand on every continent. All the fruits of progress have been preserved. Communications are swift and efficient. A worldwide telephone network, television, radio. You can always chat whenever you want to. Travel has been kept to a certain extent, but there are far fewer planes and ships. Sometimes people go on visits. We go off to the lagoons, to the rain forest that by this time has been restored. A picnic on the shores of Haliç on the Bosphorus, finding new species of animals on the banks of the River Parana, or wherever. But such visits are not everyday matters. We will swap videocassettes and once a week there is a link-up by television when all the citizens of the world can meet. With one hundred percent participation. Where some deviants are put to shame. People philosophizing. Now there is time to think about existence as such. Maybe the answers to all the most thorny issues will emerge. The long-term dispute between the concepts of infinite space and the cosmos will be one of the favorite topics, but the debate will take place in a cozy and utterly refined atmosphere. There will no longer be a problem of getting enough to eat, expansion will not cause headaches, nature will luxuriate. We will have withdrawn to inside our own borders, at the same time retaining all we've invented. How much time we will now have to analyze the past: how could it all have happened? When did science get out of control? When did we begin to regard ourselves as unpunished? What metamorphoses have taken place between the sexes and in their relations with one another? How did violence escalate? We have plenty of material on the last of these questions. We can watch all the films ever made in the evening hours, there's great material there. War films, love films, films on industrial production. Let us approach them as ethological material.

"Then you don't want to give me that little gift?"

What could I say?

I had no one to complain to. Public opinion was on the side of the woman. Blurry morning light shone in through the window and the trees were dripping with rain. The whole of nature was breathing extinction and I was expected to be game for biological optimism! It just wasn't fair. Those gray clouds, those departing migratory birds, those hapless people crouching in the potato furrows! And me here in the embrace of a mother spider! How sad were those thoughts, I remember them very well, but I was pretty young and immature at the time.

There was nowhere to retreat to.

Mankind consists of people and people impress people.

Killing a person is punished much more severely than killing a pig. You even get praise for doing the latter. They sometimes say: Peeter's a good pig-sticker! or Jaak is the number-one knifeman and bristle-scalder in our village! But people are holy, and some think that through mankind nature gains a perception of itself. But wouldn't it have been enough with one universal being doing the feeling? One human being and nature would have been able to feel, and so be left alone. Everything would be left just perfect, as it always had been. But nowadays? What must nature feel by way of 5,000,000,000 perceivers? What kind of fucking feeling is that, I'd like to ask?

At any rate, the woman's assault had offended me, and I have not quite managed to get over it to this day. There is something humiliating about being raped, and without any sexual enjoyment, without the slightest nuance, without passion, simply a demonstration of biological superiority. Simply to avenge the ego, to fill an empty existence. By some miracle, I managed to avoid making her pregnant, though she gripped me tight, in an iron clasp. I don't know where I got the strength from, otherwise I'd never have got out of her clutches, I mean under normal circumstances, under normal conditions. In one fell swoop I was at the other side of the room, one single leap, I knocked down a porcelain vase, but it didn't break. My skin seemed gray in the light of the autumn morning, and although I remembered the secret lives of hippopotami and mankind's definition of a thinking reed, and lots of other things that garnished my shame, I was still satisfied with myself because I had managed to run from Life itself. I was as pleased as a child, as if I'd managed to escape from a *vagina dentata*, or from a man-eating fish, lurking in the womb of a woman, or from other things that sensible people keep away from.

But the woman laughed.

Ha-ha-ha-haa, her mocking laughter resounded theatrically through the little house. I suppose it was meant to.

I know very well why she was laughing. She wanted to humiliate me. If only the poor woman had known I was not to be humiliated. I didn't even feel sad. Quite the opposite, I felt joyful. That time I still managed to escape.

Ha-ha-haa, the woman laughed again, and this time even more cynically. In my situation, any other man might even have started to beat her. But not me. I don't unfortunately go in for such things, I no longer have an image of myself to shatter. I went into the other room and wiped away the millions of potential offspring with a handkerchief.

Only just before, I had been a writer, even a popular one, I had been translated into several languages, but now the novel was half-finished, the protagonist had stayed for the night on the road to Liikola for all eternity, was no longer advancing or returning. What was all this about? Shame!

Was the woman guilty of this?

Woman as importunate life, as the principle of expansion, as proliferation?

She despised me for the way I thought, and no doubt felt that I wasn't manly enough, which is something that is taken in very narrow terms around here, on the border between East and West, or perhaps people just don't think about it. Anyway, such accusations are meant to hurt.

From outside wafted the smell of wet grass and wet leaves. There was some bird or other flying around, at least you could hear the rustle of wings.

Perhaps I was just in a bad mood, how else can it all be explained? It felt then, and feels now, as if my life had been ground to dust, and you can decide where this thought of tackling complex human problems led, *human bondage* as it is called, or even the *white man's burden.* True, I was trying to become a good citizen. But a wolf always makes for the woods.

I would have wished for something else.

For instance, to travel to Italy, bathing with depraved nymphs in the Trevi fountains, practicing orgiastic rites at Corinth, getting baked in the sun, on the parched grass, doing something so crazy that they themselves could never even dream of. Fleeing to Eleusis, sacrificing pregnant sows to Demeter. Or losing my human guise entirely? Sacrificing that woman? Sacrificing her to an idea that would get the world out of its dead end? That really is an idea. Go into the kitchen, take a tenderizing hammer and a bone-saw and do away with her. I would enter the room carrying them and they would glint in the moonlight or, if the moon were down, in some other source of light, perhaps the light of that same autumn morning. Anyway, they'd be glinting. Then I'd kill her and give her flesh to the hungry, her blood to the thirsty, her skin to the naked, and her bones as fuel to the frozen. Would that not be an honorable solution?

Our affair was that advanced!

Because look, my Dear, I actually took a few steps in the direction of the kitchen, I don't think that I would have taken along a tenderizing hammer and a bone-saw, I would simply have drunk some water, but behind my back I heard a kind of snorting or grunting, and when I turned round, I saw something flashing, in the light of the dawn or whatever light it was, and I felt that there were fangs. Two fangs.

Honestly.

I tiptoed into the other room.

I bolted the door and sat down on the floor.

Now and again, I would manage to get the first chapters of my new novel in the newspaper in the university town of Tartu. I would call them "fragments" and never admit to anyone that nothing more of the novel about electricity existed. And . . .

You asked me what happened to the woman.

It's not so easy to answer that question.

I was sitting there on the floor in the other room, well, I sat there for quite some time, maybe an hour or so. I thought how stupid I was being, one way or another, then I got up and went back into the bedroom.

As you can well imagine, the woman had gone.

Yes, just as if she had never existed, you're quite right, and this was indeed my first thought, but then I realized that she could have snuck out quietly, which is not polite, but does happen. Laughs, then leaves. Of course I felt hurt, but then there was nothing to be surprised about. A little later I told the story at a meeting with the kolkhozniks of the "Red Partisan" kolkhoz, and among the audience I started hearing little cries of: shame on you! shame on you! not wanting to be a father! anti-humanist! With great effort I managed to explain that I loved children a lot and have brought up plenty of them here and there in my life and the only problem is that I didn't see any particular point of doing so as I didn't believe in anything, or rather I believe in very little and there was no point in handing down all my nihilistic thought to the children—their little pouting mouths would grow hard, they would ball their fists, and tears would begin to flow. The audience agreed with me, but still remained aloof. If such a varied audience felt hurt, then why not that woman too? Later on, the most trite suspicions entered my head, whose only fault was their triteness, but were otherwise vital enough and justified: I began to look around me in panic and checked my most valuable electronic equipment and my most valuable books. *Do you believe me?* You'd have done the same. When? After chance visitors leave! But nothing was missing. The woman had been honest. She wasn't a thief. And outside a cold rain was falling. Still those black bare branches of the apple tree, those rotten pears in the yellowed couch grass, all the sweet decay, sweet autumn after autumn, for in autumn you want to eat something sweet, such as apples or potatoes baked in flames, and I now remember that that woman had also said to me, panting: when I see some tiny, sweet, red-cheeked child, I want to eat it up! But now I'd like to talk about how the first chapter of my novel did nevertheless manage to get into the paper in the university town, without the preceding and following parts, and—

Listen, why should I say any more about that woman? Those memories are so unpleasant. They're worse than unpleasant, they are embarrassing. Yes, *embarrassing*. I can't think of a better word. OK, I'll return to the day in question. And you're right when you say that day continues to torment me. I walked from room to room, from the hall into the kitchen and the weather just didn't clear up, the clouds remained very low in the sky and snow could be expected soon. I looked now out of one window, now out of the other, but it was the same in all directions: things were rotting, decaying—in other words, the same wherever you looked. You could only see the test pattern on TV, the radio was just whining to itself, and the papers didn't come. I shut my eyes and tried to let all my muscles go limp, especially around the corners of my mouth. My lips rested on my teeth, my tongue lolled back. Of course I fell asleep, of course I had a dream. I awoke in the darkness of evening. It was still raining. In fact it was raining even harder now. The rain was literally lashing against the window.

I felt even more sore. I got up off the sofa and went into the hall. I had, in fact, already managed to think that I could hear a suspicious scraping sound. There was someone on the stairs. I snuck up to the peephole in the door. Yes, a figure was moving outside. But the lights on the stairs were so dim that I couldn't see who it was. No, I didn't think this had to be that nighttime woman, no. There was supposed to be a cannibal roaming around in our town at the time who would turn up here and there. He was said to be a very daring man. He'd even been spotted on the beach at Klooga, among all that bare flesh. He had a small moustache. In broad daylight! No wonder that he dared to be outside my door in the middle of the night. The figure was leaning against the wall and stood motionless. It stood with its head hanging, in the shadows, deep in thought. One hand was in his trouser pocket, the other hanging loose. A melancholy cannibal, but he no doubt knew I was watching him. Why the theatrical pose when you're alone on the stairs? Suddenly, he straightened up and came right up to my door. I didn't jump back because I knew that the light from my hall through the peephole would betray anyone looking out into the corridor. I stood, my eye pressed to the peephole. He approached and came right up to the little tube, a centimeter or two long. We could both see only darkness. And yet we were so close to one another. Could he perhaps smell human flesh, my bionic field? He had to do so as he was an expert, no amateur. Perhaps this was a test of resistance, as we stood there like that. Like two lovers. Hero and Leander, or Pelleas and Melisande, or perhaps to be more exact Penthesilea and Achilles. When did he leave? I don't remember, it was pretty soon. At any rate he left before I did, yes, he gave up, descended the stairs, walked away quite silently. After that, I couldn't get back to sleep for a long time. I thought about my life, about my mission, about society, I tried to improve it in my thoughts, then destroy it completely, I kept on discovering problems. It was still raining and the air was sultry. I threw back the covers and stretched all I could. In the end I was lying spread-eagled on the bed; that's the last thing I remember of that long period and I still remember that the next morning, it was still raining and my mood was even blacker. So, to sum up: a banal episode but one that induced anxiety in me, made me uneasy. Later on, I tried to figure out why. The relationship was an intense one, something that is generally appreciated, and I have nothing in principle against such a relationship. True that the business with the child made me cautious, but the woman could have been joking. I remember what she said because it sometimes happens that a person affects you from afar somehow. Yes, when referring to her own past she went into unpleasant details. For instance, she mentioned that her divorced husband had drowned on a beach in the west of the country, drowned while saving a friend, drowned a hero though his body was never found and presumably the wild pigs ate his washed up body there as it lay on the shore. A sad end for a man so full of zest for life. But nothing there was too exaggerated, because in nature everything eats everything else, sad though it sounds. What was most important for me about that tale was the old Estonian adage that says that people eaten by pigs will not rise again as the last trumpet sounds. But should I worry about such information? Me, who has grown up in this world, as we all have? No. Or maybe what affected me more was what the woman said to me about liking black pudding more than anything else? Laughable, so why should that affect me? No, I just can't explain!

What was there then? There was what there was.

Some tiny but cozy little arts event, for instance watching Ibsen's *Ghosts*. It was staged in a gray and modest way, with a large window as backdrop. The still sea glittered from afar. It could also have been ice. In the third act, during the night, the sea disappeared altogether and you could imagine that it wasn't there anymore. I decided that the action was taking place in Norway, as tends to be the case with Ibsen, but during the interval a friend of mine explained that since Ibsen actually wrote in Danish, the play could even be set elsewhere. I didn't argue and waited for the dawn with which the play ends.

A merciless sun above the snowy fields lit up the dying people. A sun that rises at midnight, because that is what Osvald wants. His mother couldn't do anything to stop the sun rising. Alas, it was too late, wasn't it? The polar night had lasted too long, the artist had withered away. But why shouldn't the sun rise? Let it rise. Actually, I don't now remember whether the sun rose during that performance or not. I assume it did, because the producer wasn't the type to argue with the playwright. But I do remember that, on the way home, I for some reason pondered the question I had been asking myself quite often: who are the Albanians? Yes. Albania has fascinated me too, not just you. For years, no one knew what was going on there. Perhaps nothing is happening there, was what insistently sprang to mind. Sometimes you think that there are places on the globe where nothing happens, and you'd like to emigrate there. In *Ghosts*, Mrs. Alving had complained that the whole Earth, all around, was full of ghosts. And it's true. You wake up in the middle of the night and the air is so sultry, so unpleasant, you are surrounded by perspectives, memories, visions, remnants. In Albania, but perhaps also in Tierra del Fuego, there's nothing like that. You can breathe the fresh air with new lungs.

Apart from art I have managed to experience a thing or two in life. For instance, when I went on business to a nearby provincial town and next to me on the bus sat an unfamiliar young lady who told me the following story out of sheer boredom, no doubt, despite my timid pleas that perhaps she shouldn't tell me anything at all:

"Half a dozen years ago, I left Estonia homeless, initially went to Greenland, then Leningrad, by then the New Year was fast approaching. Me and Maara didn't manage to get in anywhere. Maara was, like me, on the road and with no roof over her head. We did know a certain Fyodor but he'd got mixed up with some criminal activities and Maara said it wouldn't be a good idea to go to his place. Well, there was also this Valeria, and some old woman too, but they didn't let us in, they ended up swearing through the door, words I couldn't even understand. Our warm clothes and our cacti had been left behind there and it's quite possible that they had sold them to some rag-and-bone man. Because we were afraid that Valeria too might have to go underground, even for quite some time, and she spent every kopeck. We went maybe four times to her door but in the end the old woman threatened to call the militia. That was all we needed, so we gave up. So there was nothing for us to do but to spend New Year's Eve at the railway station. At twelve o'clock there was some kind of salute outside, but inside the station no one wished anyone a Happy New Year, people simply ignored one another. There were one or two annoying things there: a drunk was lying in a pool of piss, and an invalid was standing up eating leftovers. But the majority of people there were quite decent really, wearing proper clothing and sleeping. Or at least pretending to be. Many no doubt were wishing they were at home, by the tree, in the company of relatives, but they didn't show their longing to anyone; quite the opposite, they seemed to blame the others, the others were, after all, those who were constantly overcrowding the trains, making travel impossible. Everyone wanted to travel, but traveling seemed unnecessary. Why are you here and not at home? Me and Maara looked for, and found, some empty places to sit, there was no room to lie down. An old man with a large beard like Tolstoy's was sitting near us and writing in a school exercise book. He had the same small, neat handwriting as some . . . I can't really say who, can't remember just at present. Without us even asking him, he told us he was keeping a diary. He asked us where we were from, then said sadly that Estonians mix one another up because they don't have patronymics. Why, oh why, children, don't you use patronymics, he asked, patting us gently on the head. Maara said that we don't regard fathers any more important than mothers. Some people don't even know their own father, and sometimes it's better that way. But you don't have matronymics either, the old man carried on, and you keep on getting all muddled up. Muddled up, muddled up, what's it got to do with you, is what we were thinking, adolescents as we then were, and replied that there were so few of us Estonians and we were individualistic, and that no one got muddled up. That remark sent the old man back off to write his diary. He was no longer interested in Estonians and their ways. Then two young whippersnappers turned up and asked us out onto the street, but I didn't want to go, because my hands were all sticky, lots of things can make your hands sticky at stations at night, jam or God knows what. He gave me his address, one of the young whippersnappers, I mean, but I threw it away and the young guys took the hint, went to see what was going on, someone was arguing and they went over to have a look, and we didn't run into them again. I didn't dare to sit on that hard bench any longer. I saw an empty counter in the corner with empty shelves and climbed over the counter and lay down on an empty shelf to get some sleep like someone on the Moon. I couldn't get to sleep, I took some drops, then I dozed off. I woke up at five o'clock, not on the shelf I had fallen asleep on, but the upper one. I woke up Maara and we thought about where you could go on New Year's morning. Igor sprang to mind and we went to his place. He was at home, but we were intimidated by a couple of drunks from the New Year's party who were standing behind him. But our cacti were there and we managed to get hold of them. So anyway, we arrived at Theater Square, we bought a kilo of plums, that much money we did have. We went by the back door into the Conservatory where we knew an old lady who let us into the organ loft. The music was playing loudly and we couldn't hear what each other was saying. We fell asleep again. When we woke, the organ was silent and the people had gone. At the station we thought of borrowing money from some Estonian or other, that was a good idea, but the only Estonians we met were carrying hunting rifles. We understood that some non-black-earth-region huntsmen's gathering had taken place, an innocent enough affair in itself, but nevertheless Estonians with guns were rather intimidating. We nevertheless had enough money to get to the Estonian border, to Narva. From there we hitchhiked and ended up in Tallinn."

As the young woman had been telling her story, I was looking absentmindedly out of the window at the woods slipping by, the darkened farmhouses, one or two stars between the clouds. I couldn't really see the girl's face properly. I could only hear her voice. We arrived at the provincial town at midnight, the ground was frozen, I shivered and rapidly disappeared into the hotel where I had booked a room. Nonetheless, the young woman's story remained in my memory word for word and I have told it to a few friends, without much success: mostly people ask what the young woman had done before and after the event, but I never answer. I simply smile mysteriously.

Anyway, as you see, life flowed sluggishly and smoothly along. I wouldn't want to claim that my thoughts have never strayed back to the subject of electricity. Sometimes at night the word sprung to mind, but didn't get me very excited. I even received fewer electric shocks, in fact, virtually none at all during the period in question. True, I had become more careful, perhaps even more crafty. I no longer stuck my fingers in places where it was not wise to do so. Higher forms of matter have always been incomprehensible to me. I have only rarely seen visions, even more rarely poltergeists, and specters and astral bodies almost never. Hasn't that been a hopelessly boring life, my Dear? Flowing steadily like a novel whose epic tautness has slackened, shuddering like a mirror being carried along a road, and much later I heard that it wasn't only me who thought like that, others too experienced what would later be termed stagnation. I didn't know this at the time, thought that I was growing old. A big misunderstanding. Life was to offer us a lot of surprises yet, about which more later.

Nevertheless, it seems to me that I have rejected a big, once-in-a-lifetime chance. I am an Estonian and, as such, not very reproductive, which is a pity, because there are so few of us and we are under constant threat of extinction, living just on the borderline of existence. But Susie! Did not some higher fate predestine her for me? Was it not intended that I, through her, would escape into the spheres, the place where life becomes a higher and more productive game? And now, after my great act of cowardice, my life remains on the back burner, a silent passing away, maybe beautiful but nonetheless shabby vis-à-vis my beloved nation. In our folk songs, cocks even eat gold and hens pewter, so how could I then be ignorant?

The chain snapped with me.

The chain of cause and effect has been broken.
Nevertheless, how noble that sounds! In the end, you have to put it into words you can accept, then the problem doesn't seem so bad.
One day, when it was raining and the trees were black.
That sounds pretty good.

The ache of loss, the pain of decision, a manly weakness, a philosophical fallacy!

Let it be said that Susie, about whom I have told You, did turn up again, on the roads of our world—if only fleetingly.

We had just been on a business trip to Poland. That country was, at the time, suffering great complications, but my political and economic education was too limited for me to appreciate all of what was going on.

At first, everything went smoothly. The three of us were put up in some sort of residence that seemed to belong to the state and was quite important: there was a soldier standing at attention at the gate and although he didn't check your documents he would salute as we passed. At first, this token of respect pleased us. After tiring negotiations the small and cozy dining room was waiting for us where just the three of us would have dinner and where we had three waiters to serve us. What was rather special was that they would fill up your vodka glass without being asked, time and time again as it was drunk empty. There was, of course, no question of a bill. The only thing that surprised us was the fact that there were only the three of us living in the residence. Where were the others, was our inevitable question! The house stood in a park, the old trees creaked in the wind, and despite the soldier, you felt uneasy at night. My knowledge of Polish is poor, but I could see from the headlines in the papers that the political situation was getting more tense. Nothing was said openly about it in the official negotiations, but it was in the air. So I was not surprised when one evening I found on the table a packet that in Russian is called a *sukhoi payok*—in other words, a packed lunch. I understood that we would be leaving for home the next day. Clearly, they didn't want to put foreigners in any danger. My companions did not believe my prediction and ate up their *sukhoi payoks*. But I packed my bags before going to sleep. I was right, of course: in the morning, three serious-looking men knocked on our doors brandishing tickets and asked politely if they could carry our bags. We had to obey. Our interpreter, *Pani* Sosnicka, stayed in the background and wept. It was not impossible that acts of terrorism were taking place somewhere or other. The car took us to the station and—after hearty farewells—the train took us over the border.

In Brest we had to wait for a day. We went into the park and walked around among the greenery that had grown wild. As always in the northern countries, it was dusk here. I think I've already mentioned that there was no snow that winter. A couple of degrees under zero Celsius, or around the freezing point. Distant locomotives whistled. A railway junction on the border. We sat on tree stumps and talked. We talked about Poland and its fate. We still had a few hours to wait.

Two men had approached us unobserved. At first, they sat some distance away, then came nearer, then quite near. In the end they struck up a conversation with us. They asked something about Poland and we understood they thought we were Polish. Stolper said we were from Lódz and were electricians. The men fell for it. Stolper went into Polish prices in quite some detail. The men nodded and shook their heads, according to the information. I kept silent as I always do in confused situations, as you will have noticed. Then Stolper asked who the men themselves might be. I had understood what was going on, right from the start. But they showed us politely where they had been detained, and their certificates of discharge from prison. They were, no doubt, from Kaliningrad or somewhere around there. Stolper asked them more about their lives. The men were talkative, the euphoria of release can make even old cons less careful about what they say. Soon I began to notice that the younger man was eyeing my wristwatch. I began to grow uneasy. I didn't let on, but knew a question was about to follow. And it came:

"Are Russian watches really better than Polish ones?"

"Ah, I just got it as a joke," I began to answer, rather confusedly, but Stolper had guessed everything.

"Talking of watches, our train'll be here soon," he said and jumped to his feet. "*Paka*—see you!"

We hurried in the direction of the station but it had already grown dark and a fine snow was falling. We weren't kids. We knew that you shouldn't try to trick *Blatnois*. They had opened their hearts to us. Luckily, no one followed and we could soon see the station building.

"Where are you running to," said Stolper in a rather forced bout of jollity, "that's far enough now, let's catch our breath!"

We stopped and lit cigarettes. We said nothing about the previous few minutes. The evening was closing in, the Brest evening, a fine snow was falling, the railway station was living a life of its own, here, beyond the bushes. Stolper couldn't calm down. He seemed to need to justify what he'd done. And lo and behold, soon he had made a new discovery.

"Gentlemen," he said, drawing nearer to the bushes, "and what might these be?"

And he picked up a yellow-checked skirt and a red-and-blue-striped blouse. Quite new, but creased, even crumpled in places. But there were no bloodstains. I suggested he throw them back where he'd found them, but that evening Stolper seemed to be hyperactive. On his suggestion, we went off to the militia post and handed over what we had found. They didn't seem particularly pleased to see us. We only just managed not to get arrested ourselves. We had to stay a good while in the bleak militia office and tell all about ourselves and give all sorts of details. It was a good thing we actually managed to make the night train! Stolper wasn't suffering much, he was at peace with himself, he had done an altruistic deed. He was talkative and kept on praising himself.

Our third companion slept. I, however, just couldn't get over the fact that that woman, i.e., Susie, had been wearing the same combination of clothes, the one who bit me in the thigh.

Of course this was pure coincidence, but it didn't reduce my pangs of conscience.

Almost a year passed.

YOUR LETTER

Do you remember when I first stepped into your life along with a hundred or so cacti, and you were very surprised, even frightened? We had exchanged letters before and you'd managed to tell me that you had an instinctive fear of all kinds of organic life, and would try to stop it spreading if it was in your power to do so. Later on, you took back some of these radical ideas and pointed out that your anger was restricted to people, but only destroying mankind wasn't enough really, because there is always the tiny likelihood that there is a modicum of truth in the theory of evolution, so you should never give up being watchful, because God only knows when some rational being could evolve again. I didn't really take your theories particularly seriously, as the whole world, at least the eastern half of it, seems to be possessed by a prevailing climate of disillusion and a lack of enthusiasm. Despising people was quite in fashion then, and I got the impression that you too had been caught in its claws. But on seeing you for the first time, I was obliged to correct my impression; well, not completely, but your misanthropy did at least take on a guise of something to be taken seriously. When you were moping there by the window in the evening and spat on the heads of those making a noise down below, even then, when you didn't suspect I was observing you, I understood that in your soul there really was some kind of void, some kind of scar that will not easily heal at your age, except by the advent of death. But I didn't want you to die because we'd only just met and I wasn't half as cynical as you. I was looking for a little happiness and peace after the years I had spent wandering all over the world, not stopping anywhere for long, never immersing myself fully in anything. I was doing research into cacti and in fact my collection was already very large, but because of difficult sea voyages, heat, or snow, a good many perished, so I only managed to get about a hundred of them into your apartment, where they still are now. You were the first man I have stayed with so long. I had had relationships, but in the long run I became convinced that men were not for me, nor for that matter women, cows, kids, or relatives. I lived with the odd man for the odd week solely out of the desire to be like the rest, to do the same as everyone else. God, what agony it was, if only you knew! Don't worry, I won't start tormenting you with all the sordid details, I'll spare you, honestly I will. Anyway, you'll no doubt remember how I came into your life and brought, apart from the cacti, flesh, blood, skin, and bone, which perhaps interested you, perhaps not, especially given your contempt for everything living that you loved to stress, time and time again, especially in your letters. I was wearing a light blue dress, a white necklace, my hair was tied back in a ponytail, and the cacti were waiting down in the taxi. You were kind enough to help me bring them up. I saw the look of fear on your face. Up to then we had met, just the two of us, with no witnesses, but now there were over a hundred, the one even more remarkable than the other. O, horror! Actually, you were in a state of panic. But now you had opened yourself up to loving me, you simply couldn't go back. Is a man afraid of cacti? Of course not! You sweated as you carried the boxes of plants up the stairs, took my succulent friends into your apartment. I still don't know whether honest protest would have suited me better at the time. Well, honesty has its own virtues, but at the time my cacti needed a home, and you were prepared to offer one. So it would be more honest of me to say that I was, and still am, very grateful for what you did. Of course the cacti didn't all fit on the windowsill, but you soon brought some tables up from the cellar and spread them out there. And a thousand thanks for doing that too! I couldn't have done anything else. All my worldly goods were scattered right across the globe, in Sonora, Madrid, Moscow, Veracruz, God knows where else. I didn't need anything except my cacti, and now you, who I began to need nearly as much as I did them. Do you remember when I told you this? I often ask whether you remember. I perhaps ask you so often because you have sometimes let it be known that you hate memory and then I have to ask whether you remember, because I don't know but maybe I'll suddenly come into the room one evening and you'll ask me in astonishment who I am, and that question wouldn't make me at all happy, because I repeat: I am me, my cacti are mine, and we all belong together, and the unit that arises from this belonging together belongs to you too, and you'd better not forget it. So, once again, do you remember? I entered your life with a hundred or so cacti, which surprised you greatly at first, even frightened you, along with flesh, blood, skin, and bones, wearing a light blue dress, and a white necklace round my neck and my hair tied up in a ponytail, and we knew that we belonged together. We were both sad when the first cactus died, just simply collapsed, couldn't cope with the dankness and spiritual chill there, although, on the other hand, I saw on your face a look of relief when the cactus corpse was dropped unceremoniously into the garbage bin: for now you had become convinced that the cacti were not invincible, that they were not capable of expansion and escalation of growth. I understood you immediately and said that cacti rarely bloomed in northern climates, especially in centrally heated apartments, because there they don't get the winter rest they need, and when they do bloom, their seeds are incredibly tiny and growing cacti from seeds is a very painstaking business that can even fail when tried by experts, and what was the most important thing was that you could never grow a human being from a cactus, whether evolution existed or not, I could even swear that from personal experience of such countries as Mexico or Ukraine, which I had wandered through both in dreams and in waking life, sleeping on shelves and in beds, performing the rituals of Indians and those belonging to Orthodox Christianity, and God knows what others. I was pleased that you took so well to the cacti, more enthusiastically than I could have hoped for, while slogging away as you were in vain at your scholastic novel about electricity, already doomed to failure, you were now actually entering into a commitment to something, and it didn't matter what: freedom for our country, cauliflowers, or dreams, the main thing was that you were committed and that the relationship was a passionate one. You adopted my way of thinking, while of course staying independent, as if it were your own and the only possible way of relating to things. Do you remember how you even wrote a short poem in which you tried to sum up your new worldview: "You relate so that feeling comes, / you feel so that passion grows. / You crow so that the whole village hears, / hears that the game has begun. / The game carries on till dusk, / after that things start to wither." Yes, I still remember that piece of doggerel because it really made me glad that we understood one another, all of us, including the cacti.

Why am I writing all this, as if your mania for writing has infected me, as if I can no longer cope out loud?

Yesterday I went to work wearing a maroon dress and my hair was curled, no longer in a ponytail. I had swapped the white necklace for a gold one, well, at least a bronze-colored one. Today, I'm going to work and don't even know what I'm going to put on. I'll be concentrating on that soon, over the next few minutes. It's hard to get used to life here, in this country, is what I'm thinking, because here everything changes so fast and at the same time doesn't change at all. But it's always been like that everywhere, it's only perhaps in the Antarctic that every new morning doesn't promise something new, at least the snow stays white, that much you know before you've even opened the curtains.

When you go for a walk, don't forget to turn off the lights, and turn on the coffeemaker, and don't forget the outside light. Electricity is crafty and jealous, it won't tolerate your being unfaithful, and it is even jealous of the cacti. You've been living with it for some time and it can't do without you. It will take time for it to get used to being alone, something quite suitable and right for electricity. Let it get over its problems. Let it get used to itself.

See you this evening.

A BEAUTIFUL AUTUMN DAY

A collision with the world around you, as always when you step out of the door into the new slums. An alluring grayness, highrise blocks where the sky is nearer (a thought of Mart Susi's). Mirages and optical illusions, vistas, the air hisses with the strange vapors of thousands of people. Smells that our noses don't recognize, at every step. I walked along, my nose to the ground as if in the imperial halls of the Tretyakov art gallery or in the pantyhose department of Stockmann's department store. I was trying to avoid having thoughts and feelings. I said: live and let live!

For that reason, I wasn't taking in what was going on around me until I had arrived at the main highway cutting through the verdant grove. This was intersected by a second highway, then ceased immediately. So a three-way crossroads was formed. But such a phenomenon of urban construction did not surprise me, nor the fact that a dog had been run over and was now almost merged with the asphalt.

Midday, the month of September, silence.

Everyone had gone off somewhere.

Out of town, to have a rest, get some relaxation, fool themselves.

Each year, I had begun to love such city districts more and more. Once I had hated them, called them unfit for human habitation. The buildings were indeed horrible, for instance the one right here in front of me: nine floors, ten entrances with four apartments per entrance, a total of 360 apartments.

But once I had begun to understand that such buildings were now our fate, that we had deserved them, with our inner refinement and everyday wishes left to our dreams, when I began to understand that we were not worthy of another type of building, the loathsome district began to take on a new, aesthetic dimension for me. A scream in the darkness, the tinkling of a window, the glass smashed to pieces in the moonlight, hundreds of people wading through the mud and taking short cuts between the blocks, the scarred features of people in the vegetable shop and the newspaper line—this became my world, my tiny *fleur du mal*. Those days, those expressionless faces, those people who had ended up in some particular place on Earth, having no notion of either excitement or fear, but who made the occasional attempt at being human, in the desire not to merge with others entirely by the choice of clothes they wore, their smiles, or their offspring, gradually became something I loved. What affected me was the way that they individually, entirely concealed from one another, raised their eyes and squinted directly into the hot sun at which it was impossible to look with the naked eye, but which did not diminish the grandeur and hidden purpose of what had been built. They did not age, were neither born nor died. They were eternal transit passengers, passing through the world as through the city. They did of course participate in something somewhere, but it would have been wrong to expect them to describe it. How hard it is to ask somebody: what did you do today? He cannot fool himself even by crying out sharply: work! Perhaps he really did do some work, but what does the word signify? Let's assume that your spouse makes a fish-grater—what should the fish think of her; if she constructs machine-guns, what should people think of her? Your opponent never cuts himself, or lets himself get shot. He is not an egotist by nature, he tries to close the gap between himself and the world, his efforts are directed outward. He attempts to make contact, perhaps by cutting or by shooting.

How can you get angry with him?

How can you get angry with cities? What should people do once they're destined for life? If we have to blame someone, then we should blame Jehovah (Genesis 1:28). But how can we blame Him?

We can't phone Him, after all!

Of course we can't; but instead I happened to notice an approaching taxi and raised my hand.

The taxi driver said:

"Fuck, all sorts of things can happen. Sometimes, fuck it, you just don't know what to make of it all. You try and make sense of it, but you don't know which way it's moving or even what it really is. What the fuck can you do in such situations? What I say is: it drives you nuts, that's what. But I don't count, fuck it, why not? Nor do they always write the whole story, perhaps they don't know themselves. Let's say you're a fisherman. You aren't? Well I fucking well am, and a good one too."

I was growing a little embarrassed by all those "fucks" but how can you interrupt a stranger and correct his use of language?

"Fuck," the taxi driver continued unabated, "where was I? Oh yes, fishing. In a word I am a fucking good fisherman. And sometimes, fuck it, all sorts of things happen. Take last summer, September I think, fuck, I don't really remember exactly. We were somewhere up Rannapungerja way, fuck, where exactly I can't say. But anyway, fuck it, it was about ten kilometers away. Well the fucking time must have been about five. There was a shower, then it stopped and we carried on fucking fishing. And suddenly—fuck!—my eyebrows began to itch as if I were being attacked by fucking mosquitoes. So I thinks, let's see what's going to fucking happen, and they go on itching, then I get an itch in my neck as well. Well, I asked my friend whether the fuck he was feeling anything. He, fuck it, was wearing a cap with a long peak. Brought back from Bulgaria or fuck knows where, and he answers, fuck it I can't feel a thing, but I was still wearing that fucking beret. Well I says to him, take off your fucking cap. At first he didn't do so, but then I told him—take the fucker off. Well, he did take off that fucking peaked cap and his hair stood on end. Well, I then took off my beret—I was still wearing that fucking beret—and he said here, it fucking well looks as if your fucking hair is standing on end. Well, OK, what can you do? Let's try and do a little fishing, When I, fuck it, raised my rod a bit, the nylon line began to make loud chirping sounds, fucking hell. Well, about five minutes passed, then my back started to itch and the skin of my ass grow tight, fuck it, and became fucking painful. Then I hear that the corrugated iron covering the prow of the boat had begun to sizzle, fucking hell. And I got fucking scared . . . The sun was shining, the water was smooth, there wasn't anybody fucking there, but everything was sizzling. And us with our fucking hair standing on end, and our backs and necks itching, even the ends of our nose. So I thought fuck, the boat is higher than the surface of the water, the metal of the boat has a good connection with the water, what're you doing, going crazy or something? We thought that fuck, soon there'll be a bang. Didn't dare to eat either, got out some fucking sandwiches, but I couldn't get them down. Really fucking weird, being there in the middle of the fucking lake and I can't remember whether we could see the shore or not. I don't think we could. Well fuck, I started to pull up the anchor, got a shock from the rope, fuck it. Tried to have a smoke, but the fucking cigarettes were also full of electricity. Would you believe it? I tried the compass to see whether there were any fucking magnetic disturbances, but not a fucking thing, everything in order. We rowed on a bit and then it fucking happened. I don't know whether it was there immediately or whether it came on gradually. As we approached the shore there was some kind of fucking rumbling to be heard, or perhaps there wasn't, fuck knows. What the fuck do you think of that? I don't know what the fuck to think either. Fucking good job we didn't fucking die."

The taxi driver fell pensively silent.

I asked him to stop the taxi in the middle of the woods near the town.

I started to walk through the woods.

I had already seen mushrooms on the market, they must logically have started appearing.

I too want mushrooms, I too am a human being.

But life didn't offer me any mushrooms. Things turned out quite differently.

ॐ

In the midst of our wearisome way through life, I suddenly found myself in a darkening wood, where I strayed from my path. When

I raised my head the hills lit up by the rays of planets were no-where to be seen—they would have calmed my nerves.

I was in a wood, and here just about anything could happen, here an event would have free room to maneuver and could ambush me from round the corner, like some neologism or other.

But at the time it was an evening in early August, it was too hot, silent, the smell of the branches, the bright patterns of light on the moss. And a good while before it had become apparent that there were no mushrooms in the woods. Of course, after a long period of drought, there's no point in searching for mushrooms, but I still couldn't just shrug off my disappointment. It was as if nature had cheated me.

What else was there to do in the woods?

Do something with soil or humus? The very thought was un-pleasant. The grass was shriveled up, ants were swarming all over the place, and so you couldn't really lie down either, regardless of how tired your feet were. All you could do was stand there, but for how long? Once you'd arrived, all you could do was walk and walk across the open country, through the wilderness.

Movement is strength. Seven horsemen went to Turkey to wage war. The prophets crossed the hills. Dostoyevsky's characters wandered through Saint Petersburg seared by shame until they arrived at their decision.

I started to hum a song to myself. I sang half aloud. Naturally, to keep malevolent animals at bay. But quietly in order not to disturb benevolent people. Both of them, the animals and the people, were somewhere in these woods near to the town. Ani-mals that dared not approach the town and people who dared not stray too far away from it. Here, around me, ran an imaginary boundary, a stretch of no-man's-land. For that reason I improvised pointless, meaningless songs. In several languages. English, for instance: *love is my business now.* Or Russian: *belye kavychki na moyei okne, strannoe zapiski ostayutsya mne.* Or German: *die Tugend kommt und geht.* Or English again*: my situation is my population, my population is my relaxation.* Such songs come to you when you're walking alone in the hot woods, devoid of mushrooms. You can't sing them with other people. The songs no doubt come up from the depths of your unconscious, they are evinced by the fragrance of the pines, the poison of the ants, the approaching autumn, the poison of the fly agaric, hidden somewhere under the moss.

I had a basket with me and in it a knife, otherwise nothing.

Little Red Riding Hood is coming from the Big Bad Wolf's cottage and has this time managed not to get gobbled up.

So I went on walking.

In fact I was already lost, but this hadn't occurred to me yet.

When you're already lost in life, it's no wonder you can also get lost in the woods near the town.

Especially if you're prone to getting lost. I should have known that there were no mushrooms in the woods. Why then did I bother to walk in them? Was it really a question of losing my way in order to get into a situation with no hope for the future for some time? Of course I value signposts and notices and prefer route maps, but one fine day you just go wild and take your basket and your knife.

This explanation sounds pretty convincing and I see no good reason to reject it.

But there's no point in explaining too much. In the woods you can get engrossed in the woods. And here there's something to see.

At first glance it's all the same and rather vague, so what if it's a shady area of green, a realm living by its own laws. When you look again, you see a system that consists of interfaces and structures and which is growing all the time, so what if the eye can't make them out? But on your third or fourth glance, your eye grows accustomed and soon you will find something or other for human beings too.

The forest is suddenly full to bursting with indications of events: look, here somebody has broken something off, here a tree was felled, and here a stump, perhaps from last year or even earlier. Individual instances are worth investigating.

The Estonian theater director Voldemar Panso once said: you have to sit on events—as you do on a tree stump.

What he was driving at was that the action of a play must be turned into something essential on stage; enough time must be given to identify the kernel of what is taking place.

But you can take his words about *sitting* literally. If you see something special here in the woods, you just sit down and watch. And don't expect anything further to happen, simply keep your eyes peeled, apply the appropriate foreknowledge. Where are the effects of acid rain? is something you will ask yourself as you inspect the tops of the pine trees. After a while you will discover branches that really have died, but as an amateur you don't know anything about what is caused by pollution, what just happens on its own, and what comes from God knows where.

And the sun beats down as if it has forgotten that it is autumn.

Before your eyes, the sea stretches wide.

When I was child the sea was exciting. When it appeared from behind the dunes, or at the end of the street, it always came up suddenly and you were always expected to do something. For instance, change into your swimming trunks. If there were changing-cabins nearby! Yes, the sea has an imperative influence on a child from the interior of the country. Swim, boy! is what it is saying through its roar. And you have to swim. Whether you like it or not. You can't ignore it, not even abroad where swimming isn't an obligation.

In Greece, at Cape Sounion, there's a temple where Lord Byron carved his initials. It may be a forgery. Maybe it isn't. But below is the sea, and the Mediterranean into the bargain. How would you describe it: blue, sapphire-hued, endless? Something like that. You're standing up there on the high cape near Lord Byron's autograph and suddenly you feel ashamed that you're not swimming, because the weather is so perfect. Your first obligation to the sea remains unfulfilled. Even more so, as there is actually someone swimming down there. Rumor has it that this is a Finn, from the same North as yourself. Did Byron swim here? In my mind, I make the hundreds of tourists disappear. What is left is a bare stretch of land, wild and agrarian Greece. Coming here by carriage, wandering down to the sea, climbing up to the temple, the sea on three sides, *ultima thule*, swimming alone, naked, under the ironic gaze of the peasant driver—being Lord Byron, afterwards to die as a freedom fighter in Mesolonghi. Interesting. Presumably he didn't swim there, just carved his name.

But as I said: before your eyes, the sea stretches wide.

Maybe I have given the impression that I had come to the sea from the woods near the town.

No. The sea came to mind when I was among pines and moss.

I was only dreaming about the sea.

And then it was time to consider the fact that I had lost my way.

It is well known that a person's right leg is a tiny bit stronger and takes a longer stride. For that reason, anyone in the woods or where he can't find his bearings by following a path will tend to return to the place he started from. When he notices this, he has lost his way. Space becomes relative whether he likes it or not. Wherever he ends up, it's always the same place as he started out. Whether he stays still or walks, the result is the same.

At that point, some people begin to shout.

I could very well be left-handed, I have never tested it and probably never will. Perhaps I'm ambidextrous. But it's not important, because I walked aimlessly and would have got lost whether I walked in a straight line or in circles.

I didn't start shouting.

I am, after all, a fully-grown man, not a tiny kid.

Who starts shouting in the woods near the town?

I stopped and listened.

The rather quiet soughing of the trees, polyphonic as ever, which is quite natural, as this voice contains the soughing of millions of branches and twigs. A soft wind, in fact. And the knocks.

The knock of the woodpecker.

Why does it knock so loudly, you can hear it for miles. Can't it manage to get its worms in some quieter manner? I daren't sing loudly, but the woodpecker is saying: I am the death-watch woodpecker, presager of death.

Can't you be quiet for just one moment!

And it was. Then, once again: the quiet soughing of the trees, the background noise of existence.

I pricked up my ears. An old proverb: he who will not hear with his ears, must hear with his ass. I listened for sounds from the town. All I could hear was a dog. I had hoped for the sound of an engine, but heard the sound of animals.

The time: nearly five.

Could I hear the grass growing, the voices of the flowers, the vibration of colors or the blinking of my own eyes, or something else? Could I . . .

I had left home at three, and really was intending to pick mushrooms. Sometimes they can appear despite the drought, though rarely. Anyway, I couldn't settle down at home. Maybe it's roughly the same phenomenon as when I was talking about swimming and the sea. My writer colleague Vaino Vahing once said something about the terror of cyclical situations. It disturbed him that you're always forced to go skiing in winter and sunbathing in summer. Who forces you? Isn't it peer pressure: *man zwingt*? The terror spreads to the other seasons: in the spring you're expected to become restless and have to contemplate the water making rivulets from the melting snow, in the autumn you can't help suffering from depression and go mushroom-picking, even if you like mushrooms and would go anyway.

An unseen authority ordered me to take a taxi and drive out from town in a westerly direction. At the first decent stretch of forest that looked at all promising, I got out and entered the woods at a right angle to the road. Without looking back. Of course I understood pretty soon that there were no mushrooms. But there was always the hope of stumbling across at least one. I walked for about half an hour, but nothing.

Until I lost my way, which could have been expected, but wasn't as terrifying as you read in fairy tales.

Anyway, there I was, lost.

In a place where the Horned Beast and the White Peril live, Silvanus too—the darling of the underdog—and, of course, Pan. Where everything grows rank and our word counts for nothing. In the woods, everything is said to be back-to-front and even voices seem to come from the wrong direction (Uno Holmberg).

The sun had sunk lower in the sky, the air was clearer, but it was still as hot as before.

Crack!

Shouldn't stay here overnight, however near the town might be.

Even though I had a knife with me.

One specific memory:

I was still a very small boy and it was already beginning to grow dark when I arrived at a spruce forest, where it was even darker than under the aspens, an old spruce forest where nothing else grew, and there in an evergreen thicket I saw a witch's circle made up of broad-headed toadstools. I knew that when night fell the forces of darkness, elves and witches, werewolves and forest fairies would all fly off to the witches' sabbath. Then somewhere quite nearby, I could hear an oriole. I squatted down under a tree and in the darkness watched what looked like a fluorescent dot: when would lightning strike, when would those and other beings fly with a rush of wings straight up into the sky? But then the oriole screeched even more threateningly and I got up and I broke into a run through the woods, which were growing visibly darker, as if I were being pursued. At our gate stood my mother and Auntie Ella who had come to visit us from town. They had been getting worried about me. The next morning, Auntie Ella, who had been sleeping in the attic, said she had heard a long, persistent rumbling in the night and had decided that lovesick cats had been banging on the attic door up there. But my father went round to the neighbors that morning and on returning told us that in the night a vehicle had driven through the woods with its lights extinguished and that a long volley of machinegun fire had been heard coming from the dark woods, but no one in their right mind stuck their nose into such matters.

The memory came to me from thirty-seven years ago, had remained in my brain for all those years, was committed to paper, and now came back to me, though there was no reason it should have done so.

Who still knows what really happened there? And who was it that saw that the vehicle's lights were switched off?

I pushed my way through the bushes, a twig poked me in the eye, grass stuck to my shoes.

When the forest was bad to people, then our forefathers would punish it. For instance: pummel pine branches with rocks, set anthills on fire, tie the tops of young trees together.

Very cruel, our forefathers.

For at first they would seriously punish it. The bushes would sway from side to side.

Perhaps on the edge of the shrub land, a spotted panther is lurking who doesn't want to retreat out of sight and is making way for the lion that is approaching, his head raised and whose sight fills me with such fear that my faith in going uphill falters and I slowly slink back into the cover of the forest.

In 1971, the following story came to mind in the mushroom woods:

I'm in the mushroom woods with a friend, and we're walking along, joking that the autumn theater season is about to start, and we'll have to see what we do with it. Both our baskets are more or less full, and for some strange reason we don't remember that there's a war going on, and we have been occupied for three weeks now. And then, in the midst of the sweetest dreams, enemy soldiers appear from behind the bushes and take us along to their headquarters. A prod in the back and we are standing before an officer. I look at the uniform of the occupier, his spectacles and thin beard and suddenly realize that standing in front of me is Balser—the dramatist who I had once seen at a conference on aesthetics in the capital when he was holding the floor and speaking in his idiosyncratically honest manner about the efforts of the Third Way, to which someone else no doubt replied. There is still hope: the intellectuals are together, though the muses are silent. The matter will end badly. My actor friend calmly utters the lie that he has played the lead role in Balser's plays, whereupon the choice is made to allow the actor to live. I have nothing to say, nor does the actor have a good word for me, simply bows to the ground, when Balser leads me off into the bushes to be shot. Balser! The same Balser who in his charming little dramas somehow managed to create a synthesis of the Brecht's social mysticism and that of Claudel, filled with pathos.

Stop! On your way! Evening is approaching!

Suddenly, the glimpse of an animal among the trees.

I froze. The first rule in such situations is: do not show panic.

The animal was behind the bushes. It was walking slowly and carefully, its pace told me that. Suddenly, I could see the color blue. A human being! was what flashed through my head. It really is, but what sort could it be? And what is he doing, what is he planning? To watch me? I'm not afraid of people.

I could no longer be bothered despising them. I felt that I would approach them from a new angle. I had realized that you couldn't blame that single consciousness, that hermetic holon, for anything. Except maybe for existing. Because despite the rebirth of a feeling of generosity on my part, a cool shiver goes through me as a branch cracks. (Sartre: when I hear a branch crack behind me, I don't immediately think that there's someone there, simply that I am vulnerable, that I have a body that can get hurt . . . that I am being watched . . .) On the other hand, you should always be prepared for a nice surprise. Better to be surprised than disappointed. As I am pleasantly surprised when someone allows others to reveal their inner thoughts before they do, just as I do when the sun rises in the morning, so I could also be prepared now for a big surprise, or else just a regular occurrence. Perhaps I have been chosen and will be allowed to see the impossible.

Perhaps some kind of crossbreed is approaching. *Wolfsmann, Wassermensch, Menschenvogel?*

No! The branches parted wide and there into the clearing emerged a man about whom it is hard to say anything.

Was this the Man Without Qualities himself emerging into the clearing?

That's what you asked.

God no, it certainly was not. I'm sorry, this novel is about imagining things and it is a little strange that, having spoken for so long about foliage and woodpeckers, I am unexpectedly avoiding a description of the man who appeared. You could well ask why he had to appear there in the clearing when we can't ask who he was and what he means.

In fact, the solution is simpler than that, and we all know it. The population of our cities is increasing every year, and the number of people who are hard to describe increases with it. There certainly are one or two of them. And now the man I mentioned wiped his eyes, simply because he had just emerged from the bushes. So he was the second real human being apart from myself. There's nothing further to say about him.

He said hello, and I didn't.

I said hello, and he didn't.

We both said hello simultaneously (out of sheer embarrassment).

The man was deaf and dumb.

We were both mushroom pickers and were disappointed that there were no mushrooms. But perhaps we'd still find some.

The man stretched out his hand and said: my name is Forest.

The man grew pale and pulled out a revolver.

Or something quite natural: we had both got lost, the only difference being that I was looking for the way into town, he for the way out to the countryside.

Nothing of the sort happened.

I raised my right hand slightly and didn't look up.

Or I did, perhaps because he was carrying a stick. I don't remember any basket.

I continued doggedly on my way and I have to say that my determination and purpose were soon rewarded.

Now I no longer met just one man, but three of them all at

once sitting round a dead campfire. They remained silent and were staring at the ground in front of them. I don't know whether they were embarrassed by me or for me. I didn't dare skirt round them, so I carried on in a straight line in order that the men would see how little they bothered me. None of the three raised his head. I could have sworn that one of them had a scar on his cheek. Otherwise I can't really say anything about them.

From that point on, I met plenty of people, tracks, and items in the woods, either out and about, or thrown away.

After the permanent joy in between, I regarded the lumber of civilization with mildness once again. Long forgotten passions floated up from childhood. Look how the discarded plastic cartons shine so brightly, how colorful are the labels! Should I pick up this litter? An intellectual of the first generation who has played with pinecones on the hills of home will never quench his thirst. I have held myself back with difficulty from rummaging through garbage cans. Just like a beggar in the alleys of Wall Street! But aren't those cartons pretty? What designs! Was it not our poet Marie Under who said that we admire truth through beauty! But in the shadow of beauty violence was lurking, just like to the left a faded yellow notice warned that you could get shot if you trespassed. A silent witness of complex and paradoxical times, which, thank goodness, are now over. The notice addressed one in familiar tones. It was right for it to *tutoyer*. You could imagine that a friendly approach would sound more credible. Politeness is nothing but a lie.

If I turned off to the left, I could lose my life, but to the right lay certain death. I avoided looking in that direction and don't know to this day what was there, and it's better not to know.

Straight ahead, through the bushes, I could see a hillock down whose gently sloping sides three children were rolling, one after the other, and I could hear their shrieks and could even make out their features, which I could describe even now, and the air was clear and transparent.

At the same time, I trod in a deep rut and I got cold bog water in my shoe, so my head was now clear, but hardly transparent.

The road was cut off by rusty barbed wire and you either had to climb over it or wriggle under it. I chose the former, but nothing happened.

A copy of a newspaper from last year had become lodged in a tree, an October issue with a nude on it. You could imagine that only a year ago this could have been the last hideout of a lonely old exhibitionist.

Impressions were positively rushing into my head!

This always happens when the countryside begins to urbanize, but how should you describe it, and is it worth the effort?

For instance, let's say: walking by a pond, the outlines of the iron constructions on its banks warped by an explosion, cogwheels and bottles in chummy juxtaposition all lying under the same pine tree, and the children again roll down the hill, and now there are four of them, all with their teeth bared; the children disappear from view, suddenly there is silence, you go on walking and you can already see straight in front of you . . . better not say what because it is unpleasant to keep on describing all kinds of things, you turn your head away, and are moved, because the hayfield billows and the sun shines on your neck and there between the hay and the sun a four-legged watchtower rises and again you feel joy at the developments—e.g., our freer national atmosphere—which now exclude them from using the familiar form of address and shooting a bullet into your head from up there, and before you realize what's happening you lower your head and see to your horror that some kind of oily water is emerging from a deep hole and think that only a madman would jump in, but you luckily aren't one, and why bother describing that hole to no purpose, it would still be a hole or an object, then you see something that really would merit literary penmanship: three black pigs with especially long slender legs. In the depths of the forest, you would certainly have started to run from these monsters. Here, however, they have lost their power since we are here in the zone influenced by the town, and so you can even describe them quite naturally, no matter if you start from their heads or rumps, with words warm or cold, the main thing is for them to be colorful, but maybe they are waiting for you, they give one or two snorts and disappear into the yellowing hay where there is no point in a solitary walker following them, neither you nor me. Then comes a stretch of nondescript brush, it would perhaps mean something to you, but you are used to more exciting incidents and ordinary nature wouldn't satisfy you. It's going to happen, you'll see soon enough, you say to yourself, and here it comes, or rather—you approach and it stands and waits, i.e., a house. It has no windows, but it's some three meters high. You circle the building and on the other side there is a bolted door, in fact everyone has left a long time ago. You can tell that from the rust and the voice inside you. You put your ear up to the keyhole and hear only the soughing of silence, nothing more. On the door are written the names: Hilja, Tolja, Silja, Kolja. It's pretty obvious that the building was once used for something that no one remembers anymore. The man who had it built was once young and successful, perhaps he even got an award for the building, he was praised for his initiative, but he has now been in prison for several years, the third of a long list of charges being the construction of that very house. *Gloria transit,* but the house still stands.

In my eagerness to tell a story, I forgot to mention that I met more and more people on the street, the great majority of short stature. From one thing to the next: were conditions in this city district worse than elsewhere, or were such people needed here, like for submarine crews where such smaller folk were required?

Stunted people instilled hope in you.

For instance, some years ago, I took an interest in acceleration. I began to wonder why people were getting ever taller. In fact, I've always been interested in this phenomenon. As a child, I was frightened by what I read in M. Ilyin and Y. Segal's book *How People Can Become Giants.* On the cover there was a woolly mammoth, on whose back was sitting a primitive human being with bared chest, waving with one hand, holding a spear in the other.

The book started depressingly:

"On this Earth lives a giant. He has such big hands that he can pick up a locomotive . . . This giant is—Man."

Only later did I realize that this was a metaphor.

It was the story of technical progress.

But they are in fact getting taller and taller. You can see a tendency over the last 130 years, and since the twenties of this century the whole thing has taken off. European statistics show that the average increase in height is one centimeter per decade, i.e., some 2.5 cm per generation. No one has yet found any reason for this. People have talked about solar radiation, an improvement of the diet, the increase of the amounts of vitamins and mineral salts found in food. Even the trauma of urbanization has been suggested. I myself have never believed in any of these theories. Nor have I found anything to put in their place. More recently, I discovered that the Soviet scientist Presman explains acceleration by a general strengthening of the electromagnetic field in the biosphere. He thinks that over the past century, where people have built high-rise blocks and installed lightning conductors, this has increased the amount of electrical discharge into the sky. And there has been an exponential increase in the electric field. Presman thinks the fact that human beings are slowly becoming giants is, in its own way, a kind of hyper-compensation for the strengthening of such fields. Incidentally, as early as 1941, a certain scientist called Treiber attributed the acceleration to the influence of radio waves, but at the time no one took any notice of his findings.

So giants are a thing of the future.

For that reason, small beings instill hope.

Above people, personages, and personalities, the autumnally dark blue sky and the low sun lit up what they had to in sharp relief, turning things that would otherwise have been painful to look at into objects of beauty by their own freshness. The Earth was tolerable, even the dusty road through the village where I finally ended up.

I am still free to turn off where I want.

I can grit my teeth and write, eyes closed:

A dusty road led through a village, past ripening fields of crops, into the distance, giving solace to my poor bare feet. Far away the forest of Saare was turning blue, a dog somewhere near began to wheeze and—

And the children?

Here they were.

At the side of the road, a group of children were playing. They were very tiny, of a conservative nature, no doubt. I didn't hear a bad word from their lips. Lately, I have met plenty of conservatively minded children, something that seems to be a new phenomenon. Children were sawing planks into equal lengths, their pouting little mouths smeared with food, tree stumps covered in resin. But their parents were also active: one man was painting his house and whistling. This was the first house I happened to spot, I mean to say the first house in which someone lived, and the man was happy, why else would he have been whistling?

And not only the man.

The train whistled too, as it emerged from the bushes and cut off my path. The boom descended. Next to me another taxi stopped at the barrier, the window on the driver's side was wound down and I could see the driver clutching the steering wheel with both hands like a drowning man would a lifebelt.

I stood there beside the tracks, basket in hand, just like a beggar, no wonder that the driver of the locomotive spat when he saw me.

As the train passes, we ask ourselves how frank we can be with other people. Other people have asked this before.

First of all: we are no longer of an age where correspondence has any particular value in itself. I don't, for instance, want to confess anything to my other self, since there could very well only be the one. Of course, notes can, in themselves, be necessary.

You can, for example, compare variants, see how the mushroom of thought ripens and reproduces, if you make a comparison with nature. A flood of words simply adds detail. Being frank sounds fine in itself, sounds like a virtue. Secretiveness isn't as good. It has suspicious moral overtones that put decent people off. On the other hand, it is good to keep silent. We are learning less, while, at the same time, noise is becoming ever more wearying. As a small child, I put up with rock concerts more or less out of a sense of duty. They were a feature of social renewal and you had to love them as you did other kinds of noise, perhaps even dodecaphony. Worst of all is, of course, the human voice. Everyone knows what it feels like to walk some evening along a peninsula with a compulsive talker, or spend an evening with one in your apartment. Voices evoke countervoices. Human stories demand things of people, they give rise to vanity. I often wonder where some people get the courage to start telling stories.

The train had long since passed.

Beyond the railway a street started with the woods on one side, houses on the other.

There is in fact no reason yet to try and understand where I am headed.

Let's drop the metaphor and say: I'm heading downtown.

I've just come from picking mushrooms and am going straight towards the town center.

That seems funny to me.

If it isn't funny, I don't know what is.

Night is still ahead.

In spite of this, they've forgotten to switch off the streetlights from yesterday.

A few days ago, a young artist visited me and told a strange story:

A few days before, his sister had got married in Pärnu, a woman not exactly in the bloom of youth, but still attractive in her own way. Her husband was said to come from the shores of Lake Peipus and nobody really knew him that well. All that people knew was that he had recently had that nasty skin disease *erysipelas* on his leg but that the cure was now complete. But after the wedding, a new and unexpected fact emerged: quite often, the groom couldn't manage to switch on lights. He would diligently press the switch, but what was expected just didn't happen. The bulbs were intact, as was the circuit, and anyone else would have succeeded right away. We laughed at this strange story and I forgot it immediately. Now, on the edge of town, where the lights had been left on, I remembered the problem of the man from the shores of Lake Peipus. I was walking along and the leaves were rustling above me and beside me. I had to resist the temptation to say: the leaves are whispering the Peipus man's story. I caught myself hoping that this husband really did exist and that the artist hadn't been forced to make up the story.

I liked almost all of the houses along the left-hand side of the road. If I had had the money, I'd have gone to live in one. But the likes of me will never manage to scrape together that much. On the other hand: an architect friend once said that the Estonian people could take up a collection and then have a special house designed for me. It would be enough for everyone to give ten copecks each. More than enough. Would you refuse to give ten copecks? asked the architect. Perhaps I wouldn't but it would no doubt be forbidden under our laws and would be put in the category of begging, was what I said, and dropped the attractive idea. I really did, because otherwise, instead of ending up in the apartment of my dreams, I'd end up in prison—you never know how they'd take it. Then you really would have gone "underground."

Yes, my thoughts keep returning to Dostoyevsky's Underground Man, no doubt because of the heat. I have seen two theatrical adaptations of this book. In one, the producer had tried to make the Underground Man a melancholy intellectual constantly in dialogue with himself, almost a decent fellow; in the other he had turned him into an unpleasant drunk, from whom you could expect nothing good. In my opinion, neither of these stagings hit the right note. The Underground Man is perhaps telling the truth, but it would still be best to keep your distance. He thinks too much of himself. If he were a real hero, he wouldn't be bullshitting so much. He would keep quiet and the last rays of the setting sun—Dostoyevsky's favorite light—would illuminate his noble face, but we would never be able to know what pains him, nor recognize him even at the Hay Market where his silent contempt of humankind has brought him.

The rays of the setting sun were lighting up my right cheek too, but this didn't change my thoughts on the subject.

As I walked along, I was taking note of what was happening that late afternoon on the edge of town.

It's really good to see how a corpulent woman takes her tub of white washing outside, how a young girl now skips forwards, now backwards and quite high into the air, how a longhaired cat sleeps its noble sleep. How the movement and billowing of net curtains betray many secrets, how many random thoughts are conveyed to people's heads by the strange TV aerial that sucks juicy pictures from the air, which a passerby cannot rid himself of. You see a mailbox from which you guess letters are gathered, or not, as the case may be, and among them are bills or death notices; you see the phlox and think plants are miracles of nature, flowering for several days in a row, and of the proliferation of plant life; so does it matter if you didn't get your mushrooms?

And then you see a few faces.

Your roving eye rests.

There, where I live, so as to fit in with everybody else, there are as many different faces as potatoes in a heap. You take one and throw the next away, you cry out with fatigue when you get onto the long-distance bus or get off.

I was on Sirmiku Street—named after the parasol mushroom.

Parasol mushrooms?

I quickened my step.

I wasn't quite so naïve as to think I could find mushrooms here, just because the street was named after some species or other.

It was just that I suddenly realized where I was.

It had seemed as if I'd lost my bearings in the woods and really had managed to get lost. The last couple of hours had passed as in a dream. Chaotic suspicions and melancholic thoughts had got the better of me. If someone had ordered me to tell them where I had actually been walking, I would have had to remain silent out of sheer helplessness. Oh sure, I knew roughly where I had been a couple of hours before, when I'd climbed out of the taxi. But I had no idea how I had suddenly arrived at Sirmiku Street where Meri lived.

This time, in real life, not simply in my mind's eye.

Anyway, Meri opened the door.

Meri and no other; it was his house, after all.

The evening was upon us, there I stood, my shoes covered in dust, my lips scabby and slightly parted.

Meri (i.e., the man Meri, not the Estonian for sea: *meri*) was no poetic abstraction, no cry of admiration from the lips of youth, but an Estonian writer, ethnographer, and historian who lived on Sirmiku Street. Thanks to my getting lost, I had ended up at his gate without even noticing.

I observed that the neatly mown lawn was a much darker green, more luxuriant and generally cleaner than all the weeds that grew in the woods, the mere sight of which makes you thirsty. Suddenly my feet felt tired.

I leaned against the stone wall.

Cool cement under my fingers.

Silence, the shadows of ancient trees, the books dreaming back there in the depths of the house.

One sole garden seat, made out of German fir, a tin of coffee on the kitchen windowsill.

My God, why couldn't I live in such happiness and peace? Why couldn't the summer come to me too, with the wind wafting the leaves in the twilight, and swaying the branches, with life constantly ahead of me? Where *über allen Gipfeln ist Ruh*? Hypotheses, children, *cordon bleu*?

I knew that there were plenty of troubles and unsolved problems in my colleague's life and the house too was showing the first signs of wear and tear. But I was clearly entertaining some kind of subconscious need to have a home of my own and the security it brought with it, and I felt a melancholic envy.

There was of course an inexplicable premonition behind all this.

Sei still, mein Herz.

As you're already at the gate, come in and visit me.

ↈ

We exchanged greetings and Lennart's eyes lit up as usual when he saw someone standing before him. No wonder, because the history of culture is the special object of his research. But who or what bears culture forward? People, no doubt, with their memories, both individual and collective. And Lennart remembers a lot. He has written:

"Central Sweden was still devoid of population when we came to the shores here in order to fish and trap. We spoke our own language of which we have kept about a thousand words that are still understood along the Volga and on the banks of the Pechora, even beyond the Urals . . . The world has very few nations that have been settled in one place for such a length of time, who have remained true to their habitat . . . There weren't many of us, about two thousand souls in all."

But he admits he doesn't remember all of them.

"Even so, we weren't the first people to come to these shores. Who came before? Maybe the Basques. Don't know, don't remember."

But he says that our arrival from the East contributed something to Europe. Namely:

"Occidental culture is especially heterogeneous and that has been, right up to the present, the motor driving science and technological development. By way of our language, we have deepened the dualism of European culture and added something of significance. Maybe the silence of the forest? The restless suspicion that in the full moon the woods become transparent?"

I took off my shoes.

There was an unfamiliar old woman sitting there in the room, and I mean an old *woman*, not an old lady.

I cautiously introduced myself and quietly pulled a chair over from the wall to the bookshelves.

Lennart came in from the kitchen with the coffee. He moved freely, lightly about the room, which was natural, as this was his own home. I noticed that the old woman followed Lennart's every movement out of the corner of her eye, but those eyes, set deep in their orbits, did not express anything in particular. I continued to peer at her. She really could have belonged to whatever tribe you like, but one thing was sure: she wasn't here purely by chance. When things turn out like this, there has to be a good reason for it. A witch, I decided, and linked her presence with Lennart's interest in shamans. But a witch, not a shaman. Although she hadn't said anything yet, I took her for an Estonian, and was rather surprised that Lennart didn't speak to her. A man who was so used to meeting people on his many travels. He has even mentioned that you can get a train to travel faster if you climb up into the engineer's cab and, apropos of nothing, when traveling through, for instance, the Rhine Valley, ask: "*Sind Sie glücklich?*" or say: "*Ich möchte gern etwas über Ihre Arbeit erfahren!*"

The old woman helped herself to sugar, but continued to maintain her stony silence.

It was hard to determine whether my arrival had interrupted their conversation or whether they had never started talking in the first place—or even that they had exhausted the topic. Lennart looked me in the eye, which could be interpreted in several ways. Perhaps he was trying to say: things'll soon get more exciting, but also: she'll be going soon.

But outside: still the same light, the sunshine, as if there wasn't an old crone in black sitting in a dark corner of the room! And the time: still so early, only seven!

Lennart struck up a conversation with me, and I replied. The old woman didn't appear to feel left out. Her head turned as did her eyes, like those of a cat. When Lennart was speaking she watched him, when I spoke, she watched me. Lennart initially spoke about the weather, but the topic didn't sound at all banal when coming from his lips. He showed me an aerial photo of a major typhoon and put his finger on the eye of the storm. I asked him whether it was true that in the eye itself there would be no wind, though there were waves the height of houses, and that the sun would be shining.

"Well, I haven't actually been in one, you know . . ." he said very simply, "but a friend of mine has, and he said that you can see the sun and the stars at one and the same time. They did not affect one other."

I looked at the patterns of cyclone and anticyclone, which rather reminded you of celestial bodies, collections of mists and spiral galaxies but, nearer the ground, mineral ornaments, sometimes marble, sometimes malachite, sometimes the iris of the human eye.

Lennart stroked the thick, shiny paper gently with the palm of his hand and looked at me quizzically. Under the steady gaze of the old woman, I too placed my palm on the paper. I shut my eyes. Yes, its surface was absolutely smooth. Suddenly, I thought that my fingers had detected the whorl of the cyclones. I started moving my fingertips in a spiral until I arrived at the eye of the storm where the sun was shining. I opened my eyes. I had not been mistaken. Lennart laughed in a friendly way. He wasn't surprised. He poured me some coffee. Patted me on the shoulder. But he was looking at the old woman. She had begun to get up with a sigh, she straightened up and left the room, her skirt rustling as she did so. The door fell shut. I looked Lennart straight in the face, perhaps you could call it an enquiring look, and Lennart understood immediately.

"Listen," he said, "I know as little about her as you do. There are things you never get a grip on."

"But . . . ?"

"I, of course, know her name, but it doesn't tell me anything. Yes . . . Maybe I'm not entirely happy with her visits, but in the end . . . these too offer the opportunity . . . of, let's say, acquainting oneself with a mentality you wouldn't find so available, otherwise . . ."

There was something odd lurking in Lennart's voice. And what was even odder: his gaze became steely. And I began to feel slightly uneasy.

At that moment the toilet was flushed. Then, the door closed again and the rustle of a skirt could be heard once more. When the old woman appeared in the doorway, I asked, as indifferently as I could:

"Will there be any mushrooms this year?"

Now the old crone smiled for the first time. She walked nimbly across the room, sat down in the same chair and beckoned to me. I looked at Lennart, to see whether I could find encouragement in his expression. I did as the old crone indicated. Now I was seated right next to her. I examined her face, but avoided her eyes. Afterwards I realized what I had been looking for. I had actually had the subconscious suspicion the whole time that I was dealing with an actress. I now realized that a couple of names even raced through my mind. I had been trying to guess whether the lines on her face were make-up or not. A wig or her own hair? You can expect anything from Lennart. Summer, the silly season, people play all sorts of practical jokes. They get up to pranks, out of sheer boredom, or want to spice up their lives a bit. Or are seeking new knowledge for the coming winter.

I looked into her round, yellowish eyes.

No reply, but I jumped when from behind me, Lennart said:

"*De tuderibus haec traduntur pecualiter*: *cum fuerint imbres autumnales, ac tonitrus crebra, tunc nasci, et maxime e tonitribus.*"

The old woman burst out laughing, her toothless mouth wide open. How did she relate to Pliny? With familiarity? Contemptuously? Sympathetically? I really didn't know!

Still laughing, she got up and went out into the hallway.

Lennart made an apologetic gesture in my direction and followed.

They stayed away for about five minutes. I thought I heard indistinct snatches of conversation, but I didn't dare approach the door. Then I heard footsteps, a door opening and closing. I went over to the window, but there was no one outside. Time passed. I began to get bored, so I wrote a poem on Lennart's typewriter.

POEM

I take hold of the flashgun and take a picture.
The woman is holding lilies, the man poppies.
They are friends.
Photos of them will remain.

In Tartu, on Cathedral Hill there is real thunder,
real lightning.
Also on Kastan Street
there's a terrible sight:
the wind has crossed electric wires,
a house is on fire
burning like a sparkler.
The employees at the pharmacy for venereal diseases
watch the globe lightning
from the yard.
Nobody is photographing anything.

In that light, this springs to mind:
Buddha once visited

the Lao Chun monastery
on Lugh mountain.
The old priest
had a cat with yellow eyes.
Sinh was his name.
With the cat's help
he would look into the future.
When the old priest died,
Buddha ordered
his soul
to enter
the cat.
Sinh's eyes changed to blue,
his tail and paws brown.

The thunderstorm is nearly over.
The woman with the lilies, the man with the poppies.
They remain friends.
Lennart is coming.

Lennart entered the room.

He was exceptionally considerate, as though he wanted to apologize for something. He sat down facing me, looked at me smiling broadly, and asked:

"Well, how did it go with those mushrooms?"

We presented our findings as if at a *viva voce*.

Lennart mentioned the fact that Sapotek shamans prayed to their gods for a good mushroom harvest on the fourth day after returning from their mushroom-picking expedition. This was, of course, the day devoted to the god of thunder, Thor (*Donnerstag*).

I mentioned the works of R. G. Wasson.

That author says that when it thunders in France, people have the habit of saying: *voilà, un bon temps pour les truffles*. I pronounce French badly and at first Lennart didn't understand what I was trying to say. I then repeated the phrase, pronouncing it "as it is written." Now Lennart understood and nodded: *oui*. Then he moved on to an even more risky subject. In Tajikistan, to the south of Samarkand, after a thunderstorm, small Tajik children would start dancing and shouting: *puri, puri, xorf!* (*puri* = flower, *xorf* = mushroom). But in the Yagnob Valley the same small Tajik children would shout in a similar situation: *katta xarcak man, pullja xarcak tau* (the big fly agaric is mine, the small one yours). I couldn't judge how good Lennart's pronunciation was. He even added a translation, which I welcomed, and I didn't bother asking him what language it was. Out of sheer satanic spite I punctuated our little colloquium with the Maori expression *whatitiri* (mushroom and thunderstorm). Neither of us had anything more to say on that occasion, I mean as regards mushrooms and thunderstorms.

The whole time I had the odd feeling that the old woman hadn't actually left. During our conversation I eased the partition door open a couple of times and peeped into the adjoining room. Of course, there was no one there.

Now I felt that enough was enough.

My heart was pounding and I was sweating, even though Lennart's room was pleasantly cool.

Why not express my worries to a man who had climbed up to the highest mountain monasteries in Tibet and descended the craters of volcanoes in Kamchatka?

I approached the subject in a roundabout way. I said that I had heard about the build-up of krypton in the atmosphere and its effect on the balance of thunderstorms throughout the globe. I asked what he thought of lightning.

Lennart said that in Ancient China there were heavenly ministries and some of these were parallel to ones on Earth. So there were ministries of, for instance, Fire, Water, Time, the Five Sacred Mountains, War, Finance, Public Works, Literature, Medicine, Exorcism of Demons, and Thunderstorms. The last of these had five gods. The greatest of these was Lei Tsu, "the patriarch of thunderstorms," a giant with three glittering eyes whose gaze could destroy, and who rode on a black unicorn. The others were the god of thunderstorms Lei Kung, the lightning queen Djan Mu, the god of wind Fen Bo and the god of rain Yui Shi. The last of these usually sat on a cloud or on the back of a dragon and held a vessel containing the rain. Djan Mu nestled amongst the clouds wearing flowery clothing, a mirror in each hand. Lightning was produced when the male and female spirits (the *yin* and the *yang*) collided and this encounter thus reverberated. But there were other sources where Lei Kung was described as one of eighty people working at the Ministry of Rain. Lei Kung had an eagle's beak, the head of an ape, the claws of a bird and held a hammer.

Lennart sat there for a while in silence. The setting sun shone on the books behind his back. The spines of the volumes of the Brockhaus encyclopedia glimmered in faded gold.

"The Bushmen believe that if virgins are struck by lightning outside their settlements they will be turned into stars," I tried timidly to interpose.

Lennart nodded vaguely. Maybe he'd seen such things himself during his travels, but as a man who loved precision, he didn't want to attach any importance to his own subjective impressions. He continued:

"In the Philippines, there were said to be a number of jealous women that once tormented a married couple. For instance, they put the stinking corpse of a goat under the house. After putting up with this for a long time, the couple decided to go up to heaven. They started off but the woman soon got tired and couldn't go on. The man and woman started to quarrel. The man wanted to press on, the woman didn't. I forgot to mention that they had a child. During the quarrel, they ripped the child in half. The man made lightning out of the one half. The woman began to cry. The man took pity on her. In order to console the woman somewhat, he turned the other half into thunder. People have come up with all sorts of psychological explanations for this story, which is just what you shouldn't do. In fact, we see something similar in what Adam and Eve did, which of course occurred when Lilith had already left paradise. By the way, the Indians of Oregon believe that thunder is a man, lightning a woman. In ancient times, the Chinese believed, something else I've forgotten to tell you, that it was the task of the goddess of lightning to accompany the god of thunder in order to prevent the latter from getting up to all kinds of mischief. The one is turned into two . . . Well, that's common in our lives too."

Lennart broke a pencil in half and handed the two pieces to me, his eyes glittering. Understanding what he was getting at, I pushed the two pieces hard against one another. For only a moment, the pencil remained whole. All I needed to do was hand it to Lennart for one half to clatter down onto the table.

"Which also had to be demonstrated," said Lennart.

I looked at him and asked casually:

"Where did she go?"

Lennart kept looking at me in silence for some time, weighing the pros and cons. Then I saw that he had decided that I would understand, so he decided to tell the truth, but only within the bounds of my question.

"She's resting in the bedroom," he said gravely.

"Long journey, eh?"

Lennart nodded and I could see from his face that he would

be happier if I didn't ask him for any more details.

"You know, I too have this feeling," I explained, "that I've been on a journey for months, rather than just having gone out to pick a few mushrooms."

He nodded.

"There are long, endless processes, like that over there, which have lasted for hundreds of years, if you can speak in their case of anything lasting." He pointed to a brass Shiva who was in permanent sexual union with a woman on the mantelpiece, his extra arms outstretched above his head.

He looked at his watch.

"I arrived here unannounced," I said, "and I didn't think of calling. Or rather, I was walking through the woods, and where in the woods would you come across a telephone booth?"

Lennart nodded.

"Console yourself with the fact that the heart of the world, its core, speaks straight to us, not via wires."

"For instance?"

Lennart gestured to outside the window.

"Look. Can you see how the leaves are turning yellow? Why are they doing so, so early? It's only early September. Maybe the world is trying to tell us something."

He looked again at his watch.

I got up from my seat.

At that moment, the telephone rang.

Lennart picked up the receiver and listened attentively.

He put his burning cigarette on the edge of the ashtray and his eyes wandered up to the sky.

"*Speak louder, please. Spell it, please. Yes, indeed. Hold the line, please.*"

He picked up his cigarette, drew on it eagerly and replaced it where it had been perching.

"*Good morning! Yes . . . Cape Canaveral? I'm so glad to hear you! How do you do? Yes . . . Allow me to congratulate you on your success . . . Yes . . . How did you make your exit from the spaceship? Fine . . . fine . . . Good for you! Did anything unforeseen happen during the landing? Oh, good!*"

I went into the corridor out of a sense of politeness, under the large glass window in the hall. Now I could only hear snatches: *long, hot summer phenomenon . . . yes, purely somatic . . . climatic pulse . . . surrounding winds . . . ecumenical understanding . . . at odd moments . . . including the asteroids . . .*

There was a steady breeze in the treetops, but on ground level, not a leaf stirred.

Of course I understood that nothing would ever be the same again. Everything is necessary for something, and something is happening somewhere all the time. A friend of mine thinks that the ground under his feet is constantly being analyzed, or at least preparations are being made for doing so. Some continents rise from the sea and polar ice is melting to an ever-greater extent, threatening to drown coastal countries—such as Estonia—solving our problems as a nation once and for all. There are married couples who grow estranged without noticing it and one day suddenly realize that they no longer have anything in common. I understood that Lennart was working for the good of future generations and wasn't just killing time like I was, someone who had for a while now neither managed to do anything good or anything bad for this Earth.

I looked for my shoes in the hall and Lennart switched on the light. I crouched down to tie my shoelaces. Lennart was standing over me and looking at me with a strange little smile. He raised his hand, pointed at the sun lamp and whispered conspiratorially:

"There's krypton in that."

Then he smiled, baring his teeth.

At that moment, the telephone rang.

Lennart went quickly into the next room.

I listened as he said:

"Hallo! *Eto Baikonur? Sem-sem-sem-vosemnadset-tri-nol-shest?*"

I hurried out through the door and tiptoed down the steps.

I went outside and waved to Lennart who was looking at me through the window, telephone receiver in hand. He was talking, but I couldn't hear and Lennart obviously didn't think it important that I heard. I went out onto the street, not onto the main road, but into the bushes behind the house.

I sat down on a broken wooden crate and kept an eye on Lennart's house. What was I actually expecting to happen? I wasn't trying to spy on anyone. I was simply envious of the fact that here something was happening, and longed to be part of it. How could anything important happen without me?

A long day, devoid of mushrooms, the woods where nothing happened, getting lost, which wasn't in fact lost, but which brought me here—could it really end so uneventfully? Even in the pale autumn sky there wasn't a single cloud. The sky was entirely transparent, but I could see nothing at all beyond it. It wasn't thinking anything, though the promise was there.

A yellow birch leaf fluttered down past me.

More and more mosquitoes were gleefully discovering my hideout. I sat there and was becoming their dinner, like some Russian language teacher. That mental association came quite unexpectedly. When in the eighth grade, I took part in a cross-country map-reading exercise. We were taken out of town, to somewhere near the shores of Lake Mustjärv, I think it was. There are lots of lakes like that in Estonia. One of those, anyway. As I was following the route on the map I discovered my Russian teacher sitting in the evening woods at one of the checkpoints. I ran past her and didn't dare look straight at her, because she was so beautiful. There were mosquitoes swarming around her. These were, of course, classical mosquitoes, from the idyll of the 1950s, *Aedes communis*, which tormented walkers and political activists at sunset alike, and got under the headmaster's shirt during collective labor in the woods. In those days, we didn't yet have *Culex pipiens molestus* in our country. In a 1967 issue of the Estonian nature magazine *Eesti Loodus* it was stated that "people have noticed the advance of these creatures into Estonian territory." They arrived in urban areas a couple of years ago. Now they are common in the towns. They fly around in the darkness, and as soon as you switch on the light they vanish. They breed in stagnant water and even in flower vases. They make their nests in the warm cellar of new houses, because they originally come from Mediterranean countries. They can transmit diseases such as yellow fever and malaria, soon they'll be carrying AIDS. But this species is, after all, relatively small and harmless. I've read that in the northern parts of Canada mosquitoes can attack with a virulence of 9,000 bites a minute, and a person can therefore lose half his blood in two hours. They cover the sky and blot out the sun. I now saw how one of billions was sucking my blood. How natural it was and how independent, as if it even had free will. I knew that it would reproduce with that stock of blood, laying several hundred eggs right in Lennart's cellar, where it was warm and peaceful. But those eggs could also come to nothing: Remy Chauvin writes that one dangerous species of fly was exterminated recently by sterilizing a large number of males with radiation, which were then released into the population of fertile females. As the female only mated once, their chances of meeting a fertile male grew smaller and smaller and in the end the species died out. We in Estonia have lost our dung beetles. Just after the war there were many of them. In the glow of the evening sun they would rise in a cloud above the village street if you so much as stretched out your hand, and then would vanish. Now they are extinct, thanks to someone they met on the way. That was what I was thinking about there by the wall of the shed, among the nettles, until the mosquito rose into the air, carrying three times its weight in blood.

Then I heard the sound of a car. I hid behind the shed, among the nettles. I was now concealed, but could see everything.

A dark limousine stopped in front of the house.

I couldn't believe my eyes: two old women in black emerged who were as like as two peas to the one who had gone the long way to take a rest in Lennart's bedroom, at least according to what he said.

They went straight into the house. From what I could see, Lennart did not come to the door to meet them. The house swallowed the old women up and I could have imagined it had all been an hallucination, if the large shiny car hadn't been standing there in the yard, and you could see the driver's silhouette vaguely through the windshield, though you couldn't make out his face.

Silence from the house. Then there were voices, but that could have been the radio. I didn't dare to light up a cigarette, afraid that the smell might betray me, especially since there was no breeze and the smoke would not dissipate quickly.

Clearly, I was not going to be let in on the secret.

Nevertheless, I stayed put. I have sat outside many doors like this, in the hope of being invited inside. My friends never did invite me in. If you go in unexpectedly, you leave a proud man. I always hoped for something. That a miracle would happen. A very rare occurrence. Actually, I'm exaggerating, I don't think it even happened once. The status of those going in and coming out is strictly determined. The longer I waited, the smaller the chance would be to go in or leave, because I had in fact made a fool of myself, proving that I wasn't good for either, that my place was somewhere on the boundary between going in and coming out.

I set myself an ultimatum: I would count up to one hundred and if nothing happened I would walk away. I didn't count the seconds, I tried to count more slowly. I remember that at forty-three another yellow leaf fluttered down past me. And that was all.

Then I said "hundred" and started making my way to the bus stop.

When I was already on my way and had disappeared round the corner from Lennart's house, a car rounded a bend in the road.

I thought that there was an old woman in black sitting next to the driver.

I waited and heard the sound of a car door slamming a few moments later.

I began running, as if I were late for something.

⁓⁓

There was no line of taxis!

It was people who were standing in line.

Waiting for taxis.

This would be impossible to explain were it not an everyday occurrence.

It took ages to get to the front of the line.

During that time, lots of things happened.

Who can be bothered describing them?

Who would bother to read such a description?

For instance:

"Around five o'clock, Peeter arrived at the taxi rank under the soughing of the lime trees, in the August evening. He was twentieth in the line, but there were even people waiting behind him, another twenty or so. A drunk was pestering everyone else with his babblings . . ."

Just like me now.

Nevertheless:

There has to be life in a novel. Key scenes writ large and grotesque dreams should alternate with lighter city scenes. This is termed "the atmosphere" of the novel. You soon get bored with too dense a text and begin to read diagonally. You have to give the reader a chance to breathe and the description of a taxi line (again!) gives you a chance to do so. What someone was like and what he did.

And yet:

I can't be bothered doing the description. So you could use an old painter's technique. They had studios in those days where younger colleagues would help the tired old master with some of the easier tasks. Painting the ground on the canvas, arranging the legs of a puppy to be painted, straightening the medals on a chest.

Or you could have written this:

"Peeter stood in the taxi line and shifted his weight lazily from foot to foot. He was in the grip of a strange restlessness . . . He wished he were already on his way . . . on the pavement, pigeons were bobbing around. Peeter watched the pigeons. He didn't like that species of bird. A grayish-yellow kind of memory was associated with them, but he couldn't really say what precisely it was. A young woman arrived with an infant. Peeter knew that the young mother had a right to jump ahead in the line, but at the same time he knew . . ."

Yes, but sometimes taxi lines can get very long, giving the impression that they are presaging something, yet don't actually, or if they do, then the event will happen privately or somewhere else: Elton John appearing at the Linnahall Concert Hall, cheese being on sale in the suburb of Mustamäe, fish being caught on the shore at Pirita.

You stand there just as if you are standing inside a glass cupola in which there is a vacuum. There are such dead points the world over, islands where time stops, whether this be Böcklin's or in the desert of the Tatars. I have seen pictures of inflated plastic bags that amidst the din of the highway give rise to an avant-garde privacy; I have seen pictures of cocaine addicts and of Vladimir and Estragon in an open space. The line manages to nudge its way forward. We have an excuse for getting home late, being late for work, for a party, for a restaurant, for the countryside, for the gambling den. No problem: a line is a line, life is life. The worst that can happen to you is getting someone's warm breath down your neck along with the question: have you got the time?

The taxi driver was a man my age, wearing yellow trousers, with a filter cigarette between his lips.

What more is there to add? Maybe that his cigarette was smoked to the stub and that he kept his yellow trousers on.

No.

The only thing that interests us is the taxi driver's story.

And this is what he said:

"Things have got to the stage where my ex-wife is taking me to court. We got divorced about six months ago, but haven't managed to move out of our apartment yet and we still live together, though in separate rooms. But she is trying to get rid of me in any way she can. So now she's taking me to court, because when I come out of the bathroom the flaps of my dressing gown are open. They want to charge me with immoral behavior. I don't think anything shows, but it could, as our dressing gowns don't have any buttons, so the two parts are crossed over with just a belt to tie up the garment with, so it's no wonder that accidents happen. But none of that counts, because if she complains that I'm showing something, then I haven't got a leg to stand on, because I have no witnesses, and she definitely wants to throw me out, and one of these days she'll succeed, what with all the slander she comes up with."

There was nothing I could say to that immediately.

In the end, I thought that it would be best to counter his story with one of my own, something I'd heard recently from a lawyer friend of mine.

I said:

"A family was living in a building where several families lived in separate apartments but shared a communal kitchen. They had taken it into their heads to drive their neighbor out of the house. They had a bathroom with the toilet in the same room. Our family thought up a wily plan, which it also carried out. It was this. One morning, the wife started doing the washing in the bathroom. It was a Sunday. She did the washing very slowly, the whole day long. Around lunchtime or just after, the neighbor asked to go to the toilet. The woman said, just wait a bit, I've got to finish my washing. She spun this out for several hours, even keeping the door latched. At about four, the woman casually unlatched the door and came into the kitchen. The neighbor stormed into the bathroom, pulled down his trousers and sat on the pot. At that point, witnesses who had been lying in ambush in the adjoining rooms emerged. They saw the man sitting there and heard the woman's cries for help. The neighbor was charged with insulting and offensive behavior and was sentenced to being thrown out of the communal apartment and never to be allowed back."

We drove past the theater.

I said to myself, not to the taxi driver:

Ah, the theater! It's right here that the audience is offered concepts that are gladly accepted. A concept means that art or its maker has an idea that he wants to share with us. For instance, in this theater I have been confronted with various thoughts: love is better than hatred, peace is better than war, truth is better than lies, nature conservation is better than pollution, an infant is better than an atom bomb, beauty is better than ugliness. I don't remember hearing on stage: kill! burn! hang! corrupt yourself!

be a villain! I love artists because they are good and human. It's part of their nature.

At this theater, they had recently been staging *Electra*. I remembered this, it might come in handy for something.

The taxi driver now explained that he had to make a detour. Why he had to do so I couldn't quite understand, who's forcing you and does it pay to give in to all kinds of compulsions? Is it democracy when you can't go the way you want to, the way you're used to? Let's drive straight there!

But the taxi driver replied that there were road repairs and we wouldn't get through with the best will in the world.

I shrugged my shoulders.

The sun was beginning to set behind the trees, the autumn shadows, yes, let's call them autumn shadows, were long and cool. We entered a slum district and you could smell fading and withering. The potato patch wasn't very far away, not that it affected me directly, children were coming from school, although my schools had long been closed down.

"Look," said the taxi driver.

We came to an involuntary stop because something was happening in front of us. Militiamen were dragging a man out of a wooden house. A crowd of bystanders had gathered outside. The taxi driver stuck his head out of the window of the cab and asked what was going on. Some children answered that they had caught a cannibal. Oh ho, replied the taxi driver. I asked him to pull up. He did so and I got out. The taxi driver went and had a smoke with some of the men and enquired about details.

It emerged that the arrest of the cannibal had been expected for some time. They had been keeping an eye on the house for several days. Someone had been peering through binoculars from over there the man said, casually pointing, for several hours at a stretch, perhaps they were waiting till he did something so they could catch him red-handed, because without proof and witnesses they didn't stand a chance in court. A detective waited there for two hours, another bystander explained, then he was replaced, another detective came to take over and at least another hour passed. The cannibal was now standing on the pavement and two men were holding him, one on each side. I asked what they were waiting for. The amiable bystander said that they were doing a house search that had no doubt been completed by now, and they were perhaps putting a seal on the door. I couldn't understand why the cannibal had to stand on the pavement in full view of everybody. He looked around fearfully. Like a wild animal that had been trapped was the insensitive comparison that sprung to mind. An animal is never guilty, never, how often do I have to repeat that, but at the time I had no one to repeat it to. I was standing in a growing crowd of people and saying to myself: come on, now it's your turn to do something. Go and defend the cannibal. You've always maintained that you support minorities, small nations, feminists, madmen, poets, homosexuals, dwarves, cats, nudists. You've always stated that everything big is anathema to you: big languages, big factories, big breasts, big countries. Schumacher's book *Small Is Beautiful* has had a great influence on you. And now here you are standing before a real minority—a cannibal. There really are very few of them. You rarely meet them on the street. This one's an exception. But his pathos is infectious. He has eaten people, beings who, to tell you the truth, I don't like very much. He has tried to reduce the species. The number he ate is not important. How many would he have been able to eat? And yet he represents a tendency. He shows that mankind is rotten inside. Foul, consuming itself; is not such a conclusion justified?

In the growing dusk, the approaching autumn, the cannibal between the militiamen.

A frightening, sad demonstration of repression, of an undemocratic society.

Let's put it this way: by arresting a cannibal, a society eats its own children.

We could put it like that because, although I don't actually share their radicalism, I have to admit that there is a grain of truth in their claims.

We inevitably start defending all sorts of minorities, all kinds of beings in danger of extinction.

Let us give him our flesh, for he hungers; let us give him our blood, for he thirsts; let us give him our skin, for he is naked; let us give him our bones as fuel, for he is cold.

Let us not keep anything for ourselves.

Let there be no more of us, nor anything else.

Expansion and development are becoming synonymous with perdition.

The fact that it is principally totalitarian régimes that promote physical prowess is no longer a secret to anyone.

And the temperance movement?

Undemocratic countries have always tried to prohibit their citizens from destroying themselves.

People are looked upon solely as economic resources.

People only take an interest in human language to the degree that it is necessary to work on the factory floor.

It is thought that people who understand one another's languages produce more and derive greater pleasure from doing so, in a word, by understanding one another they increase the speed of exhaustion of the Earth's natural resources.

And now it is evening, autumn has arrived, and the cannibal is standing there between two militiamen.

Let him go, comrades, and let him start to eat us up.

Let him find disciples, one crazier than the next, their fangs bared, their beards unshaven.

I read in the paper today that the government has announced that it has decided to start combating disease.

Who is the government trying to tell this to?

We should not utter the government's name in vain.

In the evening, in the darkness, in autumn, as I have already said several times.

In the slum, among the wooden houses, in the clear air growing chilly.

On Yablochkov Street.

The wind was making the metal stop sign above my head clatter. In the dust sat a huge fluffy cat, while another one was looking down at it from an upstairs window.

Right in front of me was a long plank fence behind which were cherry trees growing wild.

The streets had such funny names: Granite Street, Boulder Street, Brass Street, Hay Street, Grass Street, Bread Street, Bowl Street, Salt Street.

And among all these Yablochkov Street!

What do I remember about Yablochkov?

Yablochkov stood on the platform of the locomotive. In his hand a lantern was burning. Inside was a "Yablochkov candle." Two blocks of carbon burning in the electrical arc linking them. But they were never consumed. Both were coated with kaolin.

This coating gradually melted away. Yablochkov shielded his face from the biting wind with the collar of his half-length fur coat. The fire and the frost made his eyes water, but his gaze was focused and alert, his face grim. Yablochkov announced that in the future Edison would appear, and his filament lamp would push aside the Yablochkov candle. But there was still some time to go. First he would have time to conquer Europe and Asia. Yablochkov did not know what would occur in the coming seconds, but more or less knew the vague outlines of his destiny. And without foreseeing his own death from dropsy, he was surprised at a hare on the rails whose ears had been pushed flat against his head by panic, whereupon Yablochkov *"guffawed so that his beard shook, opening his large mouth with its white teeth."* Yablochkov thought that technical progress would bring mankind happiness.

Let's leave Yablochkov to Yablochkov, because just then my eyes turned to the cannibal and he began to talk uninhibitedly, and no one could stop him.

"I simply wanted to develop," said the cannibal, "wanted to understand more about myself and the world around me. It was horrible to think that this damned life and this cosmos would remain incomprehensible to me. I just couldn't cope with the thought. But fate came to my aid. I grew up in the country and my parents, simple people, kept pigs. We ate the meat from the pigs we'd raised, fresh from the slaughter, but also later on when it had been salted down. Of course, we didn't throw away the byproducts either. Our farm worked on the barter principle, and we had to make good use of everything. For instance, we boiled soup from the innards, the bones were given to the dogs, then to the children as humming-tops—if only you men would remember how they used to hum. Shall I stick to the byproducts? Tongue with peas, kidney sauce, that sort of thing? We of course didn't even throw away the brain. We simply braised it, so there you are. I only learned later on how you were supposed to serve up brains. The Yugoslavs, for instance, would stuff kohlrabi with brains. The brains were mixed with parsley and egg and stuffed into a hollowed out kohlrabi. Then it was of course put in the oven and served with smetana. I've eaten it when I was still working as a stagehand in the theater and I was taken along to the Shibenik Festival. Oh, I could give you loads of recipes: roast brains with spinach, brains fried in lots of lard, and so on and so forth, recipes I've only learned of just recently. But there's a secret to it all. Brains have to be eaten fresh. Then they have their effect. I don't suppose you've eaten brains? I mean those of an animal. They lie there warm in the skull, you feel a slight urge . . . Makes you hungry for a woman . . . By the way, I read the other day that in Southeast Asia they eat a monkey's brain. It's recommended you remove the scalp while the monkey is still alive and eat the brains with a spoon. That is the custom among refined people. What are you looking at me for? I've justified all of this and I have powerful sympathizers, for instance the Hungarian, Oscar Kiss Maerth. How do people become so wise and cruel? Where does this evolutionary upheaval come from? Why did *Homo sapiens* arise in the first place, why did he descend from the trees? Where did he get his reason from? Perhaps from eating the brains of his own species. Where did that start? Don't ask me, maybe by accident. One fine day. But that's how it went. We ate brains and we started to get to know nature's secrets. We were no longer just a meaningless speck of dust blown by the winds of the universe. We ate brains and began to control our own destiny. I'm saying all this, all you have to do is listen. It was by eating brains—which could, by the way, have started from some superstition about eating your enemy's brains and getting your strength up from doing so—by eating brains we began to become rulers of nature. We fashioned tools, soon cities arose and fields of crops sprang up. By the way, since, as I have already said, brains are a powerful aphrodisiac, then this would explain man's inordinate interest in sex in times when it isn't important for purposes of reproduction. But the story is all nonsense. Would you gentlemen be kind enough to tell me what I should expect?"

The uninhibited exhibitionism of the cannibal had made us grow anxious, even me, who always tried to be understanding about everything. His frankness rendered any character analysis impossible. I no longer understood whether it was he who was speaking, or me. The growing dusk favored the delinquent who was wavering between the pride of self-revelation and a dog-like subservience.

The middle-aged sergeant twirled his moustache, coughed and said:

"I would imagine that they'll give you the maximum sentence that our society stipulates."

The cannibal looked him straight in the eye.

"And that makes you happy, does it? Maybe your great-great-great-great-grandfather ate my great-great-great-great-grandfather. Huh?"

The militiaman spat.

"*Poekhali*," he yelled decisively.

The cannibal's hands were tied behind his back and he was led off to a waiting vehicle.

I could see that he was trying to wave in the direction of the first floor, where pale faces could be seen. Family? Victims?

Children? All of the above?

The cannibal was pushed into the vehicle and the doors slammed shut.

The vehicle took off.

Did time stop?

Again?

Several times today or over the past year?

Did the rowans become redder or more bitter during that monologue?

"What a fucker," said the taxi driver.

I was obliged to agree.

Our taxi rushed off into the sunset.

Exactly, our taxi rushed off into the sunset, past the old graveyard, rushed and rushed, I mean to say not literally into the sun, only in the direction of the sun, but that's how you say it, rushed off into the sunset, and in that low yellow light my role was to use every moment, register everything that I saw, to be open to impressions, and first of all I can say that I had got the impression that hairs were protruding from the cannibal's nostrils, but this didn't seem in any way disgusting, I could even confirm now that the cannibal was a good-looking guy or at least manly, and that was logical, because only a real man would be so fastidious about what he ate with such an inexhaustible appetite. I know a thing or two about cannibals. In that field there were lots of taboos. Some you could eat, others not. For instance, in an exogamous marriage, the husband was free to eat his wife, because the wife's totem was different from his own. The woman was still an outsider, so it was quite OK to sink your teeth into her. But try eating your own mother, your own flesh and blood, and you would never be forgiven. Nevertheless, we eat what we love and haven't we sometimes been tempted to bite the throat of the woman we love? Don't we prefer marbled lean meat to always eating pale fat? True, but I was quite excited at the time. I would be lying if I were to say that I am internally free like some unattached lover or some group-therapy enthusiast. In fact, the situation was rather piquant. When taking a good look at the cannibal, the sharp nose, which seemed to have evolved for purposes of sniffing, I remembered Kaplinski's recent claim that cannibalism is in fact the invention of white colonizers. He based this on what some ethnographer called Ahrens had claimed. It was said to be a way used by the conquerors to vilify the aborigines, to place them beyond culture and compromise them. I can believe in all kinds of nastiness perpetrated by Whites, can believe in their attempts to compromise people. But I too believe in the cannibal. Why shouldn't you be able to eat people? We've all eaten pork. It is said that pigs are vicious and stupid, especially those you find in Tibet, if you really can call them pigs, and it is said that pigs themselves are cannibals. And they are too. Yes, I really mean it, pigs are cruel, can be measured by the same yardstick. I remember that the pigs didn't want to die, especially on days when the class struggle was intensified, or when November mornings were dark or never really got light, then it would take a very long time to kill a pig. This was caused by incompetence, as far as I could tell. I couldn't detect any sadism in the postwar generation of farmers, trained back in bourgeois Estonian times, nor can I now, though there were excellent opportunities for them to be sadistic, had they wanted to. Meanwhile, the pig would be shrieking for almost a quarter of an hour, most of this time taken up with dragging the pig outside, getting it out of the yard. They were admittedly pretty indiscriminate with regard to this animal that was, after all, condemned to death by now, while the pig itself clearly felt the fear of death or something of the sort. There is something of a paradox in this, because if the pig really had felt a fear of death, it would also have been able to sense that it was being raised only to be slaughtered for food. The pigs' collective unconscious would have understood: there are lots of us, we are born one after the other, we are fattened and then are eaten up. But does such knowledge make an animal any more stoical? I can't tell, a pig's eyes really are very small and it is hard to read anything into them. Tiny eyes under fair eyelashes. I sometimes went to look at the pigs when they were hanging in the shed; they all glowed there in their individual way (why do I need plurality here?)—glowed there in the darkness and hung there alone, while in the same room men were drinking moonshine and discussing how the farms were being turned into kolkhozes, with no one against the plan, and how indeed could you be against collectivization when the government had wanted only to do good for the past several hundred years. I looked through the door of the shed and I can't say I would have felt sorry for the carcasses. Nor now, for that matter. Pigs are cannibals: they eat their own piglets like the Revolution or Saturn eat theirs, sometimes a pig will eat up its whole litter, eat them up like potato chips, as my mother would say, or so that only one survives. Yes, one survives and that one is taken indoors and allowed to live. Until it too died one evening, no doubt because of the way it is living.

Let's leave pigs where they are, but I had forgotten by then that I was still in the taxi rushing into the sunset, and then passing the old graveyard. Do you understand now where I was and what I was doing? I didn't myself. Still don't.

That whole day, so strange!

So incomprehensible!
But I did say it was autumn! Darling, I really did!
With the car rushing on!
The main thing was to get home!

The encounter with the cannibal could also have ended differently, and this is the easiest thing in the world to imagine:

The militiamen
are relaxing at home, far from here, lying on the couch,
sipping tea, water, and beer.
The first platform of the train
is empty.
Kaolin remains
what it is.
A hare disappears between the snowdrifts,
merges with the white.
Yablochkov
shuts his large mouth
with the strong white teeth.
The cannibal's window reflects the sunset.
The room is empty,
the flowers unwatered.
A cockroach wiggles its moustaches.
Between the covers of a book, in the Court of King Arthur,
a few meters or so away,

behind the round table
several empty chairs
remain empty for ever.

When I reached my door, I remembered what had happened the previous Saturday:

The evening before, I had disconnected the doorbell, just like that, I didn't want to be disturbed. In fact, I could no longer stand any kind of sudden, unexpected rings, the type you have to react to within a second. Natural bells are much gentler. From an hourglass, you can see that half your time is up. The sun never sets suddenly. But an electric bell sounds as if war has broken out, even when it makes its presence known by way of some melodic chimes. Anyway, I had wanted peace and quiet. But I now felt that enough was enough. The whole day before me, one great big tabula rasa.

I reconnected the doorbell.

It rang immediately!

I was nailed to the spot, my hair stood on end.

The ringing didn't stop.

It rang and rang.

This just wasn't natural. What did he want? But I thought that anyone could ring like that if he wanted to find out if there was anyone at home. In the end, even someone asleep would be roused by such interminable ringing.

I wavered and wavered, but finally opened the door.

As I had predicted, there was no one there. The doorbell had got stuck. I poked it out and the ringing stopped. That meant that somebody had been there in the meantime, during the evening or the night, or even just a few moments ago. And had pressed on the button quite forcefully, some child or could it even have been a giant?

I closed the door.

Now I rang the bell myself, as if to tempt fate.

Hello, is what I will say, when You open up.

I will also say something else.

But You never open. You're too lazy.

I always have to put the key in the lock and turn.

I opened the mail box in the empty entrance hall and found a letter from my mother that read:

Hello!

How are you getting on in town? I heard that you are now in town. You could come over to entertain me a bit. People shouldn't work all the time. For example, the people next door said that Tissen's (you should remember him, you were at junior school with him) nephew and family went off on holiday to the Carpathians. That was very sensible of them. But you haven't even got a car, which rather surprises people out here in the countryside. Sometimes I get the feeling that you don't even feel like going outside the house anymore. When I meet people who ask about you I've got nothing to tell them.

Since your father's death I've been very afraid of thunderstorms. And the wild pigs also worry me. They've bred a lot and on sunny days they get into our fields. They don't touch the rye or the barley, they prefer oats.

There are still problems with the young people from the pupils' work brigade. They are making the hay nearby and keep coming here the whole time to steal berries. I just don't know what to do, because we had to surrender our shotgun. It was a souvenir of your father's and he was allowed to keep the gun, but not the shot. Now we haven't even got the gun anymore. And how should I, an old woman, be able to handle a gun anyway? I couldn't pick it up nowadays even if I used both hands. The dog has grown old too and it can't tell whether you're friend or foe. Last summer you said that someone ought to tell the head of the kolkhoz, but you know nothing about real life. Can't you understand that I would never be given a new place to live now? Perhaps they would even throw me out of my house in my old age. If you go around complaining, no one will ever forgive you for it. And the authorities won't like you either if you start pestering them. So please come yourself to help me a bit with the schoolchildren from the brigade (and also with the wild pigs). I really can't manage on my own. Do they sell electric fences where you are in town?

Your Mother

࿐

Father died in the spring, which was several months ago now. Of course I knew that such sad news had to come one day, Father was well into his eighties.

But whatever the age, it's a shame, especially when it's your own father.

I've imagined several times that I would come home from a party and find him on his knees with blood trickling out of the corners of his mouth, not much, but a little bit, and somewhere a dog would surely be howling like in the novel *The Master of Dry Gulch Farm* by our well-known writer Tammsaare, which describes the suicide of a strange and savage farmer during the first years of the Estonian Republic, but a dog would have howled elsewhere at a death too, and why are we always talking about literature, it would howl in real life too, and though I haven't personally heard it do so, at any rate I've heard a dog howl sometime or other.

Anyway, I've imagined on a number of occasions that I find, coming from a party, that he has blood dripping onto his shoulders from the corners of his mouth, but the news reached me that spring, just after the snow had melted, or to be more exact when the first snowdrops were pushing up and we had gone to the zoo to see various species of cats, especially ocelots, but we didn't of course miss other animals, especially the wild horses and pigs. Of course, we didn't hear any wolves howling there at the zoo, although the news of the sad event was in the air and on its way to meet me.

I found the telegram stuck in the door. I quickly put my black suit into a bag and we got going, first by taxi, then by train, then by bus, then another taxi. Without going into every detail of the journey, I'll simply say that we arrived before sunset. Do you remember?

A dog ran to meet us, an old dog, but one that was still hale and hearty. I imagined it was feeling sad and people expected it to be, because people were later saying: you're an orphan now, and now and again you expected it to start howling. But the dog didn't howl, not even when the coffin was carried out. Someone even kicked the dog, I don't know whether out of disappointment and anger or in hopes of finally getting the poor creature to start howling. But this all happened some days later, first the old dog ran to meet us, to greet our unexpected arrival. Do you remember?

First, the old dog ran up and the landscape too was very ancient, not in primeval but in historical terms, in the ice age during the Quaternary period, now a little spring-like, but partly already summer-like, because on the slopes of the drumlins grass was already growing, which was beginning now to disappear in the dusk. Do you remember?

Later, people asked me whether there were still adequate facilities for storing father's corpse. They mentioned that usually such problems arose, they themselves had had them. Someone had had a friend with the same problem, and so on.

I said that there weren't any special circumstances, the weather being pretty cool, and that father was in the shed where he had first been put, but I didn't know quite where because I had been at the zoo at the time. One man said to me, boy, from time to time, you ought to put a cloth with some alcohol over your father's face. I did so right away, but more reluctantly later that night. The torch only lit up a small part of the shed, that is to say that the rest was in darkness. On one occasion I didn't take the coffin lid right off, just lifted up the edge and poured a drop of alcohol into the depths of the coffin. I wasn't quite at ease with myself and sat scratching the dog for a while under the old rowan trees. The trees soughed or didn't sough, I don't remember which, but at any rate I didn't see any astral bodies, though I was in the mood for doing so. The next day, I of course wet the cloth in the proper manner.

A couple of weeks later, I met a friend on the street who expressed a lively interest in my dead father. As he was standing there before me, I realized all the more that he was an aristocrat, if we can nowadays define such a race by its absurdity and endangered status. The latter quality has forced them to cling to biological life and to its manifestations. Feeling that the "water level" is rising in the world (Ortega y Gasset), suffering from their eternal rheumatism, frequent headaches, and kidney stones, they want to merge with the world in its animalistic forms. Some of them have forked dung up onto carts with gusto and have lain with devotion face down in fields of wheat. This friend of mine once told me, foaming at the mouth as he did so, about spermatozoids and the birth of his own wife. Now he was exhibiting a living interest in the death of my father. I told him that there was no trickle of blood from the corners of my father's mouth, but there was, on the other hand, one from his forehead, because he had cut it as he fell against the water barrel. Couldn't he have drowned in it, was my friend's first objective and entirely justified question.

Yes, I suppose he could, and the devil knows what else he could have done to himself.

Anyway, father died in the spring, but now in the autumn the work brigade schoolchildren were plaguing my mother and she didn't have a gun. What should I do to stop them? Youth was clearly the representative of future tendencies and to fight against them was shortsighted, even reactionary. I imagined myself lying amid the berry bushes, in the dusk, the butt of the rifle pushed tight to my shoulder, with young women and men in my sights.

Oh no, my hand would fail to squeeze the trigger. I have read Yevtushenko's poem: *kto v molodyozh ne verit, to ni vo shto ne verit!* If you don't believe in youth, you believe in nothing! Let them steal, perhaps that's good for something, or the behavior will later change into something useful!

We need this and that, but who needs *us*? Do, for instance, pigs need us? They don't even know how the light is reflected in amber. Demonstratus said that amber was nothing but solidified lynx piss. And Lennart Meri, who has suggested that the pig become the emblem for Estonia on its coat-of-arms, quotes Cassiodorus from whose tale it emerges that a delegation of Estonians (which is how we tend to translate the Latin word *aestii*) went to parley with King Theodoric in Ravenna in the year 524. The aim of the trip was economic, but the delegates also took with them amber that was "graciously accepted." Of course, you don't look a gift horse in the mouth. The same with pigs. It doesn't matter what kind of mouth accepts things, once we've been so good as to bring them.

※

But let's not get downhearted.
Home!
We're home, we've finally found shelter, we can get back to our regular lives.

Here I could hide from the world at last. There's a certain charm about living in apartments. Apartments are my favorite place on Earth. What makes them so valuable is that there are so many of them. In towns and cities you can never manage to count up all the apartments. There are some hidden away under every roof. Behind almost every door there is an apartment, behind some several of them, even several dozen. Often you can enter them by the front and back doors. Sometimes you can get to an apartment from some unexpected entrance: next to a shed, right in the middle of the garden, through a trapdoor in the roof, from the end of the cellar. The doors are locked and the curtains drawn. The walls are sufficiently thick.

Your head is spinning. You lock the door with trembling hands, press your ear against the crack between the jamb and the door, then your weary legs grow weak and you slide down the door onto the floor of the hall, straight onto the hemp matting. You are saved.

You rip off your bow tie, pull off your patent leather shoes. Your heart begins to ease. You close your eyes. You say a prayer of thanks to the apartment. You want the walls to draw nearer, the ceiling to descend. You want the room to turn into a coffin, then adopt a concave shape to accommodate your body.

This doesn't happen, but it's not important. At any rate you have a supernatural relation to space.

Where are you?

I can hear your breathing, even feel your breath on the back of my neck. Are you looking over my shoulder? Listen, and I'll explain something to you. I'm going to explain that mushroom picking was tiring, but life itself isn't. I got lost, or life led me astray. I was in the woods like a small child, but I didn't cry, are you listening? Now I must recover so I'll go and lie down on the carpet, which will adopt the shape of my body. Quite different from in the woods. No ants biting you, no beetles crawling all over you. Have you heard what people say? Never mind looking for mushrooms, fuck off, drive away, go find your damn mushrooms somewhere else! I did drive away, but the mushrooms didn't show their faces. And now you're all angry, so for instance the *Islaya* is really jealous of my *Clytobes*, *Sclerodermas*, and other cacti. And as for the *Lophophora williamsii*, you hate every *Psylocybe* around. Damn rivals, you say and spit. Am I talking too much? I've got into the mood, I'm a little euphoric. You haven't flowered the whole summer long, but with regard to the flowering of mushrooms, I still haven't really understood anything about it. Clearly they have their spores, but no one really knows anything either about how ferns flower although plenty is said about them. I myself can't stand *Psylocybes*, they're very crafty, don't expect any help from them, but they're not any cleverer than the rest; when he was young, one friend of mine ate seven whole *Amanita muscariae* and nothing happened. Only when he'd downed a bottle of vodka on top did something actually happen: he fell asleep.

So here I lie, stretched out, enjoying life, looking at you, bodies, both round ones and conical ones, I touch you with my gaze and say: despite everything, you're in pretty good shape, both the conical ones and the veiny ones and even You who are neither conical nor veiny, but smooth.

Now I look up at the ceiling and know: this is the center of the world, and that's all there is to it.

The center is where we are.

There's a man walking around on the other side of the wall, he no doubt thinks I'm talking to myself.

Let him think what he likes. The main thing is that he doesn't call a shrink. People often go crazy in this part of the city, just the other day a man from upstairs threw all his belongings out of the window into the yard. He didn't let anyone in, the militia had to climb onto the balcony and in through the window. Do you remember?

I love apartments even more than I did in my youth. This passion of mine has never left me. Luckily there's lots of them, so what if I don't own them? You can always dream, can't you?

Apartments, apartments everywhere, all kinds of apartments, the majority are admittedly overcrowded and barbaric, but some are temptingly empty, dust has collected on the tables, phones ring unanswered, or there are plates placed on the table. So many opportunities, so much potential for a new life, so many partings of the ways and secret encounters!

Ah, you think proudly, I'm still young enough, I can own whole bunches of keys and addresses, keep them for a rainy day, or here and there draw the curtains, sniff up the smells of strange kitchens, sweat into the private patterned duvet covers, send my excrement down all sorts of pipes into the distant sea.

Your thoughts grow ever more hymnal, the more wallpaper you see before your eyes.

Oh, it wouldn't do to say so aloud, but you have always collected keys, for a long time already, pick the first and the last up from the ground, because you never know when you will encounter a locked door that the key fits. When in bars you try to guess who the burglars are from their stories and their appearance, you move and sit closer to them, try to pick up every word, every story. It would take little to make you start asking them to take you along on their housebreaking expeditions. But these murky specialists smell a rat, cast suspicious glances at you, pay the bill, and move off elsewhere.

Actually, you're quite happy with what you are right now, it's just that you're in a lively mood and want a bit more. Give me anything at all, and I'll eat it up.

Here you are flying in the empty room. Here you all are, and You are too perhaps? You're not only on the windowsill, but everywhere, all at once, so that the air is pregnant with you, as was said of old. That isn't so difficult to imagine. Not seeing things or touching them is something that has never bothered me. Only I don't know how large you all are, for instance how big you or You are. Doesn't it get cramped? I've given this some thought. I haven't bought very large items of furniture, so that you have the room to be everywhere, so that you won't bang yourself on the sharp edges of cupboards; I don't have any dishes because in the long run they all get broken and you'll go and step on the pieces and cut your feet, assuming you're two-footed beings, sometimes at least, for some fleeting moment, which is something I wouldn't have anything against, it would be a more familiar feeling. I'm grateful to you because thanks to you the idea of being everything and everywhere has become natural to me. It's true that even without you, the concentration of energy in several parts of the room would be very high, so that some cacti would quickly lose their the natural shapes in trying to fight against this. You, I'm thinking, you just try to fight against it when you watch the mortal coil of that *Gymnocalycium damsii*. You have often asked the *damsii*s to mediate, mediate between you and me; that is something that I now have to admit. In general, however, I now look at you with a braver eye, since getting hold of the tone generator, when you think how primitive our old friend the galvanometer was, with its hapless cogwheels, how imprecise the scale, and yet we still have a good word or two to say about it, don't we?

Look now at what I'm doing, and You look too. I'll do the talking as I point things out.

Silence will be your token of assent.

First, let's have a look at our latest guests: one *Submatucana*, two *Escobariae* and one *Homocephala*. And when I look at your absolutely introverted spheres, I begin to calm down and think that all that occurred this past day has been nothing but a bad dream. It simply never happened. Of course it didn't! I put all the *Gymnocalycia* in a row. Can't they be all together. In my opinion they can. Look: *baldianum, bodenbenderianum, cardenasii cursuspinum, damsii, denudatum, horstii, icronthlonum, michanovichii*, another *michanovichii*, yet another *michanovichii*, this time a *rubra* admittedly, if you're not colorblind, an *occultum, ochoterenai, rogonesii, saglione, schickendantzii, stellatum* or *paucicostatum, zegarrae*. There are even four *G. friedrichii*! But one of them is being eaten up by little white maggots. Have to fight against them. In a casually playful way—is that the right expression?—I pick up the bottle of poison and pour the white foam over the maggots. They die, as we can see. They are the only victims. Some of my visitors have said that hunting is more interesting than growing cacti. I don't think so. Hunting is destructive. Could I imagine myself firing at a cactus with a shotgun? What could I imagine myself doing then? What kind of spectacle would I make of myself? Would people still respect me? Maybe I'd even get kicked out of town. No, I'm not going to start hunting.

Without you all, I would never have met You. Are you listening?

Lightbulbs near the motionless ceiling, white walls. The shadow of a fly. Outside the occasional shouts of alcoholics, then again complete silence until a lone immigrant walks past, her heels tapping, wearing spectacles, then again the silence of the grave, as if I weren't in a newly built city district where they are thinking of cramming 200,000 people, most of them asocial types, skeptics, compulsive inventors and sports persons.

Now we'll re-pot the *Lophophora williamsii*, and this time we won't start eating it. You have to leave something for a rainy day. Castaneda made friends with someone they called the Mescalito. But he ate them in exceedingly large quantities. I don't have enough *Lophophora*s to make new friends. Besides, the Mescalito was frightening: Castaneda compared his head with a green strawberry. Later on, Castaneda realized that his friend was the face of a *Lophophora*. When you all turn up, you will be prettier for sure. I'm quite convinced of that. But You?

I looked at the clock. Still plenty of time. Somewhere, something had been left undone, and something had been done badly. I couldn't get rid of the idea. Everything was wrong. Perhaps Lennart's old crones knew a way out? But they were hard to communicate with, hard to get your wishes across to. Perhaps Lennart could manage it. Maybe Lennart knows better.

Don't worry, I'm not going anywhere. Just washing my hands. Actually, that large *Tephrocactus* ought to be repotted again, though perhaps autumn isn't the best time to do so. The pot has become root-bound, have to warm some water and give the plant a real soaking. But let's leave that until the spring. The *Tephrocactus* is kept outside all summer, that's what it likes, in its home habitat, in the mountains of South America, the difference between the day and night temperatures is very great. In fact, some cacti even tolerate snow, such as, for instance, the *Opuntia* family that's managed to spread all over the place, even to Greece and Vietnam, where snow doesn't actually fall, but where the *Opuntia*s don't naturally belong.

In South America, most winters tend to be warm; snow does fall but soon melts because the temperature never drops below freezing, or very rarely at least. Last year, we had a cold winter, several days below minus-thirty in January, so what kind of winter do You think we should expect this year? A mild one, no doubt, because they tend to alternate, now a mild one, now severe, well, it used to be like that at least, but now things are getting rather confused.

I like that *Horridocactus*, I suddenly shouted, I wish I knew when You were going to start liking it.

In fact, it's one of the few cacti that leaves me quite cold, is what you would reply.

I explained that the specimen here didn't have a classical appearance to it, when we look at typical photos then we see something else, but I still value it, maybe because of its name, which sounds like the *horror! horror! horror!* as Macbeth has moaned on quite a few stages in his time.

You came late that evening. Do you remember? You'd been to auctions and fairs, bought silver and gold, potatoes and beets, exactly that—potatoes and beets, as I remember.

Why don't I go into detail about the shops where people buy potatoes and beets, why don't I make them up before your eyes as they really are?

I'm not able to.

Because at an everyday level, life in this country is simply appalling, and if you start trying to describe the horror of it, you really have to devote yourself to the task, stack up thousands of pages of all kinds of absurdities, changes in the shops' opening hours, shortages at the greengrocer's, water taps that run without stopping, thousands of people who speak a foreign language, the lack of greenery around, the wrong time zone on our clocks and watches, rudeness and ill-breeding, loud arguments on trains, shoes that fall to pieces almost immediately, standing in a line for plane tickets, millions of things, billions of obstacles that are put in the way of people here every minute, but I don't want to write about it all, and nobody would want to read it anyway. One should rather push this frustration down into the subconscious and write as Proust suggested: one of the characters doesn't close a window, doesn't wash his hands, doesn't put on his coat, doesn't say a word to introduce himself. That is a more honest and pure feeling. I don't wish to know anything about the fact that three-quarters of the potatoes in the shop are substandard or that the clerk at the savings bank will start insulting and swearing at me simply because I dare to approach his window. But I hope that fellow writers exist who are able to collate all this material and turn it into one giant mythology.

Better for me to tell you about Tissen, a man who remained true to himself and didn't conform to new trends in society, a man who still had a dream.

TISSEN

I'd felt the lack of air the whole day and yes: my ears were itching! I didn't once hear the lark, but the swallows kept flying low, of that I was quite sure. Clearly the dandelion was closing up and dreaming, but the other flowers were all the more fragrant for it. I marveled at the clear contours of positive objects and events, the high stacks of cumulus clouds collected. The wind was blowing them together. It would not have surprised me if salt grew moist in its cellars, the hair on people's heads grew limp, and the strings of musical instruments so slack that you might as well put them back in their cases. And as for moles, they were of course making high molehills and with crooked lids of earth on top.

When your ears itch, when the autumn is mild, when the air holds lots of electricity, then all the rest is not far off: I feel a sharp pain in my leg, look down and see a flame shooting out of my calf that sizzles like a damp squib. That's how it starts and we'll have to do something in order not to get killed by it, you can't just stamp out this fire, some people have managed to smother it by covering up the victim so that the fire dies from a lack of oxygen, which is what happened in 1835 to one of the few people who escaped with his life and wasn't turned into charcoal, this being the mathematics professor at Nashville University, James Hamilton. Otherwise, you could end up as a pile of ashes, yes, ashes, because this process doesn't even leave any bits of bone, which you would always find in other circumstances, however long you burn up a person in a crematorium or at the stake. Even when the temperature is some 3,000 degrees Celsius for twelve hours there are still pieces of bone left over, but here there aren't, or perhaps just a foot with a sock and shoe on it. You never know when you might burst into flame. When I read Jules Verne's novel *Captain at Fifteen* where the alcoholic chief of the savages suddenly starts burning, set alight from the punch bowl, I imagined this could only happen to smoldering alcoholics. In scientific literature there are also references made to two alcoholic noblemen who were killed by a fierce flame that shot out of their stomachs. Also the perfectly respectable mother Mary Carpenter who in 1938 was out rowing with her husband and children and burned to ashes within a few minutes before their very eyes. The boat wasn't damaged, but never mind the boat, not even their clothes were singed! Verne was no doubt inspired by the death of Countess Cornelia di Bandi in 1763. All that was left of the woman was a pile of ashes, her feet still wearing shoes plus a half-burned head between them. The chambermaid noticed that the wax of the candles in the bedroom had burned, but not the wick. Such phenomena have not been recorded in the case of animals. Why not? What is it that is so special about human beings that they can turn to ashes so melodramatically, endeavoring with such passion to become inorganic?

I've examined the problem and know that such things often happen when the magnetic field of the Earth is out of kilter, when magnetic induction rises to two gauss, and it's not for nothing that I assume that conditions are perfect right now for chance to intervene.

In fact we all live in the hope that we won't simply burn up the very next minute. At the same time we know that a roof tile could fall on our head at any moment, but always assume this will happen sometime further in the future.

We hold our breath for a moment.

What happens the next second?

One . . . two?

This time nothing has happened, although there's a magnetic storm brewing, as we could hear this morning on the radio, and our ears are itching, which means that there'll be a thunderstorm this evening, if not sooner.

I switched on the galvanometer. The hands twitched and froze in expectation. What are the *Astrophyta* telling us? And which of them should you trust the most? The *Myrostigma*—does it care about the present, current state of things? And is not the *asterias* too introverted to take any interest in the state of the atmosphere in our tiny little republic? Let's turn to the *ornatum*, and quite understandably leave aside the *senile*. Let us say that the *ornatum* cares about day-to-day problems, even flirts with them.

So, Mr. *Astrophytum ornatum*?

Mr.?

Or Mrs.?

Whatever. Binary pairs always fill the heads of human beings.

As I imagined, 2 gauss, now what?

Will someone phone, dial my number?

Dialing energetically, without hesitation, dialing the last digit this very moment.

The telephone rang.

Summer, August to be exact—who could be phoning? What does he want?

"Tissen here," says an unknown voice.

Ah yes, Tissen. Now I remember.

He was asking whether he could come round to my place. Wouldn't of course been have right to refuse. I agreed.

Tissen was a schoolmate of mine from village school who I hadn't seen for a couple of years. I remember him from a fight in the first class back in 1951. I, who don't have the habit of hitting people (though I have lightly slapped hysterical women on occasions), punched him in the school corridor where we danced ring dances during the breaks, to keep the pupils fit (e.g., "We're Going to Mow the Rye" and "The Sun Rises, Greeting You"). I think I was justified in hitting him because Tissen was spreading nasty rumors in the bleach fields of the manor, the lodge and the dairy, all part of the kolkhoz by this time, that I was getting top marks because my parents had bribed the teachers by giving them a large slaughtered pig one night! Exactly that: a slaughtered pig under cover of darkness. Me, the one who read and learned quite quickly, had bribed the school! Tissen wanted to make people despise me. He succeeded in part—at any rate dogs would attack me on my way home from school. We were both seven-year-olds at the time. I don't remember the details, but one thing is sure, Tissen slandered me and I hit him. How could I hit him? Me, who was against all violence? You have to take into account the times we were living in. Betrayal often bore fruit, and you could literally be sent to *the cold country*, i.e., Siberia, if exposed. Bribery has always been disapproved of by the state. Even in those days. OK, we took along a pig, but would we get sent to Siberia? Rumors fly, people can always find plenty of accomplices, soon the story would have reached town, the Gray House there, where such tales were desperately needed. In the periodical *Stalinist Youth* an article had just appeared whose title read: "Is There Room for Him in a Soviet School?" It doesn't matter who they were talking about, but it was clear that there was no room for him there, nor perhaps anywhere else, for that matter. He had done wrong, wanted to enter this world, peep in through the curtains of the beyond. He should have stayed here, that would have been better both for him and for us. Now he had to take his responsibility and return where he had come from, and await better times. And this was to teach us something and protect us. In the end, I didn't trust my own parents. God knows, maybe they really did take them a slaughtered pig. And at night too, when the rye was swaying in the wind, by moonlight too? Blood dripping from the belly of the pig onto the dust of the road. Just like in *Huckleberry Finn*. There the pig was a payoff by Huck's father who was an alcoholic and behaved scandalously. My father was a decent man. I got confused, and since I had to hit someone, I hit Tissen. When he was seven! My only excuse was that I too was seven.

Was it like that or not?

The devil knows.

In the old days, I remembered much more, but now I'm trying to gradually clean out my memory. I have thought that memory could be to blame for nearly everything that has happened to us. I have many friends who praise memory and want to find their roots. I don't dare to argue with them, because they could think me crazy, but in my opinion if there'd been no memory, no historical time, nothing would have gone wrong. Cyclical time is less dangerous. There, the dangerous baggage of memories is small. Science would not have been invented, or if it had, it would have been quite different, not so advanced. That's at least what I sometimes feel. On occasions, I want to know nothing at all. To be a completely free individual without any feeling of responsibility. History makes me sick. The silent witnesses of the past have hurt me. For instance, I have sometimes thought that the museum at Oswiecim should be razed to the ground, and in so doing, preventing it from serving as a prototype instead of a warning. Where do I come from, don't ask, all that was yesterday. Today the sun is shining, shining only on us.

I lay down on the couch, looked at the white ceiling and the white walls, the gray floor.

I shut my eyes.

I tried to concentrate, focus my thoughts on one topic in some depth.

Electra and her brother Orestes killed their own mother. What had their mother done wrong? Earlier, she and her lover Aegisthus had killed Electra and Orestes' father, an important military leader who had returned from the Trojan Wars not knowing what lay in store for him. When Agamemnon returned home he had brought the clairvoyant Cassandra back with him from Troy who, on seeing the sun burning red over Mycenae and the snake's eggs on the hills, foretold the looming tragedy. Cassandra was killed by Clytemnestra. Clytemnestra was Electra and Orestes's mother, whom they subsequently murdered. That's how it was. But let's return to Cassandra. She was the daughter of Priam and Hecuba. They, in turn were the descendants of Zeus and Hera. But what happens to Electra is quite different! Her mother was Pleione, one of the seven Pleiades who all got married to various deities, until they were turned into doves, then into constellations of which Electra's sister Merope is the weaker of the two, since she was ashamed of being Sisyphus' bride. But Electra's father was Atlas, a Titan who was forced in the Far Occident to carry the Earth in the orchard of the Hesperides and whose brother Menetius was struck by lightning and killed. Electra's children were Jason, Dardanus (from whom Cassandra was descended), and Harmonia. The husband of the last of these was Cadmus, the founder of Thebes, who fought with the dragon and defeated it although its teeth, on falling to the ground, sprang up to become new dragons. Their daughter was Semele, the erstwhile Phrygian earth goddess (cf. the Russian *zemlya*, earth), Zeus' paramour, to whom Zeus' wife Hera appeared in crafty guise as Semele's nurse, the good old Beroe. She sweetly encourages Semele to flatter old Zeus and ask him to appear in all his glory. Semele tells Zeus to appear in all his glory. Zeus is flattered and appears in all his glory, i.e., as the sun. So he inadvertently burned up (how can a god do anything inadvertently?) the pregnant Semele. But little Dionysus, who was six months old at the time, was saved. The grandfather to this Dionysus was Dardanus, Electra's child, his son being Erichtonius, and his son Tros, Tros's son Ilus, Ilus's Laomedon, Laomedon's Priam, Priam's daughter then Cassandra. Cassandra was taken as war booty to Thebes by Agamemnon and there she foretold the fall of the house of Atreus, which indeed occurred. Clytemnestra, along with her lover Aegisthus, killed her husband Agamemnon, for which action the children Orestes and Electra murder her in turn, and Electra, whom I've just mentioned, appeared a few years ago at our town theater in the guise of an actress. This Electra's son-in-law Cadmus was the forebear of the philosopher Thales (as some think) who, in the year 585, foretold a lunar eclipse . . .

. . . but Tissen was born in 1944, born in the countryside, near a small bog, which could be seen from my childhood home, though now trees have grown in between forming a screen. Tissen left the small village stage with great hopes.

From near his house, a drumlin sloped away. This descended gradually to the river. I had often imagined little Tissen tripping up in the long grass and rolling down to the water, with dogs barking after him, rolling and rolling, until some sheep picked him up by the scruff of the neck or some horse rolled in his way. I haven't got any evidence for this, but have allowed my imagination free rein. I don't know whether Tissen is that rustic, but he does arouse envy in me.

In other words: I too know the countryside, even if to a more limited extent.

When it comes down to it, we were brought up in the same atmosphere, surrounded by the same mentalities, so why should we differ so terribly much?

Both of us know the language, are affected by the same restlessness, the calories in our diet are the same, we walk on two legs, we shake our head for "no," are subject to the same criminal codex.

But there was no point in spinning out this train of thought any further. It just didn't appear to be a productive one.

His story, his childhood?

Ridges, a river, soapwort on the hillside. Summer.

A perfectly likely perception.

But let's go on:

Dogs far and near, the water hemlock growing up to your chest, the darkness of autumn, two sets of tracks in front, two behind, a trumpet clarion, a floating curtain, kolkhozes being set up.

And we'll explain this all ourselves, as it's not our intention to keep things secret.

Tissen could hear the dogs barking near and far. Then he waded into the hemlock patch. Autumn came, the weather grew gloomy, pitch-dark nights followed, then snow began to fall and Tissen saw hare tracks. In the winter, Tissen blew the fire-warning horn, although his parents had forbidden him from doing so. Spring arrived again. Tissen took down the inner windows; a gust of wind blew out the curtains and at the same time marked the start of the farm collectivization of the whole republic.

Are these fictions? I have experienced them myself and can swear that they were not dreams. The kolkhozes still exist. When I go outside in the country, I can see a kolkhoz about half a kilometer away. It lives its own life, there's building going on there. New housing blocks are rising up, but everyone thinks they don't belong there in the countryside. Yet they are being built and everybody is happy. At least that's the general opinion, although we don't always know exactly what people are thinking. But they should start thinking about what they will be doing, once they're built, when they're really standing there, something hard to imagine, but something you have to start doing, just like you start thinking of other things that have been even harder, such as the Cold War or porridge that burns your mouth. Me and Tissen come from the same part of the country. It was precisely in that open space that Tissen saw the hare tracks, I can say confidently when I travel to the countryside, but I can mention just about anywhere, by just relying on my memory: the hares of our childhood.

When I was a child, hares were very quick. That is something I do remember. They often leapt out from somewhere, froze for an instant, then ran off. For that reason I never managed to get a close look at them, all I ever saw was their rumps. They would disappear into the long grass or behind a snowdrift, depending on the time of year. The worst they ever did was to gnaw the bark off the apple trees, especially in the winter when the snow lay thick on the ground. For that reason, the trunks of the trees were wrapped up before winter arrived in paper or even with bundles of fir twigs. The tracks hares made were very strange: two almost side-by-side in front, two close behind. Wolves' tracks were in one straight line. Of course, the strange nature of hare footprints resulted from their jumping rather than running. I can't remember ever seeing several hares together at a time, I got the impression that they were solitary creatures. Nor do I remember ever having eaten hare: there were few hunters in postwar Estonia. When all's said and done, the past few years at that time had been critical ones in the life of our country, many had perished in the war, many had fled abroad, many had been sent to Siberia. So huntsmen were scarce and who would be shooting at hares if not huntsmen? True, there was some family somewhere or other that bred rabbits, but they weren't hares and they had red eyes, which frightened me. I just couldn't imagine eating hares, they had such vacant stares. But people said that hares were brave. That vacant stare expressed their courage. Hares would appear in dangerous places and were forced to take off, but the main thing was that they had been there. From vulgar materialist science books I learned that their long ears served as mechanisms to regulate their body heat. I don't believe this even now, just like I don't believe in evolution, and I think that hares' ears serve to prevent them from hiding from their enemies. Do hares have a lot of enemies? There's always someone who's after your life. One time it'll be an eagle, another an eagle owl or a goshawk, often a wolf, a lynx, especially a fox, and even a cat, sometimes all at the same time. So a hare can wander about and huddle under the windows of the village social club in the moon-white snow, while from inside merry waltz music can be heard, interspersed by marches, which invite you to be happy. During the hard years when the first kolkhozes were being built, the hares would sleep in the snow, forest hares even under the snow. They would often get into the headlights of cars on the main road, because they couldn't get back into the dark woods due to bright light. They could in fact run at fifty kilometers per hour, but not for long, and soon the car would catch up leaving a bloody trail from the hare causing laughter from women drivers wearing their astrakhan furs. Then the car would disappear round the bend and the hare carcass would be left lying in the road in the darkness and the soughing of the trees, with only the odd Forest Brother coming and stepping over it, or some timid women's pioneer leader with eyes like a doe's would feel sorry for it and bury the corpse in the dead grass. Me and Tissen remembered those times, although sometimes we turn them into fiction as we also do with ourselves.

Tissen is no fiction. He is completely real. He has worked in several jobs: he's been a psychology lecturer, a freelancer, a mechanic in a holograph laboratory, a theater director, then a freelancer again . . . I like his name. In my opinion it contains a quite adequate number of subtexts: in him the male and female principles are united. On the one hand breasts (*mamillae*), on the other the German weapons manufacturer Thyssen, the so-called Iron King and author of the book *I Paid Hitler*. This unity could seem mysterious to uneducated people if I didn't mention how reflection and action were united in Tissen, striding in parallel. It's as simple as that, at least to my mind, but I could be wrong because I only know Tissen very slightly, though more than I know myself, which is why I've started writing about Tissen, but not about myself as many do and quite successfully at that.

Thinking in this way, I went to bed and woke up to the ringing of the doorbell.

Tissen had promised to come at one, and he was punctual.

᠀ᠥ᠀

He was very agitated.

First of all, he made sure the lock on the outside door had clicked shut.

"Hello," I said.

He whirled around to face me.

"The Third World needs culture like a pig needs a saddle," he said forcefully.

He fell silent for a moment.

"You're not part of events around you," he said, "not only things happening in the Third World, but here too. What does a person need? Faith. What gives them faith? Knowledge. What gives you knowledge? Art. Yes, art too. Why not? I'm asking you, why not? I'll give you an example: I'm expecting you to write a sequel to that novel about your youth that deals with secondary school pupils around 1960. That work was a big event for me. In it you describe the thoughts, dreams and conflicts of your generation. Later on, you told me that this work was a lie, that people lied everywhere the whole time in those days, and that you weren't any different. Well, what do you say to that? You shouldn't shatter readers' illusions, what are they guilty of, those innocent people who read and believe? Think, weren't those times beautiful, looking back on it? Weren't those the years, when we were growing up and becoming aware of the world around us like a morning in early spring, with the song of the lark, with a bright blue hoarfrost beyond the barn—if you still remember what barns and hoarfrost are, if you still remember anything about life in the countryside! Is there any point in being so abstract? We were, after all, born into the world of flesh, shit, and blood, we, here and now!"

Midsummer, a room with white walls.

I hadn't managed to get a word in edgeways.

I thought about how Tissen's world had been born. He opened his eyes and saw the arc lamps in the maternity ward. He had the taste of his mother's womb in his mouth, a taste that surely comes to mind nowadays when he eats an egg and when the yolk meets the silver spoon in his mouth. Then he remembers his own beginnings.

A warm breeze blew in through the open window and Tissen kept on pacing back and forth, from wall to wall. I thought to myself that my apartment was too small to accommodate people from the Big Wide World. It was all right for introverted thoughts, quite ideal in fact, but a man of action would feel like a caged tiger in here.

"Anyway, it would be very interesting for the younger generation to know what happened to ours, the one from around mid-century."

"It would perhaps be interesting for us to tell them, but they tend not to be interested, just as I, in turn, haven't paid much attention to what happened to the generation previous to ours."

Tissen gave me a poisonous look.

"Perhaps you don't even know what happened to you yourself?" he asked.

"Well, I don't."

"So you think you've always been living in an ivory tower?"

"What do you mean *ivory*? I've maybe seen ivory once in my life, and the flesh attached to it or the whole elephant, on a couple of occasions."

"Stop evading the issue. Plenty of time to make jokes. Let's put it this way: do we constitute a certain Soviet generation or don't we?"

"What the fuck d'you mean by *generation*? I just don't want to hear the word!"

"You can't get round it! Everyone belongs somewhere, to some generation or other!"

"Which *gene* and which *ration*? I don't even understand the constituent parts of the word!"

"What is there to understand?"

"Well, whether you belong to it or not!"

"I don't!"

"So where then *do* you belong?"

"I don't belong anywhere!"

"What year were you born in?"

"1944."

"Well, then you belong to the Golden Sixties!"

"Belong to them yourself, if you want to!"

"I already do!"

"Good luck!"

"Why should we be arguing?"

"Let's not then," I said. "Let's start all over again: what is it you want?"

"What I want is for you to describe our generation, because in people's subconscious there are many blank spots, and these have to be got rid of!"

"Let the historians get rid of them!"

"They have a pretty hard job trying and more often than not they don't manage!"

"To get rid of them?"

"Yes!"

"The blank spots?"

"Right!"

"What are they good for, then?"

"Don't ask me!"

"Who else should I ask?"

"There isn't anyone else to ask."

"What should I do, then?"

"Write a novel about our generation!"

"Why ours?"

"Ah, now you *are* admitting you belong to it!"

"When you've been around long enough, you sometimes begin to belong a bit. But what should I then start describing besides the blank spots?"

"Our aspirations! Our rise and fall! Our idealism and our resignation!"

"Camus's death, Playa Giron, the bombing of Hanoi, the Bay of Pigs, Eleanor Rigby, the Green Berets, Twiggy, the Chelsea girls, Philip Blaiberg and Christiaan Barnard, Dubcek, Sharon Tate, *Midnight Cowboy*, my first marriage—which is, by the way, the only thing on this list that I remember experiencing personally, all the rest are things we read about and heard on the radio. Otherwise what we're talking about are things we never really experienced ourselves. Do you want me to continue with the list?" I added grimly, "Kennedy's murder, God, not just one but several Kennedys, two to be exact, and then Martin Luther King and the Cultural Revolution in China, Biafra, the death of Che Guevara, always deaths, you may notice, that's what sticks in your memory, Sergeant Pepper, who managed to stay alive. The Prague Spring and the ensuing autumn that involved our own Soviet tanks, Led Zeppelin, the storming of the 'Odeon' and the confused moments of Jean-Louis Barrault, and the confused moments when I heard about the scandal with the Rolling Stones at the Altamont concert where the Hell's Angels killed a man who had stripped naked, killed him in the name of law and order, the sky was a little cloudy, well, that was one of my clearest memories of the event, you can go on for dozens of pages, although we hardly left the little town of Tartu during the most exciting years of my generation, hardly ever went even to Tallinn and so we couldn't even watch Finnish TV as they could up there. Do you remember when they stormed the 'Odeon'?"

"On the 15th of May?"

"Come on! It was the 16th, don't you remember?"

"Course I do!"

"And Cohn-Bendit speaking?"

"He cursed everything! Malraux, the whole of culture, even Barrault! They were all sitting on the ground! With him there cursing away!"

"Cursing! Only two years before, he was defending the staging of Genet's *Screens*!"

"But by now, Genet had for him become a part of bourgeois culture!"

"Did we also curse them?"

"You mean Barrault? Or Genet?"

"We defended Genet, though we hadn't even read him then! We cursed the bourgeoisie!"

"At the Odeon?"

"Yes, at the Odeon."

"The bourgeoisie? Or the petit bourgeoisie? The nouveaux-riches? The philistines? Home-owners?"

"All of them!"

"Those in Estonia, too?"

"Estonian ones, English ones, French ones!"

"Was I cursing them too?"

"Yes, you were, everywhere you went!"

"Those were the days!"

"They certainly were, and funny that we remember them so well! But why's that cactus red?"

"That's a *Gymnocalycium michanovichii var*, a *friedrichii var*, a *rubra* no doubt cultivated by the Japanese, and which doesn't have chlorophyll, so it only grows when grafted. We have only a few of them here, but they're grown in large numbers in Scandinavia. But how did we get onto the subject of Cohn-Bendit, we could just as well have talked about the Papin Sisters, who chopped up their landlady into pieces, or about Polzunov, who is said to have invented the steam engine independently in Russia. Cohn-Bendit, can you imagine!"

I remember Cohn-Bendit, whom I've never met, I remember his speeches, which I've never heard, I remember the hall, where I've never been, I remember Paris, where I've never been, I remember my ideals, which I have never had, and I remember that four years ago, I bought a plastic pisspot at the shop round the corner in Rome for 26,000 lire when all I was allowed to change for the journey at the time, and pay for in rubles, was 32,000. I have tried to erase that information from my brain, but haven't yet managed to. I will no doubt have to remember that price to the end of my days, in the same way I'm forced to remember that once, one summer, when I was four or five years old, the thermometer showed, one misty day, 15 degrees Celsius. These memories throb in my heart, and there's simply nothing I can do with them. I'm sharing them with others, that's all I can do.

Why is there so much room in my memory?

A FRIEND'S STORY

A friend of mine once told me the following:

"As a child, I used to be afraid I would never remember what happened to me later on in life, and that others, yes, I mean other people, would have to remind me what happened. The first signs were: as a six-year-old I had to listen to my mother reminiscing about when I was two. I myself remembered nothing from those days. But you have to remember, and by yourself, yes, by yourself! I poured myself a glass of water, and, making use of the brief time I was alone in the room, I stood the glass on top of the cupboard. I thought to myself: now I'll remember this for the rest of my life, me alone, and no one else will be able to remind me of it. And my prediction was fulfilled, I will remember that glass of water and that cupboard until my dying day. Me alone."

Tissen sank panting into an armchair. His eyes were closed. I was afraid that he had passed out, or even died of a stroke. But no, he was already opening his eyes and said:

"I imagine you expect me to say more. Now I've turned up after all this time. OK, in that case, let's talk about pigs."

Looks like it's going to come to blows, I thought fearfully. Such a turn of events doesn't bode well.

"Are you thinking of those bastards who have made our wonderful society undemocratic for more years than I can remember, who have cruelly crushed every initiative, who have censored and forbidden everything so horribly and have thought obsessively about only one thing: the main thing is that nothing happens; who thought in a totally uneconomic and over-centralized way, but who totally forgot to think about people?"

I concurred, to be on the safe side. But Tissen shook his head.

"No, that's not what I mean," he said.

I was dumbstruck.

"I'm simply talking about ordinary pigs," he explained, "who've got little piggy eyes and which we kill to eat."

I nodded.

Tissen continued:

"I'll tell you a new story from real life, this time one where there is no culture of any sort involved, either that of the Third World or our own. But first a couple of words of introduction. You've not fallen asleep, have you? Should I perhaps leave? Thank you. Have you ever heard of Lõivajõe, or ever been there? No? Well, Lõivajõe is a village that was already in existence at the start of the thirteenth century. It's mentioned in the Book of Records from Danish times. But that's not what's most important. You've dealt with history in your previous works but it has remained at the level of ornamentation, has never really been thought through. So let's drop the Danish Book of Records and talk about the present day. Put your imagination to the test, try to see the reality behind my dry comments. Imagine the weather is changeable. It's 21 degrees Celsius outside. There's a westerly wind blowing. There are squalls. And this is all happening in the vicinity of Lõivajõe—the Lion's River. There have only been three claps of thunder, and those pretty far away, but all of a sudden something unusual happens. Let's say that the pig keeper is called Linda. She's feeding the pigs. There's a loud cry and something flies in through the hatch of the pigsty . . ."

"The hatch?"

"Exactly, a hatch, leading to the outside world. A hatch through which the pigs can get out into the fresh air. I'm not going to describe it in any more detail. Anyway, something flies through this hatch into the pigsty. The pig keeper throws open the door. Now don't ask me again which door. The important thing is what the woman sees. The pigs are floating up into the air like balloons. They rise up over the walls of the pen! Some even fly from the one pen to the next. Immediately, the whole sty is filled with a burning smell, so under normal circumstances you would think there had been a short circuit leading to a fire. But the electric cables are whole. This all only lasts a split second. Then she sees a fireball moving from pen to pen. Then suddenly—*badamm!* It's all over, dark, silent, the fire out. It takes a while for Linda to recover. She goes to inspect the pigs. It turns out that only one piglet has died. It is lying on its right flank in the path to the dungheap. There are no external symptoms. Only later does it go completely blue. Dissection reveals that the whole of its insides are filled with blood. But as I say, that happens later. First a patch is noticed on another pig where the globe lightning, or whatever it was, has made an orange patch, about twenty centimeters across. Lines radiate from the patch. A third pig has a triangular coal-black mark, about ten centimeters long on its left flank. No blood coming from it. The other pigs . . ."

"Knocked unconscious?"

"Nobody knows because a short while afterwards they were all moving around again. But to start with they were very frightened. They didn't eat anything until the next evening. That's the story, anyway."

Tissen looked at me triumphantly. His nostrils barely twitched. I don't know whether he was joking. The story about the pigs seemed familiar somehow. As if I had read it somewhere. Like the one about a pig's squeals triggering off Saint Elmo's fire. If that's what it does. And they are enemies, the pig and the other, after that. But why is a virtual stranger telling me all this in a white room, in the middle of summer, in the middle of the day, with the sun blazing down outside, which, thank goodness, isn't shining in through the window? Am I dreaming?

"Well?"

"Well what?"

"What happened then?"

Tissen smiled.

"I just wanted to tell a story about an adventure that took place in faraway Lõivajõe. The pig keeper woman, Linda, was shaken, as was her husband who entered the pigsty just as all this was happening. What have you got to say to that?"

"What am I supposed to say? Who ordered him to go in? You shouldn't meddle with fate."

"You're making fun of me, as always. That's the sort of sterile methods you writers use."

"I'm just not interested in such things," I said, as coldly as possible.

"What does interest you, then?" yelled Tissen. "Angst, summer neuroses, sterility, bungling! The main thing is that it's far from real events, from nature, people, and as near as possible to morbidity! Or I'll eat my words! I'll have you know that this summer, the center of the world for *me* is in Lõivajõe. Something happened there that I just can't be indifferent to. I have to take sides. On questions about pigs, the systems of life, myself. I can't stay any longer in my ivory tower. Do you understand?"

Only now did I notice that Tissen was wearing glasses. I saw how he polished them with his handkerchief. His vacant stare did not see me. Although he nevertheless consisted of flesh and blood like myself. He was worrying. He didn't want to leave. No car passed by. Everyone was on vacation. Tissen was here. Perhaps he couldn't see me at all without his glasses. Slip out, hide under the sofa?

I shut my eyes and tried to collect my thoughts. But not a thought entered my mind that would even clothe my plight in verbal terms. When I opened my eyes, Tissen was no longer in the room. I jumped up. The apartment was silent. Perhaps Tissen had never been here and the idea crossed my mind that perhaps it had only been an illusion. Keeping close to the wall, I sneaked out into the corridor. I reached the doorway, staying as quiet as a mouse. I stopped, and now I thought I could hear breathing. Tissen was standing just round the corner. I swallowed hard and stepped across the threshold. Tissen was indeed standing there. He smiled, put on his glasses, and walked past me, back into the room.

"Well, it's a hot day," he said, rubbing his hands. "And do you know what just sprang to mind? Liikola, your good old Liikola, your ordeal by fire, your touchstone. After Liikola, I too wanted to love my neighbor, but it proved to be damned difficult to do so. I'll tell you about it sometime. In a word, I'm at present trying to love this one, that one, and the other. But I just can't manage to. The more I come to think of it, the more I blame Christianity for everything. Or, to be more exact, not Christianity itself, which I like, although you can't really do anything with that sort of liking. Nietzsche said that there was only one true Christian and that was Jesus himself. The rest just aren't Christians at all. The only way to become a Christian is by imitating Christ. But who can manage, or be bothered, to do so? Where was I? Yes, I haven't got anything in particular against Christ, nothing at all really, but what is termed the Religion of the Cross does annoy me, because it doesn't help this world. If acid rain comes to our country, if it is polluted by dangerous strontium fallout, why doesn't God do something about it? And if it is true that he hears our prayers so that he has become a mere puppet in our hands, why don't we pull the strings, i.e., pray? How difficult it is to find out who the culprit is! But everything's all fucked up, that's pretty clear, and I no longer dare to put my faith in young people either. Isn't it precisely their neuroses and dithering that are to blame for everything, because they perpetually need new things to stimulate them? Always demanding new things and new fashions. Every year, there's a new style and industry has to meet their expectations, otherwise they will revolt. They can't do without them, just as people can't do without insulin. It's decrepit old people, yes, decrepit, who have to work by the sweat of their brow creating new combinations of notes and colors. No, Whites should put a stop to all this, otherwise they'll get all fucked up by the Negroes."

"War?"

"Come on," laughed Tissen, "I haven't changed that much over the years. I remain staunchly opposed to violence, that is still my conviction and I'm not retreating from it. I still love Gandhi and Francis of Assisi, as I always have done. But there are other means, because it can't be that you can't influence people at all. Every day you see how people are persuaded to move in the most disgusting directions. Does that mean that there isn't a right direction for us? There is, if only you want it badly enough!"

I noticed that Tissen had a big smile, baring all his teeth. I noticed that one of his socks was bluish, the other gray and that he hadn't shaved since yesterday. I thought about the fact that an inferiority complex (what else?) had arisen in him over the years since he always looked very manly (why did he bother?). To stress this fact, he was wearing jeans made in Romania. I checked this by looking at the back pocket while Tissen was striding back and forth expounding his theories. I know that Romania didn't use to be a particularly open country. I have traveled through it once by train, but wasn't even let out onto the platform. I would have liked to have breathed the air that Dracula had breathed, i.e., the Wallachian voivode leader, Vlad IV (1431-76) known as the Vampire, and whose skull is on display as a reliquary in a museum of curiosities in Hollywood, bought for only $3,000 in 1973. In a word, I'd have liked to breathe the air of the homeland of vampires, if only they'd let me step out onto the platform. In fact they didn't actually forbid you from stepping out onto the platform, but no transit passenger dared to show any inclination to do so. So the hinterland of Romania has remained a mystery to me, as have the jeans Tissen was wearing.

He said that he regarded Lightning as the Savior. Because the person who gives birth to you, she is also the one that saves you. As we already know, it's not impossible that lightning is to blame for the fact that we exist. He was thinking of organic life in general. Because back in 1952, Stanley L. Miller did a series of experiments where, by mixing methane, molecular hydrogen, ammonia, and water vapor (as the atmosphere of the Earth could well have been some four billion years ago) he managed to create artificial lightning, i.e., an electrical discharge. As a result of this experiment, the so-called primal soup was discovered, as we've already said, to contain substances such as gluten, alanine, and also a number of amino acids and organic compounds.

I was startled by an abrupt flicker and realized that someone had thrown something at the window, so I went to look. There was no one standing under the window. Tissen came to join me.

"Must have been a bird," he said. "Sometimes they crash right into the window pane."

He stretched forward to peer out of the window, and then nudged me in the ribs.

I looked where he was pointing, but could see nothing.

"Dead," said Tissen succinctly.

And indeed, there in the grass lay a small bird.

"Must have already been sick, there's nothing to be done," Tissen commented.

He sighed and continued:

"Well, later on, apart from lightning, people began to think of solar radiation as being the source of life, also the radioactivity of the Earth, the heat from volcanoes, meteors, and cosmic radiation. I myself believe in lightning."

He smiled amiably.

I gradually began to realize what he was driving at, but just that: only the direction, no more.

To go on a visit to a schoolmate after twenty years, and a hated one at that, and then start talking about the pigs of Lõivajõe and about the primal soup. Did he think I was simple minded? That I would let myself be taken in that easily? So what if I too was eager to have a discussion. The years have taken their toll and all my secrets have been bottled up in me these last few years.

Let's wait and see!

He wants to say that I have been provoking him! With fragments from my novel! Maybe he's right, but it doesn't really interest me, because my ideas can be used in different ways.

But lightning is something new.

I've never talked to him about lightning.

I've never told him anything, in fact.

I believe in lightning!

What was there to say against that? *I believe in music, I believe in love?* To say nothing of the gods, if you discount those who were inside, those who were interiorized already when I was still a child, and about whom I don't have a clue anymore.

I tried to change the subject.

But Tissen didn't take the bait.

He said that he was investigating the quantity of krypton in the atmosphere. Krypton is released into the air by nuclear power stations. In normal air there are only a few parts per million, but now this has risen to around 45 ppm. Krypton isn't yet a biological danger because it doesn't form part of any living organism. But it does make the air conduct electricity. In some places (above the oceans) there is a danger that such conductivity could rise to 20%. If krypton spreads throughout Earth's atmosphere, this would inhibit the formation of thunderclouds. But where do tropical countries, for instance, get their moisture from? Always from thunderstorms. On Java, for example. The city of Bogor has 322 thunderclouds per year. And all those other places: Central and West Africa, the South American interior, Southeast Asia. A reduction in thunderstorms would throw the heat exchange of the whole Earth into confusion, said Tissen finally, with an innocent look on his face.

I had quite a job holding myself back.

I wanted to interrupt and shout in one breath:

"Exactly—there are sixteen million thunderstorms on the planet per year, which means 44,000 a day. Every second there are a hundred flashes of lightning . . ."

At the last moment, I caught my words by the tail.

Why bother showing off what I knew?

As if trying to emulate Tissen.

Tissen seemed such a socialized sort of person that people envied him. In other circumstances I'm tongue-tied, but this time I too was trying to voice to my concerns about society and nature.

Times have changed.

I thought in the manner of a responsible citizen:

Former opponents shake hands before the thunder!

Tissen knew an astonishing amount about thunderstorms.

Me too.

I knew how to make thunder offstage by shaking a large metal sheet. It's done by the stagehands, occasionally by a special-effects man.

So I also knew a thing or two.

But despite my knowledge, Tissen needed to consider himself superior to me. Just for that I could have stuck my neck out—but no one would have wanted my neck. Self-respect is, of course, a fact of life. Psychologists have drawn attention to the fact that we turn Others into stereotypes and characters. Others are this type or that. For instance weirdoes, cunning people, or fanatics. We ourselves are simply Me. We are varied. We suit our partners. We are very open. We are everything. We are different from Others, are unique and special. There are of course states of mind and nation-states in this world that promote uniformity. And not everyone can permit egotism. We have survived times when it was highly thought of to spend one's days together with others in the same space. Those were the times when you stood elbow to elbow. So that we'd be brothers or something similar. Such a way of thinking was Tissen's and highly thought of in the Third World. But the Third World too needed its leaders, Egos risen from the depths of the sea. Tissen was full of love for the uneducated masses, but he wanted to be like a father to them. He would have given starving Negroes our flesh, thirsting Africans our blood, naked Bushmen our skin, and given our bones to shivering Blacks for the fires he imagined them to have.

But Africa doesn't need Tissen. There are other men there and always in uniform. They are mainly Blacks, i.e., people who belong there. No one would believe that Tissen wanted to help. And perhaps he doesn't. God knows what he wants. There's a good chance that he himself doesn't know.

At any rate, his attitude to people seemed too open.

Even here in my home.

Yes, everyone has his own "me," but a European upbringing means that it doesn't do to flaunt it too much. From that point of view, Tissen had obviously been badly brought up. So what that he knew all about Kampuchea or Mozambique. Tissen couldn't hide anything. When talking with other people he found it necessary to smile scornfully. This was a carefree flash of a smile, but Tissen found it necessary to repeat it, just to be absolutely sure. This was accompanied by boorishness: Tissen uttered sounds like those made by phantoms or Mephistopheles. These were generally regarded as bad form, but his mom, dad and party members had forgotten to mention it. It was as if Tissen hadn't really grown accustomed to observing his own behavior in the mirror, so there was a whiff of the slum about him. I often wanted to tell him: Tissen, try and be humbler with other people. Kings and princes bow to the ground, bankers help fallen little Negro boys to their feet. The Pope removes the shoes and socks from a young man in the developing world, kisses his toes and washes them. I don't know what he himself is thinking, but it is a grand gesture for all that. Humility leads to exaltation, so the humble are taken more seriously later than the exalted. These latter types are comical. They are always playing a role, but not one from tragedy, but from Feydeau's farces.

To which genre does Tissen belong?

In my opinion, he changes style in mid-text.

"You know," said Tissen, "yesterday we gathered in my studio after the break as we usually do. We had our photo taken on the steps and, as always, one of us wondered jokingly whether the photograph would have just us in it, or whether someone would also be in it that the human eye couldn't detect.

"I don't know whether I ought to tell you, but we are experimenting with art holograms and because of that, or for some strange need to compensate in some way, we were talking about astral bodies and auras. For some reason we needed such jokes, though a hologram is an entirely explicable phenomenon in materialist terms, but I suppose it makes it a bit more romantic. Anyway, we were standing on the steps, there was a fresh breeze blowing, quite strong really, and Goga was taking the picture. He does so every year, but he's never showed us any of the photos he's taken. And it isn't as if the photo itself is so important. It's simply a little ritual among us men, to help us extend the height of summer a bit. And in the name of making the summer last a bit longer, we wanted to celebrate the event. There followed another little ritual that also brought us together: we phoned the doorman and told him that we wanted to celebrate the end of summer by drinking a bottle of Scotch in our workroom, and would pay the appropriate fine for doing so the next day. After grumbling a bit, he went along with our plan. Usually you have to pay the fine the same day, especially if the fine is a large sum of money. But since we only allow ourselves this transgression once a year, and only at the end of the summer, and as there aren't any alcoholics in our group, then they generally pretend they haven't noticed. True, one captain of the militia had to smile at our behavior and said that after only a couple of strong drinks you wouldn't be able to tell the difference between anything appearing before us in a darkened room, whether it be a hologram or hallucination. This last comment was, of course, meant as a joke. In a word, everything was a joke, all this business about registering the drinking bout beforehand, and the fine."

Tissen laughed, neither a little nor a lot, and I will carry on in the same style as I have begun, without bothering to reproduce all the nuances of Tissen's use of language. In other words: I will paraphrase.

"Our laboratory is a place where both science and art are brought together. On the one hand, we are constantly improving our experimental equipment. It is, of course, an exaggeration to use the word *improve* because we aren't capable of making any fundamentally new discoveries anyway. But it's true that we do, now and again, discover some odd offshoot of scientific knowledge. None of us five dares undo the basic knot, because they are machines with balls, so to speak. You'd undo the knot, but you wouldn't be able to tie it together again without going to ask permission from Moscow. We have had to keep a notebook about the mechanisms. Our scientific work has perhaps been restricted by that activity but we do arrange holographic sessions, for a small circle of people, admittedly. Haven't you ever been to any of our evenings? A pity. Of course the publicity we make for ourselves is deliberately kept low-key, we've used uncontroversial titles such as 'Unbelievable but True' or 'Imagination and Life.'

By the way, do you actually know what a hologram is? Nothing more that an optical resonator. You've no doubt heard of an auditory resonator, like when singers smash glasses with their voices. In a word, you make a three-dimensional figure using laser beams. As in life. People have been talking about holographic art for decades now, but it's only recently that it's become a reality. To get a basic knowledge of it all, I would recommend the book *Understanding Holography* by Michael Wenyon, which has, by the way, also appeared in Russian, but of course all the information there is somewhat out of date by now."

How fluent the man can get, was what I was thinking, almost enviously. I have to admit that holograms do interest me. But on the other hand, I can't stand it when other people are so long-winded. What right does he have to fill the air with such sound vibrations? I angrily attributed it to Tissen's generation, forgetting for a moment that we had been in one and the same class at school in the village.

I said:

"I remember myself as a child being the enemy of one great big hologram. I would wrestle with it frantically. I got worked up about all sorts of sci-fi notions. In the early '60s, I happened to read an article where a man with an engineering background conjured up before our eyes pictures that were a kind of three-dimensional TV, and which would affect all our minds at the same time, figures that you could smell and even touch. By that time, Ray Bradbury's cautionary tale had already appeared, the one where lions in the TV room actually eat people up, and this technophobic story fascinated me."

Tissen wet his lips, he could evidently not wait for the end of my story, which was natural. I made a warning gesture:

"Just a minute, I'm trying to generalize here."

Tissen could not hide his disappointment, but stayed politely silent.

I continued:

"Yes, we were a generation that was all cracked inside. Two opposing tendencies were in fact mixing in the world at the time. On the one hand there was technical progress that was all of a sudden moving at a faster rate than ever before. We were in fact being affected by cosmic travel and computers. Ethical problems were out of sight, beyond our horizon. Suddenly, those years immediately following the war were forgotten, although their human dimension, which expressed itself in dreams of individual happiness, as well as in collective prison camps, nowadays capture the imagination more than all those flights to conquer space. The hero of the day was, in fact, someone who was good at general knowledge, and in my youth such people would become very full of themselves. And they had every reason to be. Physics was strengthening the defenses of quite a few countries. Atom bombs seemed the sad exception. Nevertheless, it was at that very time that here in Russia the conflict between the 'physicists' and the 'poets' took root. Proud physicists would reject poetry and all other kinds of woolly thinking. That really went too far! (Tissen yawned!) In a word, I started reacting against the technocrats by writing to the papers, evoking all the wars that were made so tangible to us by being brought into our living rooms through the TV set, including tactile bullets. This spectral prognosis seemed a very attractive one to me. By the way, Professor Kaalep, who knows a lot about the culture of classical times, supported me in this and took to task the very learned, but technocratic-minded, lecturer Scheffer, who was always bubbling over with enthusiasm. Kaalep claimed there were two opposite types of human beings—*Homo faber*, he got the expression from the title of Max Frisch's novel—and *Homo sapiens*. What this second type of being was is already evident in the name itself—on the condition that the wisdom involved is multi-facetted—while the first type would be a kind of creative person, a type who is active, in other words someone who manufactures things without really paying much attention to the consequences of his actions either in a cultural or wider context."

I fell silent.

How could such a tale interest Tissen? I had the feeling that I was trying to explain our way of life to an Australian! Even I was getting fed up with what I was saying, so I fell politely silent. But Tissen, whom I had already interrupted once, now just continued.

In the end, he smiled.

"Professor Kaalep is on our side. Times have changed. He has come along to give us talks. What you don't know is that Kaalep freed himself from his anti-scientific attitudes years ago. He has got into the computer spirit pretty well, nor is the art of warning unfamiliar to him. Yes, you heard me: the art of warning. The anti-utopias that we have planned are something that interests Professor Kaalep. He now claims that mankind is responsible for our planet. He still finds it hard, admittedly, to get used to our condition, and the people you have in your time tried to label as 'playing the system,' 'dodgy politicians,' and I don't know what else."

Tissen's tone of voice had changed. I suddenly had the feeling that before me stood a complete stranger. Or was I deliberately making him more primitive than he really was in my mind? Tissen's gaze had suddenly become more focused and penetrating, his voice more intense and quaking with excitement.

"Playing the system! I would almost say that you people are jealous. What do you know about politics or games? Have you ever been in such a position where you have to think several dozen moves ahead, sometimes in one night, and with dozens of people playing against you? Maybe you have. Let us, gentlemen, start talking now about the concept of holography, if you gentlemen will allow."

He made a slight, ironic bow.

"We started off very simply. With just some spatial object. Music. The object moves in space. Always from simplicity to complexity, from innocence to significance. I remember a bust of Che Guevara that was in a glass dome. We didn't have our own premises in those days, and our technical equipment was pretty poor. Nevertheless, we soon attracted attention, especially when the first international hologram conference had taken place in Moscow where, incidentally, such varied people took part as Andrei Konchalovski, Gene Youngblood, and Claes Oldenburg. We were then noticed, and our basic funding increased, so we could employ a couple of actors. We succeeded in rising to the occasion. I think there are no limits in practice, the only thing is how much it's all going to cost, and whether the expense is worth it."

Tissen lit up another cigarette. I was thinking what an intensive life he led, both in his own opinion and that of others, and if these opinions concurred, was this indeed not a life of intensity?

"Last year we got so far that we made a woman. An exact copy, though I don't of course know of whom, but anyway the machine made a copy and this was filmed by a computer. I really don't know who was copied. Better, more ethical, that you don't know. The woman moved in accordance with the program that was, to be honest, a pretty complex one. Three-dimensional, with her naked. You will ask: why naked? To be more convincing. People are born naked and die naked, only wearing clothes in between. Watson has said that he couldn't believe in astral bodies wearing trousers and skirts. Who could? Clothes spoil everything. So that's why that woman too was naked, not for any other reasons you may be thinking of. She stood there in the middle of the hall, we've got this small hall, fifteen meters by fifteen. Stood there, moved around in a circle about one meter in diameter, could also say something, something like: I just don't know what to do. The original woman said that too. And she would also say: oh dearie me! Just like that. That was so nice, and she herself too. A Botticelli type, but a little plumper. A kind of indescribable sadness on her lips. *Ewigweibliche*, if you'll forgive the banality of the expression, mature at any rate. We really don't know who the original could have been, and if we did, we still wouldn't say. The machine recorded her and made a three-dimensional copy. A fantastic woman. Don't know whether she was married or what habits she had. Though she seemed intelligent. By the looks of her. The illusion held, even on close inspection. Everything was very nice. Then the scandal occurred. We had this employee, a man. By the name of Murdo. You just can't imagine. Tried to have sex with Our Woman. Honest. I discovered it myself. It was at night. The building was silent. I was doing something there. I heard a knocking sound through the door of the hall and had a look inside. Murdo had switched on Our Woman, she was standing on a dais. At half-past eleven at night. Alone and naked, with her intelligent gaze, as I said before. I saw Murdo go onto the dais, take down his trousers and tried to penetrate Our Woman. But the joke is that there wasn't any flesh. There he stood with an erection in the middle of nothingness, of a mirage. Murdo did have necrophiliac tendencies, I suppose. Or, God knows, maybe some other perversion—the woman was lifelike, still is, and with that intelligent look on her face! I called the others. We could have killed Murdo, beat him till the blood flowed. Nasty business. Murdo had shit upon our most holy relic. We loved Our Woman platonically. Everyone except Murdo, that is. That's when it all started. You will ask: what? You'll hear in a minute. Let's analyze our team and the actual situation at the time. Murdo showed us our true place. That affair with Our Woman really was the last straw. However, it was all necessary, so that we could define ourselves."

Red blotches had appeared on Tissen's face. He sank down, with a slight gasp, into his armchair and crossed his legs. I felt hot and opened the window a little wider. I think it was even hotter outside than inside. I stood there looking out. This probably gave Tissen the impression that I was ruminating about his story, that I had been grabbed by it. In actual fact, I was just letting time wash over me. Sometimes it's better to treat an unexpected and unwanted guest in that manner. He thinks you're pondering his words. He didn't dare continue. But you're simply taking a breather. Gathering strength to take another volley of words. Have you ever in your life thrown someone out of your apartment? Nobody, no doubt, or at least very rarely. I shut my eyes. The warm breeze blew in my face. Behind me, Tissen was breathing heavily.

"Let's say it straight out. This woman, this stranger, is no big deal. Murdo isn't guilty of anything. He just lacked self-control. But by creating this woman—even if seducing Murdo was only a pretext, although this wasn't consciously acknowledged—aren't we using the power we have rather childishly, without thinking of any further applications? I feel I can say all this to you because I have information about you, that, among other things, you're growing alienated from aestheticism, or have been for a short time at least. I think that at such a high level of technical achievement art ought to be used for something more important. Do you know how much energy our machines use when all we do is create a woman, although there are plenty of women on this Earth, and besides, ours is nothing but the copy of an existing one, a clone if you like?"

He started and looked around for something.
"Got a phone?"
I nodded.
"Do you want to call somebody?"
"Quite the opposite."
He lifted the receiver and left it off the hook.
"Moscow's on our side, but some of our lot are putting obstacles in our way."
I smiled knowingly.
"The money is allotted from above, but what about the future?"
He looked me in the eye.
"Officially, we are now setting up a laboratory to examine the

dynamics of clouds. I suppose you already know that. *Laboratoriya dlya izucheniya dinamiki oblakov.* Period."

Tissen, why do I think I'm better than you? OK, I say to myself proudly that Tissen waddles like a duck. But who doesn't walk funny anyway? Me, you, we all do. Tissen, it's me, is what I say, and Bob's your uncle. Hello, Tissen. In fact, I have been of no use either. Melancholy had crept inside me. Small children made me cry, I got depressed eating meat, old book bindings awakened tenderness in me. Everything was disintegrating. Nothing stood the test of time, including me. Somewhere on the other shore were madness and God, sometimes both wearing a beard. Neither instilled much confidence. Of course, if you love yourself long enough, you can destroy yourself anytime, or give in to something beyond the personal. But when I want something else, I don't know how to do it, and a blind rage awakens in me. God preserve us from God.

"So, I believe in lightning," Tissen repeated now. "And you?"

Provocateur!
   What can I be accused of? Does he imagine I'm actually thinking anything? I have always thought. I was thinking then, was thinking in between, and still am thinking now. You can't punish people for doing so, although they have in fact been punished. My thoughts rarely materialized and they are hard to grasp. This isn't, of course, pride on my part. The thoughts Estonians have are often secret ones. They vanish like the tracks of fish in water. They leave behind words, but these no longer mean anything.
   When you try to do the right thing once or twice in your life, then Tissen turns up one hot noon.

In fact, he didn't succeed in throwing me off balance with that.

Don't we get used to the fact, early in life, that all kinds of people want to make us ridiculous?

On the other hand, it's more useful to give the impression of being a loser, otherwise they get angry and start attacking you. So I blushed slightly and looked down, as Tissen wanted me to do. And I'd clearly got the right idea, because Tissen smiled, maybe even victoriously, or maybe not, but he was in any case in a good mood now for some reason.

"I've heard it said that in some situations sadness can bring on a mad joy."

What was he getting at now?

Of course I have used irresponsible metaphors, but I've never said things like this.

"That's poetry."

"Maybe. I've nothing against poetry. I've even written poems myself. Usually, however, I judge things with my balls."

I have lived and worked, loved and hated, made mistakes and had successes, have been verbally abused for no reason at all, built a home for myself whatever others have said, and now he comes along, believing in lightning.

"But something has to be done. Crying into the void. Choosing freely. In big cities they spit on humanist principles, we've known that for ages. Even if the metropolises don't care about people, at least we do here in the provinces. Every individual ought to made aware of the fact that . . . You have to love. Roughly and boldly. You have to teach. So all this rubbish doesn't advance any further. But the masses will awaken, awaken one day. They'll interfere, I'm telling you."

"What's all this got to do with lightning?"

He smiled shyly.

"I thought you preferred a metaphorical use of language?"

"To hell with language usage," I answered, "and why mess around with their images?"

He wagged his finger in warning.

"Aren't you starting to suck up to me, my friend?"

What does he mean by "sucking up"? Where's he get that from? Comes in, wearing Romanian jeans, his thoughts as fuzzy as can be, every other word a hint or an allusion; I should have thrown him out long ago, and now he starts accusing me of sucking up to him.

But he was right.

Imperceptibly I had begun sucking up to Tissen.

I wanted to please him.

What a horrible, endless day—and so hot too!

As if reading my thoughts, Tissen shut the window and looked enquiringly out onto the street. Soon he'll be closing the curtains, I thought with resignation. Should never have let him in. I thought that Tissen's eyes had changed color. I don't remember what color they were before, but not as red as now.

Nevertheless, he left the curtains alone and said:

"It was I good thing I came. Now isn't yet the time to put all my cards on the table. Let's say I've just popped in to see an old friend. Renewed our acquaintance. Nothing more. But we both know that there aren't that many of us. I'll be going now. I'll tell you in more concrete terms in the autumn or towards winter, let's say when the last flowers have withered. And if I don't tell you then, you'll see or hear everything for yourself anyway. Our time will come too, one day."

He paused.

"No one can take Liikola from us, it was what it was when it was, or what should we call it? I've put down my thoughts on paper. They're quite apolitical ones, quite asocial too. You can read them. They were jotted down for you to read. Read them and you might understand that the wolf will always make for the woods, however much Little Red Riding Hood may cry out."

He opened a document file, took out an envelope and shoved it into my hand.

Tissen turned suddenly and made a rapid move towards the entrance hall. I tried to open the front door for him, but he did so himself, nodded in silence, and left. Two boys, about ten years of age, and who had been avidly listening outside the door wheeled round with surprise when the door flew open and darted down the stairs. The door clicked shut. Here in the hall there are always clicks, I thought, at that inconvenient moment: when you switched off the main light there would also be a click, which for some redundant and incomprehensible reason I found irritating. I've imagined that what happens is that something contracts as the lamp cools down. But at this moment I had no time to be thinking about such trivia. I rushed back into the room and looked down out of the window and the first thing I saw was the unfortunate bird lying on the grass, but a moment later Tissen had reached the asphalt, and I looked down on him from above and noticed that he was thinning on top.

Tissen walked disjointedly, stooping a little, and quite quickly, as though he was worried about something. Perhaps he wasn't quite at ease with me, or with himself.

Theirs or ours?

"Still too early to put all my cards on the table!"

Actually, those who claim that it doesn't matter to whom you sell or present information are wrong. A beggar wants money, but do we start investigating what he needs it for? But a good deal depends on who a spy is working for. You can't be too cynical nowadays. I don't like it either when people sell weapons to both sides in an armed conflict. You've got to choose the one you feel is closer to you, or one that's more linked to the memories of your youth.

For instance, will Tissen maybe start asking me later on about certain military installations, or exhibit an interest in troop movements? What should I do then? You have to think up some lie or other, because my betrayals will end up in a mess and no one really needs them anyway—the basic principle of the secret services is a bureaucratic one: once they've started spying, they just can't stop, sums of money exchange hands, papers are shuffled. But perhaps Tissen has honorable reasons for his work: he just simply wants to get to know a writer's mentality, to keep him from making a mistake when the need arises.

No, there's something more to this than meets the eye. He has well-advanced plans because he was talking a bit too much about lightning. That can't be a coincidence.

"Remember Liikola!"

Well, I still remember you!

On the other hand: it's always nice to have a devoted reader.

I went into the kitchen, rubbed my eyes, spotted the coffee mill and began to grind some coffee beans. So here you are, I said to myself: you've tamed electricity and are using it to get the miraculous mill working. You want for nothing. Oh, and what other things were there? From the ceiling, an Ilyich bulb was dangling, on the walls there were black plug sockets. The leads came out of a panel on the wall, you couldn't actually see them, but I knew their geometrical layout, triangles and cubes that they formed around me. And there was a stove with three hotplates, in other words the Magical Fry-It-Yourself machine. In the corner stood Old Father Fridge in which we kept foodstuffs that were likely to go off quickly, and lo and behold, they didn't go off. And next to the front door the Self-Ring-Bell instead of a dog.

I hadn't had enough sleep and felt a bit tired. The sun was shining, but the streets were empty. This was because it was a Sunday. I felt envious of the Pueblo Indians who would describe phenomena in nature for their own pleasure. Their Chief Ochwiay Biano told Jung that the sun stays in the sky thanks to the efforts of the Pueblo Indians. If they were to stop performing their sun rituals, eternal night would ensue about ten years later. We tend to smile at the naïve assumptions of the Indians out of sheer envy, as Jung himself noted.

A coffee machine will stop if we don't do what's necessary, if we don't fulfill our duties as a citizen, if we just let everything go. The hotplates will stay cold and eternal night will ensue.

These were exciting times, as they always are, by the way. There were rumors flying about again that there was a cannibal in town! It's true that there are always such rumors flying about and, as always, people could name the victims. The militia made efforts to catch the cannibal, but then sat on their hands out of sheer hopelessness. The wind was blowing from the east, and as the folk saying goes: *when the wind is in the east, 'tis good for neither man nor beast.* Voltaire pointed out that Charles the First's head was chopped off when there was an easterly wind. In Arabia the percentage of serotonin in urine increases when the *sirocco* is blowing, and the *sirocco* blows from the east, as far as I know. So Tissen's threat was amplified willy-nilly.

The cacti were muttering to themselves, actually via a Hatsumoto device. How can I help it if nature runs its course, stores up electricity and thus prepares for lightning? Why do I always get angry when the Gauss readings climb? For instance, the *Gymnocalycium occultum*, a real yeller if ever there was one, mews like a cat. What are you yelling about, I'm not going to disperse the clouds! It's all superfluous panic because lightning doesn't strike inside these buildings, just the stray globes, i.e., globe lightning—I tend to call them globes to myself in a rather familiar way, although I've never actually seen one myself. One of these globes is not exactly likely to come whizzing in through some crack in the window, I'll give you that, but you also make a pretty good globe yourself, old *occultum*, so I can't really say that your *occultatio* has been particularly successful, as you crouch there pregnant with meaning on the windowsill, and will no doubt defend yourself ably against the other globe, so we'll have to see who comes off best.

Oh that comb-shaped vanity, that pathological luxuriance of forms and the peeping via the tone generators that goes with it, the instinct for self-preservation that, in extreme circumstances, will accumulate outside! Who ordered the overabundance of individualization, who ordered the development of characteristics to advance so far that the fear of death becomes too great? Could have stayed humble, lower than the grass, then you'd have had no fear of lightning! Now you'll have to pay for your originality!

Ahaa, the old *Astrophytum* has raised its voice, and the tension between heaven and earth is increasing.

One, two, three . . .

Then came the first flash of lightning.

The sun was still shining, but very mournfully by now.

OK, get going if you have to, I thought morosely, and I disconnected the TV aerial, a habit from my childhood, and shut the window. Then I sat down to watch what would happen. The wind rose and whirled litter about. I was behind glass, protected therefore. I had never heard that any storm at our latitude had ever got the better of any of our prefabricated concrete high-rise blocks of apartments, however mediocre they otherwise are. I pressed my chin against the windowsill. I remembered those poppies and lilies that always spring to mind when someone makes lightning himself, i.e., is taking snapshots with flashbulbs. I have seen such photos taken with flashbulbs of friends in among poppies and lilies. We've drifted apart, to be sure, but I can't say that I've ever completely lost touch with the friends I've made in my time. Anyway, the poppies and lilies, but these were flowering inside me, there weren't any flowers outside, just the yellowing grass, because autumn was not far off, in fact it wasn't far off any time of year, as spring wasn't, or winter. The year is so short, what else is there but things that are near? Anyway, the second lightning flash and the raindrops start falling. Sages have said that rain is sacrificial fire, the wind is its fuel, the clouds its smoke, lightning its flames, thunder stones its coal, and hail its sparks. Nice images, but there's no time to think about them now, as with other metaphors, because now the leader falls to earth with a rustling sound, clearing the road, and an impulse follows, or several, which you can't of course actually see. People say that there are usually two or three of them, but sometimes you can count up to fifty, not of course with the naked eye but with the suitable equipment, and maybe experts have such equipment, but where they get it from they themselves don't really know, when it comes down to it. If they can't get it produced locally, they can always buy it from abroad. For ordinary people like me, all those impulses merge into one whole. I'm alone. The Tissens of this world have left, random passersby cast their shadows, over the large block of apartments the shadow of a gigantic wing descends, that's what I'm saying, the wing of a giant bird, lightning keeps on flashing, far away at first, then nearer, until in the end it is pretty close; a chestnut tree gets split in half, I'm blinded just before that happens, or maybe it was the other way round: the bright flash blinds me, I close my eyes again, now there is a clap of thunder that fills my ears, and when I open my eyes again, the chestnut tree is in two halves, split in two, but there is no fire or smoke to be seen, and my hearing comes back little by little and with it the patter of the rain. And that's how it goes on: a dreadful thunderstorm, a rare thunderstorm, a thunderstorm that is always a thunderstorm . . .

Where was I?

Oh yes! At around three o'clock the thunderstorm started and lightning split the chestnut tree in our yard in two. I was sitting by the window and followed the course of the storm from beginning to end.

When the world had been cleansed and the sun came out again, I went onto the balcony and happened to hear what a little child on the neighbors' balcony was saying.

"You say," reasoned the child, cramming a jam patty into its mouth and presumably addressing its parents, "that the lightning killed the tree. How could it be allowed to? If I wanted to kill our

Edik from this block, then you wouldn't let me. And the tree has done nothing wrong, it was just growing there happily, as you say, and when the builders wanted to chop it down in the spring, you wrote a letter to someone saying the tree was very valuable to us and don't touch it, and the tree stayed where it was. But Edik isn't valuable, he steals everyone's bicycles and wrecks them, and forbidding him doesn't stop him. If I now want to kill Edik, I'm not allowed to, but the thunderstorm comes along, the sky's dead sure about what it wants, and nobody has a bad word to say about the thunderstorm. Why is the world so unfair, can you explain that to me? Well, I'm telling you that if you can't explain, then I'll kill Edik tomorrow, yes tomorrow, because I'm not going out again today, it's wet outside, but I really will, tomorrow. And you just try saying anything bad to me."

"Wipe the jam off your mouth," replied the mother. "And you've got jam all over your front, why can't you use a napkin, how many times do I have to tell you, can't take you anywhere, because you never know what you might go and do."

Then I remembered Tissen's letter, which was lying on the hall table.

Dear Mr. Writer!

I always hold it against you that you pour quite un-necessary scorn on your own first novel, where you de-scribed the way your generation thought, their dreams and conflicts. You have said afterwards that the book was one big lie, that people lied everywhere all the time, and that you couldn't act any differently. You shouldn't be allowed to disillusion the reader like that, because what is the poor reader guilty of? He is who he is; you can't go around 'taking back' what you said, like Tammsaare in his novel *Old Nick from Hell's Deep*, who wanted all of man-kind taken back because it wasn't going to get salvation. Cloudy term that word 'salvation,' but our propaganda machine has deliberately muddied the meanings of vari-ous religious terms. For instance, no distinction is made between 'belief' and 'religion.' Lenin always talked about religion in his atheist works, because he was specifically against religion, but religion has always been translated as 'belief' into our language, a word that, as far as I know, Lenin never had anything against. And all in all, people have more recently viewed religion as an inevitable psychological state of human beings, to be regarded as a link between knowledge and practical activity. It is not simply knowledge, but knowledge fertilized by the will of human beings, their feelings and strivings, which has turned into conviction! Believe you me, atheism isn't some kind of doctrine of disbelief but what it literally means, i.e., the disavowal of God. Assuming we get something positive out of the destruction of religion in the human psyche, in other words achieve a state of disbelief, we could when bringing up our children arrive at such absurd results, because we mix up religion as a social phenomenon and forget that true atheism is a positive definition, whether you like it or not, the possession of conflicting tenets, belief in them, being convinced of them. Without giving human beings positive values, without embracing them with an inner conviction, all we end up with when bringing up our young people is an increase in nihilism, cynicism, and a spiritual void.

And so: you have to believe in something.

For instance in Conscience.

Yes sir!

These last few days, I've been thinking a good deal, and am pretty sure that you have to offer people catharsis, and in large doses. Isn't it true that the presence of the atom bomb has prevented large-scale wars from breaking out in Europe? People, even if they are generals, are afraid. We need fewer joys in life, small doses are enough, but regular ones. May joys appear before you, in bas-relief, so you can eye them and feel them, a little like sweets in a bowl that never empties, because someone always buys more. But fear should resemble suffocation or drowning, yes, like a little death from which it appears as though you won't come back, but actually you always do. But we live on, in the knowledge that life is a short enterprise, mankind is a risky kind of group, nature is very vulnerable and death is always ready and waiting just around the corner. That's how someone might eat candies from the bowl on the table. A shadow has fallen over his subconscious and it never goes away. The grimmer the shadow, the better. Paratroopers by the supermarket holding flamethrowers; a tsunami reaching up to Toompea Hill; snakes forcing their way inside houses through the drain in the bathtub; a naked man with a knife outside the balcony window in the moonlight. *Memento mori.* There is always slight unease, you move along as on thin ice, you are no longer so proud, it is a sin to be so, as you know. The ancient Egyptians dressed their mummies for a banquet in order to remind people how brief pleasure and happiness are, we have to think up something else if we want to exist, if we want to keep a balance at all costs, if we want whatever it is we want just now, because without humility nothing will ever be achieved. A proud person sticks his nose into everything and is most satisfied with himself. He thinks he has been given the right to this, that, and the other thing. People speak a great deal and with enormous stupidity, they assume that in public they can shoot off their mouths without any inhibition, have opinions on everything when listening to what others have to say. Always cracking crude jokes, some people just can't do without jokes. True, I did see a man on the Moscow train recently who had a file full of facts. The first wasn't a fact, but a question: what is a zero diet? The answer was supposed to be: starvation. Apart from that you got to know how much cold a goose can stand, and the answer was something like 120 degrees below, and the goose would still be alive. People talk about such things in a loud voice, and if that isn't pride, I don't know what is. *Trägheit des Herzens?* I was reading, I think it was Ortega y Gasset, where he said that a Roman soldier would have to do his guard duty at night with his index finger resting on his lips in order not to fall asleep. This man served as a warning to all proud people by demonstrating that in the silence of the night he was demanding an even greater silence. We should have such a guy in our subconscious, but where would you get one from? Always well organized and ready to scare us. Let's say it straight out. You have to scare people, and everyone at once. Not the way the Iranians are scaring the Iraqis, or the Estonians the Russians. Let's leave nations aside for a moment. You have to sap the foundations of existence, have to penetrate people's nightly dreams, but when doing the penetrating you have to use pre-existing structures and organizations, even creating them if need be. And you need helpers, collaborators. Especially collaborators, bright and lively people who are interested in what they're doing, and in doing it effectively, and who retain their determination. My own thoughts are extremely fickle. I think one thing today, another tomorrow, I'm well known for that. Overnight, my thoughts can do a 180-degree turn. Today I will call black white, tomorrow yellow or purple. That is, of course, human, but my personal disposition increases this tendency. I've often described myself as a pragmatist, but in doing so I don't touch the core of my being, because today, for instance, I think I don't believe in God: in my opinion He may exist, or may not, but if this notion of gods brings with it certain consequences, I think it's sensible to tackle these consequences once they've arisen, whatever may ensue. Anyway, my assistants would preserve any chance idea of mine, would stick to it and never be able to change direction. They would be stubborn as mules, wouldn't rest until they had achieved something. They would feel that it was a sad thing to give up before the results are there. They would avoid exhaustion and skepticism. Damn it, if we had taken on some challenge we'd be God knows where by now. We'd have sown the seed and only watched them from the corner of our eye as they flourished. Lord knows if I ever want to see the fruits of my labors: they will have removed themselves so far from my initial impulses! But still—it is precisely in my helpers, or, in broad terms, Others that I have the only support for my existence, my only chance. Being fickle, I wouldn't really exist if I wasn't embodied in my disciples, where I at least achieve some kind of temporary constancy. Being new, I can look at my assistants and think: this is me. I am your Conscience.

So as you see, I know no sadness or surprise, I simply do not exist. I am merely the arena or the stage at the theater, where current events come to a head, but I lack a center. To put it in theatrical terms: I lack a core to my role, something that Stanislavsky and Panso so desperately pursued. I lack the wholeness of a human being, I am simply the ever-changing aspects of a conglomerate entity. A strange story, isn't it? I'm happy to tell it, to see what a face you pull, because even I like to check up on myself now and again. Your expression waivers, which is quite understandable: you can't listen to such a tale looking someone candidly in the eye. You began to believe me, you're already convinced that someone with endless potential, boundless opportunities is speaking to you and you find it difficult to relate to me as a human being. A Me-You relationship. But you can rest assured that I'm not cooking up any plans for you, I don't have any hidden agenda this evening, I too just want to take it easy sometimes, let's put it this way: an empty stage also wants to confess. That I remember from the time I was a theater director for a year, when I had just left the university, before I started working for the institute. The night stage creaked, it had something on its mind. Me too, my friend. My heart is creaking and I want to confess.

Kind regards,
Tissen

The letter made me anxious.

That same night I replied in diffuse but urgent style:

Dear Tissen!

Have you thought everything through? I beg you, don't do anything before you tell me what you're planning.

Tissen, if you've got problems, call me. I'm ready to help you.

Kind regards,

(. . .)

ঞ৳

No reply came.

And me and you all, especially me and You, used the pleasant times we had left profitably.

You came late that evening, you had met someone, seen something, I distinctly remember. You talked about it at length.

"My dear, don't keep going on about that Tissen, he isn't interesting enough for me to want to get to know him better, even through your descriptions. Leave him alone, don't get so worked up about him, and next time don't let people in so easily, we do after all have a spy-hole in the door, you should use it. When he talks a lot and paces back and forth, he's just plain boring, but before you know it he's drained you of all your energy for the rest of the day. I know many such people and always avoid them. They are like eternal Communist youth pioneers, always agitated about something, always deep in thought, their hair mussed up, banging on the table with their fists and planning something progressive. Staging a coup to overthrow the government, or trying to fight for artistic freedom, or how to save the soul of some fallen woman or other. Let's keep out of their way, my dear, they are dangerous and always very active. Remember electricity, which you used to be so in love with in your youth—it would move at the speed of lightning from one place to the next, it was here one minute, there the next, always there when you wanted to iron your shirt, do the washing, or boil some tea; in that same way a paranoid person, someone who wants to save the world, arrives at a place within a split second, there where injustice is rife, where the secret police are on the rampage, where an inferior race is suffering. He is as quick as a goblin, except that all he wants is good. Oh, what am I talking about? A goblin also wants good, tries to function in as effective a way as possible, one that has results. He isn't guilty of anything himself. Nor am I saying that your Tissen is guilty of anything either. Yes, I perhaps hurt him without meaning to do so, even I don't know why myself, why I suggested to you that he just isn't a very interesting person and he isn't worth knowing. But you just can't avoid the fact that he poisons the atmosphere in the room and drains my energy, I can feel it already. Get thee hence Satan, do your evil deeds, but leave me alone! Now you will feel that he has gone, that my cursing him has been sufficient. Do you really want me to tell you what I saw today? I went out early, while You were still sleeping. The sun had risen, which isn't such a miracle because it's only late autumn. The trees hadn't yet shed their leaves and a fresh breeze was blowing. It all sounds so matter-of-fact, but I am happy that I'm a human being, and that you exist, so what if you don't at all appreciate mankind as a whole? Those feelings that arise, whether in spring or autumn, cannot be overrated or commented on too much. Of course the wind gets lost somewhere, for mankind's benefit, and I'm thinking: it blows and billows and how little of it is needed to power windmills or power stations; it blows through empty spaces, it ends up everywhere and no one can catch hold of it, grasp it and in the end it simply grows weak, as it meets no resistance, and dies down in some gravel pit or other. What do you remember of where it's gone? Vain strivings, gnawing at your soul, aren't they? Useless energy, like us who also erode cliffs and heap up *barhan* dunes, also for God knows who, but we talk and talk about it in the way that the wind soughs and sighs. There's something beautiful about that, though I don't really know what beauty means, but it keeps getting used, so I don't see why I shouldn't use the word myself. I can, can't I? Thank you. Anyway, I went out early, there was a breeze and the swallows were sitting there on the power lines, getting ready to migrate southwards, perhaps to Italy, where they are a popular dish, but where they always seem to fly off to. In Italy, the *Opuntia* flourishes, they imported it at some time or other, with some plan or other in mind no doubt, but one that nobody any longer remembers. They lounge around near hot white walls like droopy old dragons. They don't go anywhere, they don't migrate southwards. Chop off one of their heads and seven will sprout in its place. Our Estonian culture could also be like that. If you close down the classical philology department at our university, then seven spring up in its place. Why aren't you listening to me? I'm not talking nonsense, I've got my reasons for saying all this, and soon I'll get to the point. Anyway, I got down onto the street, a breeze was blowing, swallows were sitting on the power lines overhead, and I went into a shop. It had a high ceiling and there were a few swallows flying around inside, frantically trying to find their way out to their companions. They twittered and threw themselves against the windows, but they were very high up and I couldn't do anything to help them. Downstairs, food was being sold. I waited at the meat counter. There were eight chunks of meat there, all of them of equally poor quality. That's why they were still there in the shop; otherwise they'd have been sold long ago. We in Estonia like meat, but there's little available. When there's plenty of meat, people prefer fruit and vegetables. But there's no meat, and we like it. Then you take what you get, don't you? Eight abandoned chunks of meat were lying there on an enamel tray. A little blood had seeped from them all or some other red liquid, and up under the eaves the swallows were shrieking. Why don't people buy meat when it's there, I was asking myself. Meanwhile I went over to have a look at the dry goods counter, but I couldn't get those eight chunks of meat out of my mind, so I went back to the meat counter. I had to find a solution, but what? And do you know what, I asked which one of those chunks of meat was the best. The shop assistant simply didn't understand the question. *Shto*, was her reply, *chevo khochesh*? I politely repeated the question in Russian: *kakoye myaso samoeluchsheye*? And she replied, and I'll translate it quickly here: every piece of meat is the best, *vsyo myaso khorosheye*, there isn't one piece of meat here that isn't the best. And suddenly I realized that she was right. At first I thought that one piece with the bone attached was worse than the others because you'd get less meat. But so what? Wasn't bone also substance, couldn't you eat it too, so why should I turn my nose up at it, and if it proved to be inedible I could find some other use for it, otherwise why would it exist in the first place? *Khochesh myaso*? asked the shop assistant, and I nodded. I shut my eyes as she picked out a piece and wrapped it up. I paid, I don't remember how much, and left the shop. *Vsyo myaso khorosheye* was still ringing in my ears. I'd always wanted to hear that, my whole life. I had always known that such a reply existed somewhere, but it had somehow never reached me. Now it had. And I knew what to do. I went up to the first dustbin I could find and put the packet in it. I closed the lid and was just about to leave when I was stopped from doing so by the sudden thought of the flies that would attack the meat right away. I bought that day's paper from the same kiosk and went back to the dustbin. I opened the lid and wrapped up the meat in the newspaper. It was really funny, at least for me. A couple of children were watching me and I almost thought of saying to them: *vsyo myaso khorosheye*, but what held me back was the idea that what I was doing was my little secret, which I oughtn't to share with just anyone. Let them consult the oracle themselves and get their own answer. I'm not some middleman or messenger. You I'm telling straight, but the rest of them will just have to do without my explanation. What have we got to eat for today? Only sausage? OK, I agree. You can fry sausage, you can eat it as it is, cold. Is the sausage expensive or cheap? Cheap? OK, let it be cheap, I now know for sure that *vsyo myaso khorosheye*: every piece of meat is the best."

Je ne connais guère, non, sinon les anges,
Je ne connais guère d'animal plus nu!
—Francis Ponge

During those years when the systems that were dominating our world began to change and threatened to turn into their diametric opposites, and about which the public had no clear ideas, I used to relate to people in various different ways. Sometimes I would view them from the inside, i.e., I would also see myself as a human being, while at other times I was an observer. Both positions had their pros and cons, so it was difficult to regard one method as preferable to the other. Sometimes it didn't seem to matter what you thought. The only thing that tended to annoy me was the way people kept their outward form. What irritated me more than the systems at work in society (whose real essence was pretty obscure, as I've said) was the fact that everyone had two legs and two arms and one head. There were much more interesting things to be seen in animated films where characters made out of plasticine would change now into a ball, now into a plate, now into a piece of string. That is a kind of life worth living, I said to myself. It was quite another matter to follow all those political meetings or serious discussion programs on TV. A man who wanted a change of government would always breathe through both nostrils; a person who called the life that we were living a bad dream would cross his legs. There were no surprises.

So the days went by and winter was already approaching, although it did so in its usual way, through darkness and sadness, not exactly surprising anyone, but hardly making them any happier either.

Well, in that way, winter grew nearer and nearer, and there was nothing that could be done about it. You could now imagine that soon snow would be falling, and there was nothing that could be done about it.

There are specific systems in nature, ones that are almost certain to occur.

Winter doesn't arrive by chance.

You can more or less be sure that it's going to come.

Chance occurrences are a completely different story.

Eddington has said about events that they don't happen, but rather we collide with them. And it has also been said that events are already there in the world like on a strip of film, and all we have to do is watch.

If events weren't often so unpleasant, you'd be able to think more about them.

But the doorbell? How could you love that? How rare it is that there's an interesting person waiting outside the door!

Events in all their varieties have triggered off varied thoughts in great people.

The Estonian stage director Panso has said that one of the features about playing events in a play is the ability to "stand with your back to the events, that is, not actually be aware that the table is expecting a letter to land on it."

And it is true that we don't know that it's expecting it.

Only the actors know, and not always them either.

Professor Lotman claims that an event is a revolutionary element (in reactionary times, there is no news in the papers).

My dear, I came back from the shop where hungry people were buying meat, thirsty people buying blood, pig's blood to be exact, made into blood pudding or just straight, many were dressed for the approaching winter and all those who were cold had only bones to burn, but there was no other kind of fuel being sold.

My dear, winter is approaching again and sometimes it bodes ill, sometimes not, in fact it just sounds like what you want it to sound like, because almost everything is in your own hands except chance, but when you must, you're able to forecast even that.

And now I'll go on telling you what happened.

On 13th December 1981, marshal law was declared in Poland.

A day later we were summoned to the command post from which Tallinn's electricity grid was controlled.

There was no time to go there before evening. This and that happened, this person and that one arrived. So I took a taxi and drove with a couple of friends in a direction I can't reveal here. I'll just say that the command post was outside of town.

Dusk was falling, snow was drifting, we were in an elated mood.

We talked about various things.

The taxi driver interrupted our conversation; he had his own story to tell:

"I was alone in the sauna quite recently. Late in the evening, so I thought I'd throw plenty of water on the stove and work up a good hot steam. The stove was an electric one, so I switched it on all the way. I sat there and started pouring water on the stones. There I am pouring and pouring, but then when I wanted to leave the sauna, I couldn't get out. I pushed and pushed at the door, but it wouldn't budge, as if someone was holding it shut from the outside, pushing his shoulder against it. I yelled for him to open the door and to stop fucking around, it was nearly 120 degrees in there. No one answered. I pushed with all my might, but then I understood what was going on. There was lots of water on the floor, the drain had got blocked. The water was flowing over the threshold and collecting outside. A small plank of wood had floated up with the water and got wedged between the door and the wall, and the door opened outwards. The piece of wood was jamming it. The switch was outside in the changing room; you couldn't get at it from where I was. The heat just kept on rising!"

We arrived at the command post without really noticing. We paid the taxi driver and got out.

One of us asked whether it wasn't impolite not to have asked the man how he managed to get out of the sauna alive.

Obviously he had managed to get out, said another, otherwise we wouldn't have been riding in his taxi.

The water level dropped in the changing room by itself, just like that, I interrupted, but it's hard to surmise why it should have done so. At the same time it's quite likely that someone else who wanted to take a sauna came along and rescued the man. In which case that sauna-goer certainly arrived in the nick of time.

He may not have survived, in which case the taxi driver was a zombie, one of us said with a smile.

Actually, the taxi driver's story came at rather the wrong time, because in the cellar of the command post itself there was also a sauna, and people would tend to take a sauna when visiting the command post. We assured one another that there were several of us and we could help one another in an emergency.

As always there were quite a few people there, some we'd never seen before. The others seemed to know one another. And really, what a miracle it is if you know everybody. Because you take one and reject the other. Not such a big difference among them, if you know one you already know most of them.

In the sauna there were only men to start with and the conversation was polite. I don't know why that bothered me. I come from the countryside and to this day I've never got used to large groups of sauna-goers. I don't understand why naked men sit around philosophizing or criticizing the economy. On the other hand, I'm not so vulgar that I think sauna talk should be reduced to only swearing. No, I don't think like that either. Perhaps you shouldn't talk in the sauna but mutter, groan, snort. I want to hear animal sounds, feel how close we are to nature. When you've taken off your clothes, why not also throw culture out of your brain? Why not be free, be natural. Why force yourself to be like you are in a café. Compare your penises, wrestle, laugh. That would be more honest. Why be pretentious in there. Everyone on Earth demands something, who's got time to listen to all the demands?

The first water had been thrown onto the stones of the stove, the steam level had risen, and the head of the command post arranged a little excursion for us, as he always did as far as I know.

A couple of dozen naked men in the bluish light of the sun lamps, standing amid the equipment—what a fascinating sight. I enjoyed looking at the fragile bodies in between all that glass and nickel. How mortal people are—was what I wanted to yell, out of sheer enthusiasm. The boss rested his oversized belly on the edge of the console. From here the whole electricity grid for the town and the surrounding area is controlled, he said with conviction. I suppose he had the right, as he knew even more about this business than we did. But one drunken man didn't believe him. One of them really went over the top.

"Let's switch off the circuit for Nõmme," he yelled, "then my wife'll know where I am now! Or, even better: switch it off three times in a row, because when I get home I always ring the doorbell three times! Where's the knob?"

The boss said nothing.

The man watched the flickering lamps and the slowly moving needles of the dials.

Water was dripping onto the floor from his legs.

He had hairy shoulders.

Why did he want to give his wife a signal?

What had he to say to her?

And another of the men, who was suddenly sitting there on the wax-cloth of the console, had spots on his back. I've nothing against spots, everyone has them now and again. It was just so unexpected, the sight of decaying flesh crouching in front of a computer. Such things simply don't fit together.

Gradually, a kind of awe began to seize hold of the assembled company.

People began to involuntarily look at the huge uncurtained window, beyond which loomed the dark night.

People began to fear the inspector, or worse, the revenge of the electricity itself, I thought to myself, riding away on my own hobbyhorse.

But the married man took no notice.

"I'll press this one here and Anna'll recognize me for sure!" he yelled triumphantly and staggered towards the console.

The boss managed to reach him in time and the man calmed down.

"Actually, you wouldn't have achieved anything, because a layman would stand practically no chance of really getting access to the city power supply," the boss kindly commented. "You have to know the theoretical side of how the system works."

The man said grimly that he'd only been joking and shrugged his shoulders.

I tried to find out from the boss whether this theory was so difficult to grasp and what it roughly consisted of. The boss smiled and answered politely that the rules unfortunately didn't allowed him to go into such details with visitors.

It would be interesting to know whether the boss knew of my one-time interest in energy, and electricity in particular. Did he know that I knew Tissen? Did he know Tissen's name? He had to. I'll get round to saying why in a minute.

Though first: the dials quivered, the buttons tempted, there were lamps of various colors. Yes, no sensible person would touch them.

I could hardly keep my hands off.

You always want to get involved and interfere.

The boss looked me briefly, but seriously, in the eye.

I could do no more than shrug my shoulders and return with the others to the sauna.

There the boss kept on casting ladles of water onto the stones.

He was a man who enjoyed life; I remembered him from school.

In the dim light of the mixed sauna, I heard a woman's soft voice through the hiss of the water on the sauna stones. The voice complained about everything, asking whether the steam was hot enough, saying someone ought to bring some cold water, wondering whether the heat didn't flay your skin or make your hair fall out.

The voice was very familiar to me. But I didn't understand how Susie could have ended up here. What was she doing?

Through the thicket of naked bodies I reached out towards that voice, but again the hiss of the water drowned out everything else. The lightbulb, surrounded by wire mesh, was dim and lit the sauna poorly.

Then a volley of conversation buried Susie's voice altogether. Someone was telling people about his life, someone else was contradicting him, anger was rising. I moved to a cooler corner, a cool draft blew onto my ass from the gaps between floor and walls, and I don't know how long I would have sat there in the darkness if I hadn't suddenly heard a man's voice: and now for a splash!

There was movement, quarrels were thrown aside, washbowls were knocked over. From the open door a thickish white vapor wafted in. Then I think I stood up and rushed over to the others. Some were shouting hurray, and I went through the motions, just in case.

I knew that some hundred meters from the command post was a pool where coolant water collected. I had once quenched the heat of my body in this water that came straight from the transformers, warm and a little rusty in color.

Like one big happy family we ran across the snowy space outside. Several spotlights were shining against a black sky. Somewhere in the distance a dog was barking. The man in front splashed my naked body with slush as he ran. You could feel a few snowflakes falling from the heavens. The women shrieked out of excitement and joy. The first bodies plunged headfirst into the water with a splash.

After a short moment of hesitation, I too jumped into the dark pit, into the whitish steam. The water was up to our chests and felt very warm. Snowflakes melted on our naked shoulders. Stars peeped out now and again from among the clouds above. But down here it was impossible to make out who was who. Susie too had fallen silent and was bathing somewhere unseen. I had already understood that she was a social person at times, but at others could withdraw into herself.

In one corner a wide tunnel led away down into the depths. This was presumably the drainage channel, but luckily there was an iron grille in front. You could feel a current, especially down at foot level.

We splashed around in silence, though a few people muttered with pleasure.

But as always, in the most inappropriate situations, under the distant gaze of the stars and the planets, eye to eye with eternity, in the warm womb of the collection pool, when there are both sexes present, someone starts causing trouble. We all knew who it was. Let's leave his name out of it because he has high status in society, and his word carries a lot of weight. He is known for his philosophical bent. But he's that type of person whose cultural veneer wears away when he's drunk. Such people never fail to start swearing and spewing and it's funny how everyone else manages to forgive them for it! How they belch and slurp when eating soup and how, when so doing, they never fail to mention the fact that they come from a long line of intellectuals! Oh, they're everywhere, no point in going into detail, we ought of course to preserve them because such people are very necessary for our world. Anyway, may God forgive him but he suddenly started bawling out in one dark corner of the pool. *Drink! Drink! Drink!* were, at any rate, his first words, he no doubt imagined himself to be in some warm pub or other, or God knows where, anyway he started bawling, and went on bawling, but his syntax was all up the spout and you couldn't make most of his words out either, except for the fact that they were filled with aggression. This man was like an animal, waving his arms about so that he took up more room than usual. Then he withdrew to a corner. We listened wearily to the endless stream of swearing, but he didn't seem to want to stop.

The man went on cursing away:

"What do you really think, what kind of life is that, you're satisfied with yourself, couldn't want anything better, everyone pulls faces, and everything's all right! But secretly, round the corner, in cells and dens, in offices too, what the fuck happens there? I'm telling you now: the emperor's naked and I'm the first who says so without beating about the bush. I am telling you right now, the emperor's new clothes, the emperor is naked, and I'm the first to dare to say so! I'll grab everyone and yell: get out of here, you renegade! What is it? What is it, I ask myself? It's all one dirty great big pile of shit and everyone is lazy and no one gives a fuck about anything. Kick 'em all up the ass, that's what I say, that would be better for them, better for you! First I'll go and drown myself and then the rest of you, you'll see! Cowards!"

The man dived into the water and it took quite some effort to get him back onto dry land.

(I must add here that you wouldn't have recognized him as

the same person afterwards when he was serving coffee to the ladies in the sauna clubroom and cracking weak jokes.)

My God!

I was up to my neck in water.

Out of the watery mass, black as birch oil, a firm white throat appeared, on top of which a large pile of hair that melted into the steam, so far as I could make out in the foggy, snowy light. Did it have eyes and what was reflected in them: the stars, the guard hut, the windows, the snowflakes? Yes, the snowflakes that were falling on my shoulders and melting.

Down, very deep in the warm water, where there was a weightless being that confirmed Archimedes's Principle, a hand with a temperature the same as that of the water closed on my penis in a grip that was firm, but not at all painful. This all happened far away, in the dusk, the pitch darkness in fact, in another world, but not hell, that would be an exaggeration and wouldn't be suitable in this context. What it was that got me excited is not necessary to explain, the most important thing was the warm and slippery mass out of which only my head stuck. With some exaggeration you could say that it was like being in a kind of huge womb, up to my neck in a warm vulva, within which a vulva that was a hand was moving back and forth.

Around me people were talking, commenting on the recent tirade, talking about their private lives. Behind me someone was talking about the Green movement, but my pleasure was increasing to the extent that I couldn't hold back any more. At the moment I ejaculated I sank unwillingly under the surface of the water, or Susie pulled me, if it was her, because I hadn't managed to get a good look at her.

When I rose spluttering to the surface, the mysterious figure had disappeared. I was immediately seized by panic. There were several other women in the collection pool, among them a couple of young girls. I thought that there were some 300,000,000 of my spermatozoa swimming around in the warm water and with a bit of good luck they could inseminate all the women in the collection tank!

It was too late for regrets, but I nonetheless decided to flee the scene of the crime.

I muttered to the first shadow in front of me something about having work to do and climbed with great effort up the iron ladder.

The dogs were barking as before, the light from the spotlights was cold and motionless. From below, as if from an open collective grave, there was the murmur of conversation.

I walked alone in the melting snow across to the command post.

A young man, no doubt the night-shift operator who had just turned up for work, looked at me with indifference and offered me a cigarette.

I refused his offer, got dressed and went home.

On the way, sitting at the back of the last bus, I thought with relief: life could not be preserved in water when there was a high-tension electrical field all around. But then again, the "water of life" was produced using magnets.

Clearly, it all depends on the wavelength.

How mournful the start of winter, how devoid of hope my meditations!

It was a silent sadness, still ignorant of the catastrophe that was now on the horizon.

As Samuel Beckett once said, there's nothing more comical than accidents. He himself is someone that the quip could very well apply to. No one could at any rate doubt his sincerity. Yes, it's funny if someone loses control of his own behavior and his freedom. Why is it comical? Just as it's comical when someone slips on a banana skin: so self-important before, married, carrying his briefcase, and suddenly falls on his face in the mud. Is that funny? I don't know, but people tend to laugh at such things, don't they? And now, at the onset of winter, when it was already getting dark at four, when asocial people were yelling their self-centered slogans in triumph into the icy air, when mothers with many children took special pride in slamming shut the taxi door with the back of their hand, when the papers were discussing the promotion of private business initiatives, when on a clear night you could see the Big Dipper—then arose the firm conviction that someone or something had gone wrong, that soon an accident would occur that would end up like all other accidents: someone or something would set right the mistake and bring the world back to its former state.

Vous savez, ces princesses hindoues, ces intouchables, qu'il
suffissait d'effleurer pour mourir? Bien. J'aime assez ça.

—Francis Ponge

On the first of January, my birthday, we still didn't suspect anything was wrong, we just put on thicker winter clothes. I held a
short speech for the cacti, in which I said that no one ever gets any
younger, but there's no real reason to start talking about time
unless there is a pressing need to do so. I said that they were
guests here in this country but were keeping themselves pretty
well. I also said a few other things. Actually, that same evening I
did begin to worry. My birthday guests hadn't turned up and the
radiators were cold. The lights wouldn't switch on and the electric
stove wouldn't heat up. The doorbell wouldn't ring. I paced from
room to room.

"Well, that's what you wanted," You said, "technology has been
switched off. Life now has a hold on us."

"Why would this have to happen on my birthday, of all days?"

"It's congratulating you."

"What is?"

"Life, of course."

"I think it's congratulating everybody except me. Otherwise we wouldn't be sitting here in the cold and dark."

True, I could see no lights in the growing darkness.

"The main thing is that the two of us are here together."

That was some consolation, but I felt it didn't really correspond to the truth. The colder it got, the more visitors seemed to be entering the room. They were, admittedly, invisible. But one of them was breathing right in my face. The unease increased. I checked the Hatsumoto device but there was no electricity, therefore no sound. The level of the galvanometer had dropped noticeably. The cacti were turned in on themselves, had taken up defensive postures. A fly was sitting down by one of the plant pots. I swiped at it and it fell on its back. What had Life done wrong to it? Was not the fly Life too? Who was fighting whom? I too am not giving up that easily. There's no mysticism at work here, the heating and lighting engineers simply got drunk over the New Year. That's not Life but Insolence. They deserve some kind of punishment. They'll get a fine or will be fired on the spot. Then things will get warmer again. But when? It's fourteen degrees Celsius in the room. That wouldn't be so bad in summer. Quite the opposite, it'd be very pleasant. But the temperature outside was dropping too. We couldn't see the thermometer outside the window, the pane was covered in ice. With flowers, ferns, crystals. I blew on the windowpane, but my heart was cold, the magic forest did not thaw. You could still see out through the center part of the window. Snow was blowing off the tops of the drifts like smoke. No one had put on the lights, neither to the left nor right if you looked out of the window.

No point in getting panicked, I was saying to myself, although I knew that panic was the easiest way out. You start howling, wake up covered in sweat, and it's morning. That's how it always ends. But I felt ashamed in front of You. I had to keep a grip on myself, more or less anyway. Not only for You, but for the invisible guests. Father Christmas or Old Father Cold had a hundred pairs of eyes, even on their backs. I had to deceive myself, You, the cacti, the grim gods, and common sense.

Take one simple thought:

I light a fire right in the middle of the floor. Why shouldn't I? How did our forefathers manage? Pile up the novel in the middle of the room and set it on fire. Spared from all the pain and agonizing! Now it's already thirteen degrees in the room! What's that got to do with a dialogue where you don't understand who is who when reading it, when it's me and when it's someone else! Getting that power station at Liikola operating, that would at least be something in such times as these. Lying there behind the shed on a warm summer night, a bomb packed in your rucksack!

I was astonished at how easily I was betraying my own principles.

But You were standing at the kitchen door, half your face in the last rays of the setting sun, on the other cheek a frosty glow, which reflected the snow down below in the deserted yard. You were standing there without any protective layer of fat, a thick plaid wrapped round You, Your eyes wide open and calm. I went over to you and put my hand on your cheek. Yes, Your body temperature was also dropping. But You shouldn't admit to such things.

"Normal," I said in a carefree tone of voice.

"True," You said smiling, "I thought I was running a temperature."

How could I tell her that it was quite the opposite?

"The guests won't be coming anyway," I said and walked over to the cupboard. I took out a bottle of cognac, opened it, deliberated over whether to take a swig or not, decided not to and poured the bitter-smelling drink into a soup dish. I struck a match and half a meter of flame rose in the air. It crackled and was translucent, but gave no light.

When, by nighttime, the bottle was empty, the temperature had risen back to about fifteen degrees. I had no more alcohol at home, I had hoped that the guests were going to bring some. Now the air was sweet and foul. That frightened away the spirits and we fell into a restless sleep.

ॐ

The next morning, I tried to set light to other liquids. Milk did not ignite, nor cooking oil. It was, after all, too cold. And the smell of eau-de-Cologne is disgusting in excess. I didn't yet care to start vague dialogues lacking both subject and object, and their smoke—as that of the chairs and tables—would perhaps be too black and suffocating. I couldn't after all open the windows!

Throughout the day I stood at the window and didn't see one person. Not even the most disgusting people who lack culture, humanism and a native land. I was beginning to imagine that I had always lived alone in this Land of Sleeping Beauty (along with You).

On the evening of the 2nd of January we collected together all the cacti and put them on the floor of the room. In the darkness I tripped over the rug and fell on all fours, but nothing worse happened, only perhaps the fact that one ugly *Stetsonia* fell out of its pot. I had tripped over the rug because we had already removed it and rolled it up so that we could put the candles on the bare parquet flooring. The melting wax did of course run down onto the floor. I remembered doing this sort of thing before, but only with a couple of candles. Now there were twenty or so to keep an eye on. That wasn't all that many but we had to think about replacements, and I calculated there'd only be enough for three batches. I couldn't get any more candles from anywhere. Maybe there were some hidden away, but where?

Anyhow, there they all were on the floor with a circle of candles around them. I didn't know exactly how many there were, still don't, though now there are a few more. But not so many more as I would have wanted, because you have to replace cacti, now and again one of them dies however carefully you nurse them. The most sensitive cacti are unfortunately the ones from Vilnius that are more exotic than any other, but the majority are grafted onto *Selenicerei* or *Pereskiae*, so they don't last that long. Another city for cacti is Moscow: you can always manage to buy some of the tougher species on the Arbat, ones that don't intend to die. Moscow cacti tend to have their own roots, or they are largely used as bases for grafting. I have sometimes thought that in Moscow cacti remain some traces of old Russian culture, the nobility, Tolstoy and Pushkin. The Vilnius cacti on the other hand express the polyvalence of a small people thrown to the winds of the world, let's say the painful frictions of local aristocracy, Marxism, a Baltic identity, Catholicism, and being European.

Whatever the case, they were all in danger now.

Actually, I should have constructed some sort of tent over the cacti, some kind of bivouac, or perhaps we too should have gone and lain down there among them, thus uniting with the cacti in their struggle. But we didn't have any pieces of material big enough nor did we have things to use as struts, grating or frame.

The fifth floor of a concrete apartment block is not really the place to go looking for things when you suddenly need them!

Any tent would have had to be sufficiently high so that the candle flames didn't set the fabric on fire.

And a tent would have had to be wide enough, with a large diameter, otherwise we wouldn't have fitted in along with the cacti, although You didn't in my opinion take up that much room, not that I've noticed anyway!

I'm telling You, to comfort You, that You are being very brave:

We're not afraid of anything, because things have been bad before now, and in the end something always happened to set them right. A builder or a militiaman or your father turned up.

I'm telling You: the moon is shining in through the window!

Today, the 2nd of January one could say for sure that the moon was a cold earthly globe and there was no help to be got from it. It looked down on us, didn't come to help us, yes, and this too: it had done so in the past, but now its gaze was so mocking, so merciless! I remember the moon from here and there, above rivers in summer or shining enchantingly through the window of an observatory, but now it was making You afraid, in extreme circumstances even angry. We could do nothing but light those pathetic candles because such a huge object remains indifferent. In fact no one cares about us except ourselves, not even some other being in the sky, or even a god.

Are You still listening to what I'm saying? It isn't too cold for You? Don't for God's sake leave. Just stay right there wherever You are. Don't let Yourself be frightened that easily! Do at least give some sign to show where You are, knock over a vase or something, or let a broomstick fall.

"I can hear everything you're saying, and I'm not too cold. Of course I'm not going anywhere, I'm right here, wherever you yourself happen to be. I don't get scared easily. I'm not going to start knocking over any vases or broomsticks, I'll snuggle up to you, and am even considering the possibility that we might die together, which would of course be the worst case scenario, but you have to be prepared for anything."

Anyway, the second day of darkness and cold, still the 2nd of January, today during daylight hours the sun shone pleasantly in through the pretty ice flowers on the window and I peeped outside to see what was going on, but nothing was, just the bright light of a winter's day. I saw no one, nor was anyone moving about on the stairs outside the apartment.

As expected, today, the 2nd of January, the sun began to set again soon after lunch—if it *was* a sunset. At any rate, it began to get dark, and the electric lighting still didn't come on.

The temperature in our apartment had still not dropped below twelve degrees Celsius.

Sociologists and propagandists had been telling us for years that in the big cities we should somehow rise above the mutual alienation that is so prevalent there, that we should start circles that would bring together people living in the various apartments, whole floors, blocks, nationalities, and even whole housing developments. Soccer matches had been arranged between streets, and toboggan races between blocks of apartments. We had ignored them all because we didn't feel like getting to know anyone, we thought that we already had enough friends. I said to myself: Should you get to know some woman from the next entrance just because she happens to be a human being?

Now we were paying the price.

We didn't know anyone living in any of the apartments in our block. In our time of need, we couldn't reach out to anyone, and no one was interested in us.

Upstairs lived two men, two brothers I suppose, who would usually come home together every evening roaring drunk, and we would peep through the spyhole in the door when we heard their heavy footsteps on the stairs, and on those rare occasions that our paths did cross, they would greet us over-effusively, while we would simply grunt indifferently in reply—if only I could now go to their door, ring the bell and say the magic words: friend, tell the truth, what the hell is going on? They would no doubt have replied: citizen, you are confined to your little ivory tower, so if the world no longer speaks to you, then it serves you right for being silent to the world, so get the hell out of here.

But I wasn't in the mood for cracking jokes.

We were used to handling information.

We were used to picking up hints, we were used to interpreting things from the tone of voice.

Local radio was off the air and we could get no picture of the processes taking place, their development, or any possible escalation.

The political agitators, who were otherwise so enthusiastic about showing up at our door and encouraging us to vote in some election or other, had given up in despair.

My own sense of reason and powers of perception told me nothing more than that the whole town was cold and dark.

Because judging by the arc of what I could see from the window, there were no electric lights switched on anywhere.

There was no glow above the city some distance away.

The radiators were cold.

The electric stove would not heat up.

The coffee machine and the electric razor had stopped working.

And if anyone were to ask what else wasn't working then I could simply say: just about everything except us.

And above the huge apartment buildings the Moon, about which some learned men have once said, if in fact they did, but clearly they did, that the Moon reminds one of our Earth when viewed from the cosmos. There is the Man in the Moon, a very lonely man, and no one else, and we today on this Earth are just as lonely, and the Moon acts like a vacuum cleaner, a very quiet one, a silent suction pump, an utterly mute machine that sucks up our energy. It is dangerous to stand too long at the window. Your heart will be empty and turn to ice.

Is this the Third World War, I asked myself at one point, is this the major cataclysm that so many people have imagined, pictured in their minds, seen depicted as a major event in films, something that will put an end to our burgeoning development?

Is this the dreaded nuclear winter?

But where is the cacophony of war, where are the shouts of battle when the fighters and bombers roar across the sky, the detonations of bombs, the paratroopers descending?

If no one is fighting anyone else, is this war?

Or was everything happening somewhere far away, silently and swiftly, with matters decided in a matter of moments, the air around us now filled with radiation, and everyone dead except us? And is that why there's no heating or electricity, because it's no longer needed?

We have been forgotten.

No, not forgotten.

There's simply no one left to remember us.

Foreign radio stations were also acting as if nothing had happened. They could talk thanks to the batteries we had, but were as lively and self-assured as always. We could hear music, political discussions, programs about art but not a word about what had really happened.

There was no doubt about the fact that the water pipes would soon freeze up. I could see a layer of ice and hoarfrost forming on the bathroom wall. This had risen up from the baseboard and had expanded by about a dozen centimeters and was now nearing the water pipe.

There was still cold water, but for how long?

The pipes bringing our water would soon be frozen, as well as the outlet pipes.

Then they would get blocked and if this happened we wouldn't be able to use them.

Perhaps some things would pass through, perhaps not, but excrement wouldn't get through the pipes.

Assuming that the temperature falls to around minus 15 degrees at night and there's snow and hail, it will be accompanied by a powerful thunderstorm. In such conditions not only will the *Opuntiae* survive, but others will hold out, such as the *Tephrocactus*, the *Gymnocalycium hubutense*, and the *Austrocactus bertinii*. I have read somewhere how fate struck one particular man. The famous Czech cactus expert Alberto Fric lost thousands of cacti in 1899. A careless student of his had forgotten to turn on the heating. Fric traveled to South America to collect cacti. He restocked his collection and it became bigger than ever before. In the winter of 1939, there was no heating because of the war and he lost 30,000 more cacti. But still he didn't give up. He is said to have kept weapons for the resistance movement in his greenhouses. Grenades in flowerpots! I've heard this from other sources as well. My late friend, the Jesuit Aleksander Kurtna, once said that he too had kept bombs for the resistance in flowerpots in Rome in 1942. So is this how flowers turn into bombs in difficult times? In a Boccaccio story, a woman hides the severed head of her lover in a pot of basil and the basil flourished. The artist Lembit Sarapuu created a *ready-made* work of art where a blond pigtail grew out of a flowerpot. Joachim Ringelnatz has described the unavoidable nature of cacti as follows: *Wer aber mit Absicht oder versehentlich / Sich Einmal auf dich / Setzte, vergisst dich nie.* And more philosophically, Hans Harbeck has said: *Dorne sichern seine Schale / Stachlich ist sein Panzerkleid. / Er verkörpert die reale / Bittere Notwendigkeit.* Then we fell silent for a short while, in the empty, dead city, forgotten by everyone. I carried on thinking and remembered that *Toymeya papyracantha* and *Trichocereus chilensis* could survive under snow. And also the

Ferocactus wislizenii. We didn't have any of those species of cactus. But we did have one or two that were very susceptible to cold: a couple of blue *Myrtillocacti*, some hairy *Cephalocerei*, some capricious *Melocacti*, as well as two *Epithelanthae*. Things were already too much for them now. When it's cold, you feel that there's no end to it. The cold is like a sea, you drown in it, and sink ever further, and no one comes to your rescue.

Were we cold? Of course we were!

Why shouldn't we have felt the cold? We were very cold, but that wasn't the most important thing.

How long is it going to stay cold?—that was the question.

Why is it cold?—that too was the question.

There are people, even whole races, that have grown accustomed to the cold. But how do we actually know what goes on within them? How do the Chukchi relate to the cold? Even Kafka asked why they live where they do. He didn't know the answer, but simply supposed that things had to be that way, everything was as it was and the Chukchi lived where they lived. Or what about Tierra del Fuego and the people who live there? I read that they live, or used to live some time ago, naked. They sheltered themselves behind screens of plaited twigs and branches. And how the wind blew through these screens! I have seen a photo of *Opuntiae* in the snow in Tierra del Fuego. Didn't they feel the cold? You can never tell. I remember a winter's day in 1964, but where this was I don't remember. I mistakenly said that it was a winter's day, but in fact it was a winter's night and after a short thaw or period of rain, then the freezing returned, the branches of trees were coated with ice that looked like glass. We were walking under such branches and the most sensitive person among us wondered whether the trees weren't feeling pain. Kaplinski smiled sympathetically and looked the person who'd asked the question in the eye. Well, don't they? asked the same person again. Kaplinski shook his head slowly. No one said any more on the subject. Why did Kaplinski smile with such sympathy, why was he so sure that the branches weren't feeling any pain? Is pain a moral category? And if not, why shouldn't branches have views about cold, just as we have views about them?

We thought the cold was dangerous for us.

We were not hardened to it.

Water from a spring ran into the river on whose banks I grew up, and its waters were very cold. Nevertheless, people went swimming there in one of the few deeper spots, and I have the feeling that between the years 1958 and 1962, they did so with more confidence and courage. I didn't care about the cold, used to swim there before the village feast or an evening dance, and I felt that I would improve my manly image by swimming in the icy water. There was something very sexually charged in the whole atmosphere when the evening sun gilded the tops of the fir trees and I stood drying myself in the long grass, swatting at the mosquitoes, my skin covered in goose bumps, and practicing flirtatious phrases, not gentle but rough ones, to say to some unknown girl, but it had to be a slim one. In the distance, the cattle were lowing, old women were yelling, but as time went by silence fell, the shadows grew longer and I would walk through the darkening wood in the hope of losing my virginity not with some girl I met by accident, but with someone I was destined to be in love with, someone I could meet on the dark boards of the open-air dance floor, dancing to the sound of popular songs, in the moonlight or the darkness of August, whenever, but once at least.

Swedish radio announced that for some unknown reason there had been a catastrophe in the northwestern part of the Soviet Union. It was said that contact with their correspondents had been lost. Telephone and radio links had been cut off. The Soviet news agency had mentioned nothing about the catastrophe. It was presumed that the Soviet government had not arrived at a united view as to what had happened. Perhaps the government itself hadn't even got the full picture. A member of the Swedish Academy was interviewed who drew parallels with the meteorite that fell in the Tungus region at the turn of the century, but thought that this time the problem was more widespread. He said:

"It is a psychological phenomenon in the life of individuals as well as whole nations that the most terrifying events of the past or of the present may be displaced into the subconscious mind . . ."

The radio announcer expressed the hope that the world would soon be informed of what had happened.

After that, a right-wing writer spoke and said that he had always been convinced that the countries of the Eastern Bloc simply didn't exist, that they were dealing with a phantom, a collective hallucination. And now everyone could see that he had been proved right. "It's not surprising that they don't answer," he explained, "there has never been anyone or anything over there."

What are you doing there, have you been overtaken by sleep? A fly already gets torpid if the temperature drops by two degrees. And a human being, when naked, will soon feel the cold if the temperature drops below 25 degrees Celsius. Our body temperature is around 38 degrees, and isn't it strange that around the whole globe the body temperature of mammals stays roughly at the same level? Whether you're living in the Arctic or at the Equator, it's always the same, always that constant level. But nature has equipped its various species differently. For instance the polar fox doesn't feel cold even when the temperature is as low as minus 50 degrees. It has that kind of coat. But pigs! Pigs are as naked as human beings. They have thin bristles that can't keep in the heat. And yet in a severe winter in Alaska, pigs feel fine. Their blood circulation is very efficient. In cold air, their circulation drops in the outer layers of their bodies so that the surface tissue turns into one big layer of insulation. Their metabolism speeds up as soon as the surrounding temperature drops below freezing. Pigs don't have many problems. I have heard that when scientists took readings on a pig at minus 12 degrees, its body tissue had cooled down to a depth of ten centimeters, in other words, its layer of fatty tissue had cooled down, but underneath it was still warm.

In the mid-1960s, I heard of SS experiments with concentration camp prisoners in which doctors with a sick imagination determined if the body temperatures of men who had been in cold water could be raised by putting them in the same bed as women prisoners.

In the late 1960s, I was sleeping with a colleague in a chilly house where everyone had celebrated Christmas or the New Year. The temperature outside must have been around minus 30 and the hoarfrost shimmered bluish, the sky was a dark blue that we could have seen from the window of the old wooden house if we hadn't have been so busy trying to keep warm, which was very difficult to accomplish because there wasn't any firewood in the house and so we had to burn chairs and tables, feeling ashamed for many years afterwards vis-à-vis the occupants, but the fear of freezing to death was enormous and our instinct for self-preservation got the better of us.

But there was electricity there. So what if the bulbs were cold, there was still electricity; so what if there was no electric stove in the house, there was still electricity and people living fairly nearby, but not just across the road as is always the case in town.

But now I simply know nothing.

You don't either, do you?

In my opinion it's dark and cold across the whole of the Estonian capital, maybe across the whole of Estonia, maybe even the whole so-called non-black-earth region of the Soviet Union, maybe the whole world. Maybe electricity has disappeared from the whole globe, just as unexpectedly as it once came. Gone somewhere else, off to other planets. Or burned itself to ash by spontaneous combustion like Mary Carpenter in the boat before the very eyes of her own family.

Went off!

As if we haven't got enough to worry about as it is.

Today, fear of snow comes to mind.

In the first instance, of course, the abominable snowman who never, even at an altitude higher than the mountain monasteries, under the heavens themselves, ever feels the cold.

If the government is powerless and the situation doesn't change, the abominable snowmen will soon be coming to Tallinn.

They will take over many empty apartments, full of frozen meat.

But abominable snowmen alone don't really make you feel worried.

I have no doubt mentioned the unease you feel looking out at night onto the snows of the steppe, white in the moonlight, with no lights visible from the train window.

Ghostly landscapes unfold when looking from a plane in the stratosphere in the moonlight: cloudscapes above all, but also other things as we could see in the film *The Twilight Zone* when some being (some *thing*) was sitting on the wingtip of the plane making faces at the passengers.

The refrigerator had begun to thaw, because the electricity was off, but now it is beginning to freeze again because the room is so cold.

The Russian cold has defeated foreigners who have tried to conquer the country. We have all seen movies depicting Napoleon's retreating troops as they froze to death, and the same with the German army in documentaries. They have covered themselves up to their ears in shawls and are hopping from one foot to the other and are clapping their hands. From afar, a small group of locals looks on grimly, most of them old women because the men are at the front and the young women are working in the factories in the nearby town.

In Lapland, people are trying out luxury cars. They charge along through the snow flurries in the light of the setting sun. Who is driving them is something we'll never find out.

I grew up in the age of radio, but in recent years my view of the world has become more visual, thanks to television.

For the fourth day in a row I've not been able to watch TV.

Twilight over the land.

This simply meant that you didn't have to light the kerosene lamp right away, you waited till it got completely dark.

Many people don't believe that the kerosene lamp existed, but I'm prepared to swear that it did. Not only a kerosene lamp, there was also a gas lamp where you had a sleeve instead of a wick and you had to pump it to keep it going. It had a very bright glare and it was lit on special days; though not at Christmas when candles were burnt.

Kerosene lamps or gas lamps were all right but they were replaced by electricity in country villages in Estonia by the 1960s.

And these pre-electric lamps were never used except when it was completely dark. In other words, in June you would never light them at all unless there was good reason to do so.

I've heard from others that during twilight people would hold discussions. I've heard that people used to talk about traditions or morals for the good of the children.

But from what I remember, we used just to keep silent, although sometimes my father used to whistle, low and sadly; he was no doubt miles away in his thoughts, in realms inaccessible, presumably thinking about times and places long vanished.

But what did we care that our parents weren't taking any notice of us but were instead escaping in the gloaming to somewhere far, far away? We could sit there as night fell, and as it got ever darker, and finally became completely dark.

With your burnt-out brains and nerves you feel like an orphan in the city, isn't that so?

What's the temperature?

Still five degrees, it hasn't dropped below, thank God, that's because there's no wind. If there were, we and our belongings would have had it, and the cacti even earlier, let's have a look inside the tent with the burning candles.

Ten? Maybe we'll survive the night but we can't just go to sleep, there could be a fire or the cold could get us, one or the other, and we'd never wake up again.

We have to keep watch in turns.

Have we switched everything on so that we'll notice immediately if the power comes back?

Oh, I know it won't come back this evening, or perhaps only the lights, not the heating; but it's best to be prepared.

And have we locked the door, though I can't believe that anyone, not even the most evil person, the cruelest, most degenerate, would be out tonight, he's more likely to be wrapped up in furs and watching the moon as we are, but with quite different thoughts in his head than ours.

And now we are watching to see how low our candles have burned.

Jesus, we've surely not used up one batch already?

And I can hear a blizzard starting outside!

But that can't be the case because just a short time ago the moon was shining and I was just saying how arrogant it looked.

It is arrogant, look, it's still shining but not very brightly, there must be a snowstorm rising.

Oh well, can't be helped, once everything's bad, then it's not surprising that things get worse. As usual, accidents always come in droves. Once it's dark and cold, then the wind has to start howling, and it would be even better if that howling reminded you of the lamentation of sinful souls or something equally interesting.

We huddle together under a fur coat and watch the hideous shadows looming on the wall and we forget how sweet shadows were only a week ago.

So many on this Earth have lost their lives or loves and all we've lost is the power supply, so why shouldn't we remember those who've departed this evening with a kind word or two?

Close your eyes, all of you, only don't fall asleep, because we've read that those who fall asleep in a snowdrift fall prey to Old Father Cold.

Close Your eyes, only don't fall asleep, because You have read that those who fall asleep in a snowdrift fall prey to Old Father Cold.

Look, this night, electricity, made by human hand, is hardly around us at all. Or to be more specific: there's very little of it. It's gone. That's a sad thing. We too are sad. But not just sad! It's worth breathing in the atmosphere; things are so rarely like this all around us!

It's two o'clock and the temperature is dropping, which is natural, because outside it's thirty degrees below and the blocks of apartments weren't designed to ever be without heating for a single moment. They were built pretty recently, but their design stems from the time when crude oil was incredibly cheap. Look, in the middle of the room it's already nine degrees Celsius. By the morning it'll be at freezing point and then that'll be the end.

Suddenly before me in the darkness I saw how Yablochkov was laughing out loud, his beard trembling, opening his big mouth showing his strong teeth.

It is now the third of January, and if the power and the heating don't come on, there's at least three months of winter ahead.

We can't start burning the furniture, because we'd suffocate in the smoke.

And we can't open the window, because then there'd be no point in starting a fire.

We can't go anywhere without a car, and outside it's completely deserted, there's nothing, just the darkness, no one is
driving around, there's just the Moon, or whatever it is, shining,
because you can't be sure what could have taken on its guise. And
all that's happening in a country that tends to be so safe, where
the occupying forces are so well-intentioned, if you like, where
there are no poisonous snakes! Look for yourself, moving out is
simply impossible, you can't just go out into the snow carrying
the cacti in your bare hands, that really would be the end, and a
quick one too!

Let's resign ourselves to our predicament as did Alberto Fric
who had the strength later on to still take part in the resistance
movement.

No, let's not resign ourselves! I'm going outside, or even onto
the street!

Something has to be done, even if the situation is hopeless!

Listen, I'm going out!
Don't go!
Wait for me!
Come back soon!
I'm coming!
I'm waiting for you!
Take care of yourself!

※

I fumbled my way down the stairs. I stopped on every landing
and listened. There wasn't a sound coming from any of the other
apartments. Had they left? They couldn't have died after only
three days of frost! Or did they rush to their doors on hearing

footsteps and were quiet as a mouse now? It's quite believable that the cold will bring with it random murderers, polar bears, beings that have been in summer hibernation for hundreds if not thousands of years.

I didn't want to frighten anybody and went downstairs as quickly as I could. I forced open the snowed-up outside door and was standing there in the moonlight.

Hello, absence of blizzard. Hello, silent night. Hello, strange cold snap.

The first thing I saw was the Moon.

It had perhaps been crying, but its tears were frozen.

Ungaretti: what are you doing there in the sky, O Earth?

In front of the building, the virgin snowdrifts billowed, no, shimmered. Just as in Siberia, in the taiga, where I have never been in my waking hours.

From our windows there was a faint gleam of candlelight.

All the blocks of apartments across the open stretch of ground were in darkness.

Shadows several hundred meters in length fell diagonally across the space.

When I waded through the drifts towards the main road, I remembered my class back at the village school where I had to walk the three kilometers there and back every day. In those days, it was just after World War II and under a kolkhoz regime, and they didn't use snowplows, time stood still and it was good, after the snow that had fallen during the night, to walk past at least a few fresh deer tracks. And in those days you had to watch out for real wolves, forest wolves. They probably wouldn't have eaten me up, but they were lurking out there and could have frightened me. I was, after all, only a child. And now here I was wading through the snowdrifts in a housing project! I glanced back involuntarily, as if still afraid of wolves.

And I did see some.

They were gyrating around each other in the virgin snow, lit by the moon, jumping high in the air, mostly both at once, sometimes singly, and silver snowflakes whirled in flurries around them. They paid me no attention, were engrossed in their game or dance, two wolves from my childhood days, but they could of course have been dogs, I tried to reassure myself. At any rate, I didn't have to pass by them, the way to the main road was free.

Yes, they were dogs, they were barking! And yelping they suddenly took off, side by side into the distance, and disappeared beyond the houses.

When I arrived at the main road, I didn't dare raise my eyes because I didn't know what I was more afraid of: whether to see all the cubes of the apartment blocks in darkness or one small, lone and bright light on a top floor, the one chilling exception. The latter wasn't the case. Everything was dark. Luckily, the wind wasn't blowing, and the frost was bearable, perhaps because of the excitement and my being alone. My beard frosted up immediately, and icicles formed from my nostrils down into my moustache. An empty world! The city belonged to me—and I have to admit that my first thought was: shouldn't I go and steal something? If every human being has gone, if hundreds of thousands have evaporated into thin air, shouldn't you take what there was to be taken? No, no, not jewels or furniture, perhaps something more cultural such as books, Jung's works maybe, especially since it was Jung who said somewhere (I'm quoting from memory): people shouldn't enlighten others by thinking of the light, but rather by being aware of the darkness. Why should Jung's books fall prey to cockroaches if no one ever came back? For twenty years I've been waiting for some admirer from South Africa or Monaco to send me his collected works and this hasn't happened yet, and the hope has begun to fade, because life is short. But not only Jung: also Runge's or Chagall's paintings that could be hidden out there somewhere in the colossal black blocks of apartments, or even a few bottles of whisky that would warm you up if things get really bad. Do I have the moral right to war booty? If I take the things myself, then I do!

But I didn't take the liberty of doing so.

Why not?

I listened and I suddenly thought I heard a train, a bird singing, but no: my fear had raised my blood pressure and my ears were ringing.

The Bermuda Triangle came to mind.

Had I won? The world grown empty, at least what you could see of it. Had the human ants scattered elsewhere?

Yes, I had won, and yet I felt a sweet sadness—you wanted it, now you've got it, and yet melancholy surges over you, you want everything back, yet you don't; in an eternal winter, the longing for apple-tree blossoms sometimes begins to bother you, you'd like to hear the chugging of a taxi engine or the babbling of a child and you know that they are never coming back, and then you grow wistful, and that has its own bittersweet beauty.

You live alone, from day to day, in the darkness and the pallor of death, you grow old and weary, you hope and love, but in that hopelessness that gives you strength, you are worn down at length, although you could make songs from the experience that you sing to yourself, such as: *my loneliness is my destiny now!* Or: *Nieder mit dem Bruderschaft! Es lebe Einsamkeit!*

So you sing and get on with life.

Any maybe you're even happy.

For once in your life!

(. . .)

When I had rolled a cigarette and begun to wrestle with the thought that there was nothing to do but to return inside, I suddenly heard human sounds, expressed by the creaking of boots in the snow and breathing. A figure was moving in my direction. In the darkness, I couldn't see his face, it was black in the moonlight, because he had the moon behind him. A somber, gloomy phenomenon, someone in distress. If the world had been normal, I would have fled towards the entrance to the apartments. But now things were quite different and I didn't move.

The man reached me, leaned panting on my shoulder for a moment and I felt his frozen beard against my cheek. He said nothing. The situation was so uncanny that all I could do was wait and see. Did *he* know everything, and *me* nothing?

Obviously, everyone except me had got clear-cut points of view about what had happened. The matter was clear to everyone except me. So it wasn't the right thing to ask: what's wrong? What's going on?

I could easily be laughed at with such expressions as: and where were you when the whole nation was suffering? You think you're so exceptional that the worries of everyone else just don't concern you? But apart from any lack of political or moral correctness, I would simply have been making a fool of myself if I'd simply asked: where have you been sleeping, then?

There is still the hope that this serious and wholesome individual will help, that you can trust in him and his solutions.

When we had stood for a little while like that, cheek to cheek, as if meeting on the Elbe or honoring some sunken flagship, I could no longer resist the temptation to ask:

"You've got to tell me, what's going on?

"But who are *you*?"

"Does it matter?"

"I don't know whether it matters or not, but why are you asking me questions?"

"Fuck, you're the first person I've seen for ages, can't I even ask what's wrong here in town? Where is everybody? What's everybody else doing? Is the government still in office? When will the heating be turned on?"

The man took a couple of steps backwards.

His beard was covered in ice.

Yablochkov? The idea flashed though my mind. Out of the frying pan, into the fire.

Soon the large mouth with the healthy teeth will open!

He'll burst into laughter and the lights will go on.

A long and tense pause.

But the man seemed to calm down and we shook hands.

"Oh hell, I'm telling you that the people aren't fools. I've seen a lot. I was in the air force, a partisan, and in Siberia, at a kolkhoz, and down in the mines. I've seen everything. You don't believe me? We say: please, you can keep your Islamic revolutions, go to the moon and let the Führer call the faithful back to the Fatherland—but you don't fool us. Do you want me to tell you? I can tell you a lot about what I saw in town. I could go on until morning. It's a story really worth listening to, if you've got the guts to listen. Do you want to hear it?"

I nodded.

Who else was there to listen to?

"Talk. Where have you just come from?"

The man's eyes brightened and he straightened up. All of a sudden his voice became firm and clear, as if we weren't standing in a yard in a dead city but at some political rally or other.

"From the center! I hoped I'd find something there, you understand? Some mannequins were lying at the side of the road. I don't know which sex they were, you couldn't see in the moonlight! I mean wooden mannequins. Someone had stolen them from a shop, ripped off their clothes and dumped the mannequin, I mean mannequins, there were several of them, in the ditch, in the snow! Obviously stolen them yesterday. There aren't many robbers around today. I did happen to meet a few, nearly ran into them, well, turned off left, always to the left, let me think now, yes, left, and now a new danger presented itself: a vague thumping sound, thump, thump, I, listening and thump, thump, they were obviously beating someone and shouting too, and the shouts were shouts of joy, so I slowed down and had a look: torches, light here and there, well, I went a bit nearer—the flour store was being robbed, great fun, flour flying around all over the shop, mixed in with the blizzard, you can imagine: flour and whirling snow all mixed up together, that really is something, men white from both, I mean from both the snow and the flour, but the women were urging them on from behind: Go on! Get some! Hurry! And: quicker, quicker! With their high voices, get what I mean? And more bags down and more flour in the air and again mixed up with the snow! I got flour up my nose, ice-cold flour, but no one came out on account of me and so I continued on my way and thought quite sadly to myself: dead right for them to steal that flour, but how are they going to cook a meal with it, the poor bastards? How will they be able to bake bread if the stove at home is stone cold? When the power comes back and it begins to warm up, then they'll all feel ashamed that they have stolen things and haven't the appetite left to eat it! Maybe they'll even be thrown into prison! That's also possible. Regret sets in, but fear too—maybe they'll get mean, beat them up and push them into the bread oven alive—no! I hurried along, through the dark night, through snow and cold, I crossed Narva Road and walked towards the center of Tallinn, turned into Anvelt Street, but that scared me, went back out onto Narva Road and walked off in the direction of the center. Then a new thought struck me: don't go straight there, make a detour! So I made a detour and approached Lomonossov Street . . ."

Trying to calm him down, I interrupted:

"A friend of mine lived on Lomonossov Street, but also the scientist Richmann who was born in Pärnu the son of a Swedish lessee. He studied in Tallinn, Halle, Jena, worked in Saint Petersburg as a private tutor, became a professor. In 1752 word got to him about Franklin's experiments with lightning: you had to put a metal spike on the roof and attach wire to it that led down into his laboratory and on the end of this was an iron plate and a silk thread. On one occasion, Richmann was standing by his equipment during a thunderstorm. A fist-sized ball of pale blue globe lightning emerged from his equipment and hit him on the forehead. He fell over. There was a bang and the whole room was filled with smoke. Lomonossov was too late. When he reached his friend, he was dead. This happened in 1753. Now I am on Lomonossov Street, the former Maximov Street, named after a Russian merchant who had once lived there. In 1876 it was re-named Gonsiorstraße after some German councilor and it got the name Lomonossov in 1950, and later, in 1955 I think it was, they erected an iron TV antenna, with cables that led to Television House. Sorry I interrupted you. What happened then? What did you see in the city center?"

"What did I see, what did I see?! I didn't exactly see people, or didn't take them for human beings, now it feels as if the city was completely empty, and do you know, then the horrible, horrible world had left me all alone! I've never been very sociable, but what had happened now was horrible! I wondered whether this wasn't all a dream—you, the department store with the lights out, or you, the bus that had run into a wall and was half-covered in snow or you, the post office, dark with icicles hanging from the façade? How swiftly everything changes, how quickly civilization disintegrates; it was there just a while ago, now no longer! Only the wind and the cold and no waking up from that, I am thinking, no waking up from the dream, usually you wake up at the last minute, but now you're not going to! What are dreams, I thought to myself angrily, you can imagine, I would have cursed someone or kicked them, but who, but what? And the Intourist Hotel, that damned place of amusement, full of sinful pleasures intended only for foreigners, which we locals can never hope to share, a den of vice barred to Soviet citizens, that was also deserted and dark! How is it possible, I am thinking, but then I understood that the Finns had fled that evening across the gulf because the ship had its own engines and you can always get fuel oil from some-where, what do you think? Perhaps the Finns even sent oil over to get their tourist compatriots out of their predicament. Huh? And the opera house! And the street lighting! Was this the end of the world, I'm thinking, really, what was I expected to think? Anyway, I went into the Old Town. Nobody there! The snow was whirling around the narrow streets. I'm walking and walking and walking . . . and do you know what happened?

I shook my head.
 "Guess what!"
 "I can't."

"Nobody could have guessed: suddenly, just like that, quite un-expectedly, without any reason and unpredictably, the city lights came on! It was as if the sun had risen! Fuck, I crashed into a wall, as if someone was attacking me. When my eyes grew accustomed to it, I saw that all the streetlamps were on. There was light in every window! God! What a nightmare! But it only lasted a few seconds. Hardly had anyone, you know, hardly had anyone some-where in the center begun cheering, shouting "hurray," hardly had the shouts gone up, when the city was plunged back into darkness as if had been stuffed into a black bag. Complete and utter darkness—you can understand yourself that your eyes have grown unaccustomed and so you can't even see the white of the snow—in this unexpected darkness I heard the cheers change to moans, just like a gramophone record winding down. I carried on groping my way along! Groping your way in the dark, have you experienced that in your childhood, or in the war, or in prison? Have you? I feel this wall . . . I feel the roughness of the wall through my gloves! Then suddenly! Horrible, horrible—some-thing soft, alive . . . ! My hand froze where it was, I didn't dare take my hand away, I kept on touching it, touching . . . ! Then,

I think it was a man's voice said: well, it's come and gone again! And I said back, my voice shaking: gone, sure, sure! Gradually, my eyes began to make out that beside me was a little runt of a man who had turned up just at the moment of that shock with the lights. Perhaps there was a door in the wall there. Wearing a tall Russian hat, stamping from foot to foot, you understand?"

"I understand . . ."

"You don't understand anything! He also said something! He said that this was a question of the Pelissier Effect or the Bubenstrauch Effect, he even suggested that Pelissier or Bubenstrauch were part of all this! He said that Mogilyov had fallen and that Warsaw was next! I thought, war, but what I said to him was: it's not a war, just a power outage! Then he offered me some vodka, I took a swig, he did too, then he put the bottle back in his pocket. He shrugged his shoulders, and went on to say that Bubenstrauch had explained that the power grid would collapse like a pack of cards stood on end and the more you try to stop it, the worse it will get. It's a paradox: the biggest power failure comes when there's nothing much left to fail! At zero the situation gets completely hopeless, then there's nothing more you can do, do you understand? The electricity supply is at that stage now, was what the man said, shrugged his shoulders again and vanished. Yes, he actually went off! I thought about how it was Warsaw's turn right now, about the steppe and the taiga, I thought about a hell of a lot of things, about my life and that of those around me, and why I had abandoned my dear children, that was years before, but still—why did I do it? Now God was punishing me, maybe he wasn't punishing others, because others couldn't see, they were perhaps very satisfied that the man they just saw wasn't very unhappy—anyway, I've been punished, because my world is in darkness, isn't it? My world!"

This was what the stranger told me in front of the block of apartments in Lasnamäe, behind whose back the moon was shining and whose face I hadn't yet seen, perhaps didn't even want to.

He was an outcast and had been punished!

But why should I be punished?

Because I was interested in electricity?

Who could I ask for forgiveness?

And apart from that there was still the central heating!

That too didn't, of course, work if there was no electricity.

We were both hopping from foot to foot, but didn't yet want to leave.

I asked:

"So, what happened then? Where did you go then?"

The man was happy to explain:

"I walked along Karja Street out of the Old Town! Pärnu Avenue was open, dark and pristine, no footprints at all! The Estonia Theater was in darkness—that surprised me! A theater should always be lit up!"

I nodded:

"Of course a theater should be lit up, because that's where Electra works, whose forefather was Tantalus who tried to feed his son's flesh to the gods. The gods didn't eat anything, apart from Demeter, that is, who had a piece of shoulder. But that was replaced later on. What was going through Tantalus's head? He wanted to know whether the gods were omniscient. For that inquisitiveness he was sentenced to eternal thirst. Tantalus is a drinker, like all people are, because he made claims on the gods. He's a drinker who they don't give spirits to because he's committed a mortal sin. He didn't listen to a word the gods said. Now he's suffering, and his children and their children are too, maybe even Electra, and at the theater where all this should be being performed, the power has gone off!"

I wouldn't say that what I was telling the man interested him. He shrugged his shoulders. Dogs were howling off in the distance, or were they wolves? The sound reminded you of people crying. A cold shudder went down my spine. But my companion continued:

"Well, what happened next I don't know! First I ran round the outside of the theater, I wanted to see whether the republic's leaders were still there at Communist Party headquarters or whether they'd all been evacuated, whether the helmsmen were still running the show. I hoped that our leaders were still here and they were too, can you imagine, and that meant something! There were lights, cars were turning up, sirens were wailing! My first thought was that they were carrying off files and safes to the waiting vehicles, and that a trek would ensue over the ice across the Gulf of Finland! To Leningrad, as in those days, during the war, but on looking more closely I saw that there was no reason for panic! Couriers were running in and out! I went up closer, but there was a rope and the militia stopped me! Not allowed, *uydi, get out of here*, they said, and back I went into the darkness, I wasn't insulted in the slightest, because in a crisis situation the authorities have to keep clear heads and concentrate calmly on what they have to do! You shouldn't interfere, should you, otherwise there'll be another *faux pas* and then you'd only have yourself to blame. Well anyway, I started going on foot in this direction, but it is, after all, some ten kilometers from the city center to where I live! I wanted to see the kids, I wanted . . . it's hard to explain what it was I wanted! I started running! I ran faster and faster! I ran with all my might . . . ! Running along, I even forgot all about the disaster our country was in, I just ran like a runner who knew nothing but how to run, not even how to walk any longer, if you see what I mean? I was flying along! The children, the children, I was saying to myself. Warsaw will fall, soon it'll be Berlin, no escape, and I'm coming to you, and I'm abandoning you to return to you, if you see what I'm driving at, abandon them to be able to get back to them, that's what I said to myself, that felt the most accurate thing to say, so what if that isn't exactly right grammatically, but that's my business, don't you agree? And everything was cold and dark, only one ship freezing out there in the Bay of Tallinn, in the icy slurry of the sea and there was one light to be seen there, a crazy light to my mind, but perhaps they had good reason not to put out the light, oh and those big factories, but never mind the factories, what about the zoo where the apes were dying, and the crocodiles, the elephants . . . ! Well, I can't really remember much else and I woke up in the snow, about one bus stop further, at the side of the road. I'd sprained my ankle, but otherwise was all right, no broken bones . . . ! Perhaps a car had taken me there, then dumped me, sometimes it's like that, people are helpful to start with, then they spit on you when you don't know the way, where now, for fuck's sake . . ."

"Who then . . . ?"

"Don't fucking ask." The man spat. "But I'll tell you this, they'll pay for it! The way they treat people, and not only here, but also, for example, down south, like in Sri Lanka! In other words: everywhere! No use talking about it."

He looked at his watch.

I noticed that he was wearing an electric watch with a little bulb inside that lit up when you pressed a button. If I hadn't been fed up with the man, I'd have broached the subject and made a joke about it. But the man himself was getting worked up.

"Fuck, half-past two!"

Without even saying goodbye he scuttled off, limping slightly, and disappeared round the corner of a nine-story block.

Silence reigned.

༄༅

As I climbed the stairs, Tissen came quite involuntarily to mind.

What is Tissen doing? Is he happy, now that the world was so deserted? True, there are still a couple of Bubestrauchs around, even a militia car driving past rounding up the remaining Buben-strauchs, but the mass of people with its demands and its consumerism had now vanished. It had vanished into thin air. Whole populations and immigrants had proved to be balloons that were good things to burst. Those concentrations of population had actually been a little like a dream. Tissen had of course been right.

It's quite true that I am on Tissen's side today, I am supporting him now that people have either run away or frozen to death. Spread out more! Disperse! That would be normal. Porshnev thought that, apart from suggestion or influence, people also possess the power of counter-suggestion, i.e., a defense reflex, and that the inner life of human beings came into being thanks to counter-suggestion. Elementary counter-suggestion is a question of keeping away from one another. Porshnev argues that after coming into being (and how this "coming into being" arose is certainly interesting) people spread out over the globe for that very reason. They wanted to be alone for a time. But no, that didn't last long.

I would have phoned Tissen and said that I now shared his anti-humanist ideas, but obviously the telephone booth was out of order.

In my mind, I said goodbye to the cacti. In fact, I no longer really wanted to go home. It was all over. I could still take a sleeping tablet and go to sleep, until the spring, hibernate. My earthly remains wouldn't rot before the spring.

The windows on the stairs were thick with ice, occasionally the ice would reflect the moonlight. The large sewage pipe that ran down the stairwell had clearly got blocked up because down the outside wall a lumpy liquid was flowing.

On the stairs I started thinking mechanically in self-defense:

The *Parodia* hadn't started ailing for nothing! Why was it ill? The root stalk seemed perfectly OK, perhaps the roots themselves had started to rot. But that *Parodia* had been strange right from the start, too elongated, too tall, perhaps too full of life. Why was it so elongated? Is it in fact a *Parodia*, although its alveoli grow in a spiral, though that doesn't mean anything! We'll have to repot it tomorrow, perhaps wash it a bit before we do so, then dry it . . . *Parodia, Parodia,* named after Parodi, we can do something, still do something . . .

(. . .)

Someone coughed.
"Is that you?" I asked, my mouth dry.

"Of course it's me," replied a low hoarse voice, which sounded as if it were coming from several mouths at the same time, "are you afraid? Do you remember when we both went swimming together? You weren't afraid then!"

I wasn't.
Susie is emitting a blue light from within.
She has a blue pig's head and the body of a woman.
Susie, why are you doing this?
All I realized was my freedom to choose, nothing more!

Is that a knife, curved like a sickle moon in your raised right hand?
Is it glittering like a diamond?
Is your left hand holding a skull-shaped beaker?
Is it really full of blood?
Is blood really a constituent part of a man's sperm?
Has the dualism of the symbol and its bearer fallen away?
I don't want this!
I'm not guilty!
Who said that?
You, Susie?
Don't ask for forgiveness, Susie.
You aren't, of course, guilty of anything.

You're just imagining that I'm imagining, here in the icy, shining corridor that you are imagining, that I am imagining in the moonlight, that in the deserted city I am imagining that

he imagines that a feminine deity, which esoterically personifies his own will, springs from the top of his head and stands before him, sword in hand.

With one stroke she cuts off the head of the celebrant. Then, while troops of ghouls come round for the feast, she skins him and rips open his belly. The bowels fall out, the blood flows like a river, and the hideous guests bite here and there, masticate noisily while the celebrant excites and urges them on with the liturgical words of unreserved surrender:

"I give my flesh to the hungry, my blood to the thirsty, my skin to clothe those who are naked, my bones as fuel to those who suffer from cold, I give my happiness to the unhappy ones . . ."

Now he must imagine that he has become a small heap of charred human bones that emerges from a lake of black mud—the mud of misery, of moral defilement, and the harmful deeds to which he is lost in the night of time . . .

In fact, he has nothing to give away because he is nothing.

That silent renunciation of the ascetic who realizes that he holds nothing that he can renounce, and who utterly relinquishes the elaboration springing from the idea of sacrifice, closes the rite.

—*Alexandra David-Néel,* Magic and Mystery in Tibet

At that precise moment, water began to drip from the eaves and the ice melted on the windows. When the sun rose, the earth in front of our block was beginning to peep through the snow. And before the absent inhabitants were back, children made all kinds of fortresses out of the melting snow. Around ten o'clock the temperature was already above zero.

On the third of January an unexpected thaw set in, are you listening to what I'm saying dear?

It is true that there wasn't yet any electricity, but the radiators were becoming lukewarm, something was gurgling inside them, the ice around the pipes melted and around twelve it was already plus seven degrees outside.

Yes, that's what You told me, when you came to visit me in the hospital.

As far as I know, You did come. What do You mean You didn't?

I don't remember everything exactly either.

I got "rose-face," that I remember.

Did you bring me the roses?

No, You took the roses away. That other rose, rose-face.

Thanks for doing so.

Three *Opuntae* had died.

They had sacrificed themselves. They had already sacrificed themselves when You found me on the stairs.

They, non-prickly, seemingly innocent cacti are dangerous to pigs because they have glochides, i.e., spines you can hardly see with the naked eye, and if only thirty-two percent of them are digested, a mucous layer forms inside animals that gives rise to a deadly inflammation of the stomach and intestines. It is said that a friend of Jack London's, one Luther Burbank, tried to cultivate glochides for animal fodder, but the results of his efforts are shrouded in mystery: was the patent annulled by people who wished him ill or did the glochides appear again later . . .

Nevertheless, I will say egotistically: I survived.

Where did the cannibal get to, and why did he turn up in the first place? What connection has he to electricity, to Tissen, to the Diamond Sow? Why was there a power outage in the city? Can you get erysipelas, so-called "rose face," from cold and darkness, and is the disease accompanied by hallucinations? Did I start this novel or did it start me?

What a mass of questions arise in a worker as he reads, as Bertolt Brecht once commented.

In me too.

I am thrashing from side to side.

At night, in the country, in the woods.

The dogs begin to bark. One of them starts up and its woof-woof is carried over to others through the howling of the autumn wind. Another joins in. Then our own dog too, right here in the yard. It barks desperately. The others lend it support from afar. You get up and look through the curtains into the darkness. You can just make out the roof of the barn looming there in the darkness, maybe the woods beyond. But you can see nothing else.

Clouds are obscuring the moon. It is an October night. Then someone or something thumps on the wall outside. With its tail or body, more likely its whole body. You wait and the sound repeats itself. It is repeated only once, but weaker. The dog continues howling, you can sense its feelings. There you lie in the darkness. Sometimes you think about electricity, sometimes even about Tissen. But inside you, you are cautious. Then everything goes quiet, the dogs stop barking, the danger has passed. At three o'clock, sleep will arrive, or maybe not, you don't dare put on the light, because the curtains are not drawn and the electricity will give us away.

In the morning you will find some explanations.

Summer had come again in all its glory, and I went to take a bath.

I lay there in the water with my head hovering above the surface.

The businessman Leonard Orr did as follows: he got into the bathtub, put out the light and waited to sink into an embryonic state and then spontaneously experience his birth all over again. The temperature of the water had to be near to that of his body. Orr's method was later used elsewhere. It was termed the *Theta rebirth experience*. Poorer people could practice the method on their own by lying in a dry bathtub. But each officially patented therapy session did, of course, cost a fortune.

I too was lying in the bath.

But I'm not Orr, my aims are different.

First, I lay there in the water, I was something like Estonia, which is similarly surrounded by water on all sides and whose coastline is around 3,780 kilometers in length.

But that's not something to boast about because some people think that only Communists live in Estonia, others think only fascists, and others again have never heard of Estonia, which doesn't prevent them from living full and productive lives.

My dear, I would have liked you to have got with me into the bathtub, sat on the edge of the bath and said that you had dreamed an old tale, it was distorted by dreaming, but in reality it was much more straightforward and alive.

And I would have wanted to hear it.

I would have listened.

Would have been like an air bubble underwater or a submarine in the depths, like an empty coffin under the earth from which the corpse had gone.

I lay there alone and didn't care.

I didn't care to whom my flesh, blood, skin, and bones belonged.

In reality you came in at that very moment and said, as you will remember:

"I saw you in a dream. You were going somewhere, perhaps out into the fields or the woods, at any rate this wasn't happening in town, this was the countryside, it was flat, that's how I saw it. And suddenly some horrible monsters jumped out, some sort of either slimy or hairy ones, creatures, pretty big, bigger than humans and obviously very strong. They coaxed you into a cage or a chest, you said, saying come here, here'll be fine for you, and you believed them, naïve as you are, you're not very verbal as you say yourself, and you went voluntarily into that cage or chest. But once inside, you were immediately tied to the wall, whereupon you started laughing idiotically or acting like a martyr, it was hard to tell just from watching. For some reason I didn't feel too frightened, as if there was still hope, otherwise I would have cried out and woken up. You were very angry in that cage, but you only had yourself to blame, because the monsters didn't use force. Well, and a short while later, this giant cat appeared, with whiskers that quivered in the breeze, at first glance a really giant cat and it ordered you to pull at its whiskers. This wish made me suspicious: a real cat would never ask such a thing, not even a jaguar or the like. You became wary and didn't do what the pseudocat asked. The cat, or rather the loathsome creature—an evil belief or something similar—saw that it'd been exposed for what it was and began to roar. I don't know what it was planning to do, whether it would make do with that cry, or whether it was planning something worse, but at that very moment all the birds began to sing: come hither, come hither, come hither. In a word, they were inviting all creatures to come, and so they came. Especially clever were the mice who gnawed through the ropes, while the cattle dashed the cage to pieces. You started running away. The monsters, the slimy or hairy ones, that had dozed off at the edge of the glade, leapt to their feet and were after you! Both you and the monsters underwent some kind of metamorphosis—that's a common feature of fairy tales, isn't it?—anyway, in the end you turned into a cactus. Then we went home together, over some stream or other, through a hayfield, the horseflies were biting, someone was screaming crazily in the bushes, but suddenly fell silent, we just kept on going, and I don't remember whether you were still a cactus or whether you had now taken on a human shape."

"What a story!"
"What's wrong with it?"
"All mixed up."

"But interesting. And what's more, it's about You, isn't it? Isn't that interesting?"

Of course it's interesting.

Living in the dreams and fantasies of others, living your own lives without having a clue, only others—what more could you hope for?

To be what you yourself don't know!

A fivesome.

I got out of the bath and dried myself and thought that I had been thinking less about death with every day that passed.

There were peonies, cats, and combs before I existed and they'll be there after I've gone.

Leave your hair flowing loose, my dear.

I want to snatch at it with my teeth in the void.

I want to convince myself that I am alone.

To express my love.

And now for a little more literature. What about a little excerpt from my half-finished novel, from the dialogue, of course?

Here you are:

–What became of that man in whose presence electricity wouldn't work; the man who came from the shores of Lake Peipus and married some girl from Pärnu?

–Oh, you know, I haven't heard anything about him for some time. Maybe he moved somewhere else, joined some Communist shock-worker building program, emigrated or got run over, or perhaps electricity started working in his presence again and there's nothing more to be said, and he ceased to be a topic of conversation, at least in those circles I move around in.

–Pity, he was obviously an interesting person, his life held much promise. But that's how it goes: one minute you're at the height of your reputation, electricity doesn't work; then a year passes, the electricity comes on and you're thrown in the wastepaper basket!

–My dear, this man was a collective fantasy, the stuff of dreams, and what can I say about him? From time to time, people turn up who have a very intimate relationship with electricity, but I've never met any of them. I read lately about an American housewife who would short-circuit everything: clothing irons, electric stoves, radios and TV sets, everything she came in contact with . . . Poor woman! But what more can I say?

–But that woman there at the command post, where all those indicators where whirring . . . I mean, where the lamps were flashing and the dials were moving, and that horrible collection pool?

–Oh, that too is a bit dubious . . .

–Like that one about the pigs eating up a man and . . .

–That one's true.

–And that she went and cut off your head?

–That's true too.

–So it's all true?

–Not everything.

–Well, what is?

–That the pigs gobbled things up and she cut off my head.

–And the rest is all lies?

–Well, let's say so.

–And cutting off your head, that's true then?

–That's what I said!

–Bullshit!

–Look at the scars on my neck!

–What about them?

–That's from the diamond knife.

–A glass knife?

–Call it what you like.

–But how did you get your head back?

–That's a long story.

–You don't want to have a real discussion with me, do you?

–Yes I do.

–Why don't you say then how you got your head back?

–I feel ashamed.

–And this is what you call a discussion?

–What else is it?

–Fuck knows what it is.

–In my opinion this is dialogue.

–It is, is it?

–It is, and, by the way, very good dialogue too.

–Who are you to make pronouncements on such things?

–And who are you?

(. . .)

A sultry, sweaty day: what dialogues were you expounding and for whom? Go wherever you like, even to the riverbank, but is it different there? Where are things different? By the banks of the river. What is it that is different? A lot is different. Is there more freedom there? Yes, there is. Is it colder there? It feels so. Are there little boys there in swimming trunks, yellow dog daisies and dried turds? In my opinion, yes. What else is there? Oh, there's lots there. A rainbow, the waterworks, a fire extinguisher, maybe even things Estonians have in common? Oh, don't ask so much, I'm going for a walk. I want to see whether the ozone layer is still there in the sky and whether they're selling copies of the New York Estonian Communist paper *Uus Ilm*—i.e., "New World"—at the newspaper kiosk; I want to see the light at the end of the tunnel, buy ice cream, especially with chocolate shells. I'm going to the park and sit on a bench. Then someone will come and talk and talk and talk and everyone except me would have left ages ago but there aren't any other people listening except me. Anyhow, I want to go to the park but before I get there someone turns up. We're already nearing the park and finally arrive, there are squirrels and he's talking and talking there, though I no longer know about what. I open the gate and am walking on the pliant asphalt until there in the distance I spot the Investigator coming towards me.

ॐ

I could see from some distance that the Investigator was heading towards me. As always, he was walking a little hunched up, as if into the wind. It was too late to avoid him, and there was no point, I had been thinking a lot about him lately. So I walked up to him and he didn't change direction either, and we greeted one another and shook hands.

We decided to go and sit down in that same park. We found a bench that was a little distance away from the others and sat down. The Investigator put the traditional large bulging briefcase next to him and wiped the sweat off his brow.

Behind a tree a squirrel appeared and its dark eyes closely followed the Investigator's every movement.

The Investigator didn't notice.

He again wiped the sweat off his forehead and put away his handkerchief.

"Well, the summer's still pretty hot! And to think that the winter was so cold . . . By the way, there are those who think that others are guilty in addition to Tissen and his laboratory. It is said that not even his damned bomb is innocent. Of course, it burnt through the cables and relays, but why did the weather happen to be so cold, as if planned? Who arranged that cold snap? Many deny that it was a coincidence, that it could have been sheer chance, a pure case of synchronicity. As you know, there are rumors that behind the unexpected thaw is Lennart Meri and those international organizations that he is known to represent and whose names are only uttered in a whisper and which sensible people don't have anything to do with. When it comes down to it, that thaw saved Europe from the predicament it was in. But how the organizations and powers managed to trigger off the thaw, overnight and at the critical moment, when a worldwide problem was not far off, that is what some doubters are asking now, and where did the unexpected freeze come from? Couldn't those organizations have set that off too? Of course, no one is so crazy as to see any direct connection between Tissen's machine and the cold winter. Tissen's laboratory operated pretty discreetly, hidden from view, and the intelligence community could hardly have had any interest in what he did. *Laboratoriya dlya izucheniya dinamiki oblakov*—who could have suspected any wrongdoing there? And Tissen himself didn't know what was going to happen either! He imagined that he would be linking up with the other side, with all mankind or at least with those who saw the results of his activities. He hoped to point the world in a better direction. Can you imagine: on the slope of the hill at Lasnamäe, on the high limestone cliff there at the stroke of midnight on New Year's Eve, the Thunderstorm of Conscience was supposed to be set in motion. Wasn't that an original thought for that man to have? The machine itself would have reminded you of a large tree made out of iron, about seven meters high, in fact not really that big if I'm honest, but what didn't it contain! Thirty lasers, two one-million-watt trompes l'oeil, fifteen resonators plus that equipment for evaporating metal that was supposed to ultimately turn the machine into gas when the program had been completed, about ten minutes afterwards, but the program was very complex, covering everything from the ethics of the ozone layer to history itself. Cables led to it from all directions, from all sorts of places! Tissen's Conscience was like a spider's web. His tentacles ranged over the whole city. Even the power of a military equipment factory was included in all this, and up to now it has been painful and idiotically difficult to find out where he had managed to wangle permission from, but he no doubt used some kind of demagogy and somehow persuaded the government to go along with his plan. Everything did indeed give people the impression at the start that this was all some kind of trivial nonsense, Bengal lights, that sort of thing. And why not have a few bangs on New Year's Eve? No one really understood the full scope of the project! Anyway, Tissen was thinking of some kind of breakthrough or God knows what, he hoped that mankind would get a shock, its own *memento mori*, its New Impulse. That's how his primitive little mind worked, and perhaps he wasn't alone, at least in his diaries there are references to your novel, perfectly innocent in itself, an excerpt of it appeared in the district newspaper, if my memory serves me well, so that, if you'll forgive me, you also played a part in this whole business, because at the time you were also promoting the liberation of mankind, inviting them to anarchy. Be that as it may, but Tissen himself didn't have the slightest idea what was going to happen on New Year's Eve. They were all semi-artistic people, at least that's what they called themselves, in a word, their ambitions were those of intellectuals, and they knew pretty little about electricity. There were, true enough, a couple of lads with a bit of a technical education, but although they might even have regarded themselves as engineers, they hadn't in fact had clue about how much current this infernal machine would amass. It was supposed to emit one huge impulse. But look what happened! What they also forgot was that they had chosen a time of romance—New Year's Eve—to of course make the shock all the greater, that would seem quite logical, from Tissen's point of view. But you can imagine the scene on New Year's Eve! Families at home, all of them baking and roasting, all the lights burning . . . It was in just that kind of situation that Tissen wanted to set off his Conscience Machine. The power grid was already overstretched as it was. And then that damned Bubenstrauch or Pelissier effect, or a combination of the two, would have to start up, and you've seen for yourself what happened then. But Tissen simply wasn't prepared for such things to happen, nor was Meri, for that matter, so there couldn't have been any collusion on their part, and anyway how could Meri have colluded with Tissen, and why would he have done so? Although nowadays, the most unlikely characters can conspire, joining together in some game or other and disappearing off God-knows-where, as if nothing has happened. But in this case it would have been impossible. I might add that Meri hadn't even heard of Tissen and his *"laboratoriya."* But as is always the case when something extreme happens, rumors start to fly. People want to know the ins and outs of all correlations, that's an old problem of theirs, going back to the time when the principle of cause-and-effect was first discovered. They can never imagine that things occur just like that. Of course there does exist what Hippocrates termed "the sympathy of all things,"

συμπαδηια τῶν ὅλων

and that can be used to explain away almost anything where there is the slightest desire to do so, like when in Pico della Mirandola's opinion the whole world is the mystical body of God, the *corpus mysticum*, where very little room has been left for causality. But it doesn't pay to go so far, because it's pretty difficult to get any change out of that, as I myself have observed. You're looking at me a little oddly and I think I know why. You happen to know that you were working for the *"laboratoriya"* as a very distant partner, let's say as an innocent catalyst, and you know that I know Meri and his aspirations, though only in general terms, of course. No doubt you thought for a moment that you were the cause of it all and, you know, sometimes I had the same fear. But that can't be true. At any rate it's not worth worrying about because you can't remember everything the way it happened, you find it very difficult to give the order of events as they happen. You never were any good at doing so, even back when you were a child. Do you remember that when you were a schoolboy you had to pay a fine to the conductor on the bus because it never entered your head that you had to pay for the ticket *before* the journey, not afterwards. In your opinion, it was quite all right to pay afterwards, but the conductor simply didn't understand what you meant. Anyhow, if you are guilty then not intentionally, and no one will ever know what went on in your subconscious. Now, at least, you are of the opinion that every individual should develop as much as he is able without fear of spreading himself too thin, grow too expansive. You are supposed to say to everybody: get on with it! Thrive! Be as significant as you possibly can! Since we can't diminish the masses, we'll change them into individual beings, atomize and pluralize them—a solution that's rarely actually arrived at, although formally speaking the idea is cultivated here and there. Most properly developed people don't need a leader or a person to point them in any direction, no didactics, nothing but themselves. That's at least what you think, but as you know, you are inconsistent in your thinking and there's no guarantee that these ideas will last for very long. At any rate, they are dominant for the present and you are acting in accordance with them. You have to instill self-assurance in people. Call everyone a genius. We too are busy working out suitable ways and means to put this into practice in real life."

The squirrel had come out from behind the tree and was sneaking up to our bench. The creature's gaze was fixed as before, and it was ready to flee at the slightest hint of danger.

The Investigator wiped the sweat off his brow.

"There are very easy ways, such as sending messages. Overwhelm mailboxes with anonymous or unsigned compliments and suggestive proposals, even though these are connected with mere appearances, selling things or people's careers. You're a good-looking fellow. Go on learning, go to university. You've got a good voice, talk more. I'd like to sleep with you. Next year you'll be earning a fortune. You have interesting thoughts. And so on, and so forth. Unfortunately I can't reveal the more complex methods involved, but I do have a whole string of assistants who are working on the case right now and will continue doing so even when I myself move to new stalking grounds."

Oh what a beautiful summer, the soughing of the treetops, the faithful squirrel, the flowing conversation in a flowing world, the flecks of sunlight on the grass, the knowledge that winter was far away!

The Investigator stroked his pepper-and-salt beard with his thin, almost transparent hand, paused for quite some while, then finally gave a deep sigh.

"But, for all that, you prefer clarity to chaos. It's true that I can't stand chaos either, and Tissen, for instance, is a typical example of a muddlehead. He didn't even know whether that Conscience Machine was real or merely a hologram, an illusion. Standing by his pile of tubes he couldn't understand which factor was the determining one!

"That was Tissen's destiny and what could he do against it? He perhaps wasn't able to interpret certain signs as being part and parcel of his fate. An interest in the problems of his generation, enthusiasm about new technical ideas, suspicions about the true path of development, a desire to be committed to something, to help people—he thought of all these things as natural impulses and didn't realize that this could lead to disaster until the very last moment. It is quite likely that in his own estimation he loved people, at least he would tell himself that: I love people, maybe the whole of mankind. We've often heard strange people talking like that, not only about love, but also about compassion, tenderness, generally positive attitudes to people, and we have seen them thirst for human goodness and burn with the desire to do good. Tissen was a great romantic! Though here we ought to ask: what did he mean by mankind, this or that, open or secret, were these compassionate people and do-gooders, awake or asleep? Who was Tissen thinking of when he was looking you straight in the face last summer? Not you, of course! You have to understand that he came to you as a colleague, to sound out a potential comrade-in-arms, he allowed himself to tell you 'when the last leaves have withered, then our time will have come.' But no news came! You were hiding in your ivory tower and Tissen was disappointed with you! He had expected more from someone of his own generation. He was depending on you as an ally. But why? Because of Liikola? Because of the friendship between members of the same generation? Yes. And he felt let down. He proceeded alone. On his chosen way. Right to the end."

He put his head in his hands and fell silent.

The squirrel had plucked up the courage to jump into the Investigator's lap and, with a graceful white hand, he began stroking the creature mournfully.

A pause ensued.

"What will happen to him?" I asked.

The Investigator shrugged his shoulders.

"Hard to tell. You know yourself how hard it is to draw a line between art and crime. Oh, this will still require a long, long investigation, with principled criteria as the point of departure, as you will understand . . . The matter is even more complicated. Tissen was a link in the chain, but he ended up causing a national disaster, with the best of intentions, but a disaster nevertheless. It could have taken on global proportions. But Lennart Meri used his powers, which also surprised us. He saved the situation, linking information from the West, the East, and, from the Third World, certain . . ."

"Was it all because of him?"

"We have reliable evidence that proves it was."

"Go on . . ."

"Anyway. Lennart saved the world . . . but how should one deal with such precedents? If, on another occasion, snow starts falling in the middle of summer, as it did, for instance, in Bulgakov's *Fatal Eggs*, what then? Will we need to create some new department, special patrol, or parliament? Oh, my friend, it's all so hard . . ."

"But how do people see *me*?"

"You mean in this matter? I can tell you that the investigation has already been concluded with regard to yourself."

"Really? I'm not too pleased with that."

"What would you have wanted?"

"I could still be kept under investigation."

The Investigator rose to his feet.

"My good man, that's always possible. We could draw up a psychiatric report on your case . . . By the way, we have a file on your case that we have been thinking to send to the psychiatrists. It's not been compiled just to cover you individually, so don't get bigheaded about it. It covers the abnormal writer in general. Do you want a memento?"

I shrugged my shoulders.

"Have this."

He rummaged in his briefcase, pulled out a sheet of paper and handed it to me.

"A good investigation. I have to go now."

He rose and the squirrel leapt back onto the tree.

We shook hands.

I stayed seated on the bench and read:

—did the writer understand the possible significance of his actions during the time of the crime under investigation?

—during the time of the crime under investigation was the writer in control of his own actions?

—was the writer during the time of the crime under investigation suffering from any form of chronic mental disorder or temporary breakdown?

—is the writer a chronic alcoholic or drug addict? If so, could this state have any bearing on the perpetration of the crime under investigation or not, as the case may be?

—is the writer, should he be an alcoholic or a drug addict, in need of forcible treatment as set out in the Criminal Codex of the Estonian Soviet Socialist Republic, paragraph 60?

—does what the writer terms his "calling" or "mission" remain within the bounds of normal psychology, or is this an instance of a morbid delusion?

—is the writer, because of his special psychological make-up, particularly impressionable and is this phenomenon under control, or could he possibly exploit others?

—is the writer, because of his special mentality, capable of forming a group of followers, an organization, maintain the position of leader, by way of which he could trigger mass criminality in society?

—what role does the upbringing of the writer play in the crime under investigation and how would this manifest itself?

—in the work of the said writer, are there moments of auto-aggression or socio-aggression and how do they manifest themselves and do such instances have any dynamic pattern about them?

—is the writer, in his present psychological and physical state, capable of appearing before a court of law and be held responsible for his actions before the court?

—is it necessary to submit the writer to forcible medical treatment as denoted in the Crim. Cod. E.S.S.R, paragraph 59?

—The writer is charged under paragraphs 66, 67 and 68 of the Crim. Cod. E.S.S.R. In these proceedings, experts are warned against making a wrong judgment or refusing judgment as set out in Crim. Cod. E.S.S.R, paragraphs 173 and 175.

A shadow fell across the sheet of paper. The Investigator had returned.

"I can tell you this much," he said, "I don't believe a fucking word of your version of events. I don't believe in your hallucinations that night on the stairs in the cold, nor do I, for that matter, believe that Lennart Meri is a shaman and has connections with Cape Canaveral. This world is clearly far more pregnant than that. Nothing here fits, I'll have to resign. I must admit that I did put my hopes in you for quite some time, especially with regard to that letter you wrote to Tissen. But . . ."

He shrugged his shoulders and strolled off.

He had finally gone out of my life.

I never saw him again. Had he really nothing more to investigate about me?

I have tried to get in touch with the Investigator by way of the *Ferocactus* since the other cacti have failed to react to him. I don't know whether the *Ferocactus* will really react. A distant cheeping . . . expectant bird song, as if coming from the world . . . indifferent . . . incomprehensible . . .

ᴈᴉᴇ

My dear, we arrived at the ceremony at midday to commemorate the dead.

There was already a closely parked ring of cars around a cemetery that was situated in a flat rye field. Just like a pearl necklace as You said and I had to agree.

The cemetery, yes, in the middle of a flat field, on the ridge of a drumlin, at a random location like a real Isle of the Dead ought to be, the church at one edge, oaks swaying in the wind.

The ceremony had not yet started.

Many people were using the time to tidy nearby graves. Near the gate there was a shed containing tools for this work (spades, rakes, hoes); there was also a big pile of sand, with state-owned wheelbarrows to transport it in.

Cars had driven up to the gates of the cemetery, and from these products that were scarce in Estonia were being sold (sausage, ham, coffee), but also products that were less in demand (lemonade, shampoo, pastries). Long lines of people formed near the cars. When a fierce but short downpour started, none of the mourners even bothered to leave, they stood there in the line, and I can understand why, when you think of how little agricultural produce can be found in rural shops. Country folk don't know what happens to the fruits of their labors. It disappears some-where, that they can see, but no more than that. Now the stuff was there in front of their noses. You have to use such good luck profitably. And they certainly did. Even I stood in a line in the hope of getting a pack of coffee.

Half an hour later, a brass band struck up, but I hadn't got much nearer my coffee. Thinking the most obscene curses, I left the line and went over to the graveyard under the shelter of the trees.

A women's choir was singing.

They sang about the soil filled with bones. They sang spon-taneously and with great sadness.

When this had finished and the choir had withdrawn, a man started speaking, talking about how many there were buried here in the earth: a little child who had not even lived long enough to utter the word "mommy," who had not had the time to put its tiny arms around its father's neck, and would have been a joy to its parents in their old age, the apple of their eye; an old mother whose gnarled hands were always ready to caress and whose joyful singing voice would bring tears to your eyes; a beloved husband who always found time and kind words for all the family and whose hands were never idle; an old schoolmistress, a great friend of the people and teacher, a tireless worker in the field of culture, giving old and young alike support and hope; men, who had never lain down their arms when the enemy marched into our beloved native land and who carried out surprise attacks from the woods at night, men who died with the words on their lips: long live our native land, long live a free Soviet Estonia, men whose children waited in vain for them at the gates of the farm when the war was over and the skies had once again grown quiet; the enemy whom propaganda had led astray and who perished for the wrong side and when he died there was neither friend nor acquaintance to close his eyelids.

The orchestra played "Ema südant"—"The Heart of a Mother."

A lot of people sang along.

Across the graveyard a succession of light and shadow rolled as the clouds scudded by very rapidly; occasionally the sun went in, then appeared again.

Ferns swayed in the wind, old women cried, a drummer drummed.

Mother had not come over to listen to the speech and was sitting on father's grave.

The speech was amplified by means of a loudspeaker.

The man continued to talk.

I kept on hearing:

let us remember, we must bear in mind, may we not forget, let us recall—

years, people, events, sons, daughters, homes, lives, war, spring days, weddings, losses, victories, sufferings, parents, children, journeys, years, events—

at length, for long, always, endlessly, thankfully, sadly, gladly, selflessly, with tears in their eyes—

in our hearts, in our thoughts, in our minds, in our souls, in our bosom, in our memory, every day.

Here and there, the begonias were in bloom, the lilies of the valley, the tulips, the lilacs, the marigolds, the stonecrop, the forget-me-nots.

The trees were flourishing and I remembered how we'd once put an Asian liana creeper in a pot filled with fish-heads under the soil so that it would grow better.

People were crying, imagining themselves part of an endless pearl necklace, pearl next to pearl, whose pearls stretched back in time and forwards into the future. They were sobbing as they thought about their grandparents, parents, and children—an endless continuum. They wiped away the tears, knowing that they were right at the border between the past and the future.

When the ceremony had ended, there were no packs of coffee left either. Another opportunity lost, but it had to be borne in mind that we were standing in a place of eternity, while coffee was very much something quite ephemeral. A specialist friend of mine had even once claimed that the effect of coffee as a stimulant lasted three to four hours at most. The graveyard had been here for at least three hundred years, maybe even longer. Several generations lay buried here. What was a little coffee compared with that! Although the drink also appeared in Estonia in the early eighteenth century.

Anyway, there was no coffee left, which was in itself a bad sign, a clear signal from Moscow—the Soviet metropolis—that we weren't needed on this Earth, that we were just getting in the way, and that they had decided to stop meeting our requirements. But that made me neither suffer nor cry. We had, when it came down to it, collected here, lived together and had enough to eat for the time being, and apart from that, I had, over the years, got acquainted with cookbooks and knew several recipes where you could make reasonably tasty dishes out of the most banal of ingredients. I had a few botany reference books, I knew more than the average Estonian about wild plants and herbs and knew how to cook them. The books were still available from bookshops at the time in Estonian, Russian and German.

There were still a few months to go to winter, and no information reaching us suggested that anyone intended in the near future to appeal to our conscience or put new ideas into our heads, and equally little information suggested that anyone would try to save us from them.

For the time being, however, we were standing near the cemetery wall, which was as tall as I was. The wall had recently been painted, and the shadows of branches moved across it. Mother sat down on a bench. I pushed aside a stone with my foot. Under it an earthworm wriggled that had come up from the realm of the dead. It looked at me, though it didn't in fact have any eyes. Then it went back into its hole. I pushed the stone back in place, closing the entrance to hell. Around me the sun shone brightly. I could see thunderclouds on the horizon, but there was no fear of rain or hail before the evening. Now and again, thunderclouds drift across the sky, cover half of it, then disappear again. Just like earthworms.

Beyond the wall, the music had stopped.

A low murmur could be heard. The sound of trees, clothing, spades, worms, bushes and rakes.

I said to You:

"It's really difficult loving someone, but I love you nonetheless, even though it's a scorching day today."

You replied:

"It's going to rain this evening."

"Not before," I agreed.

"Then it'll get cooler."

"Yes, it will."

I saw your shadow move across the wall as if the sun had swayed slightly in the sky.

Mother raised her head.

"When the rest get here, we'll leave," she said.

It was half-past two.

For some time now, I had noticed movement in the distant fields of crops. Black dots dispersed, then converged, but they were coming towards us. They were running, they were in a hurry. They were people approaching the cemetery, up to their chests in the rye, and at first I thought that they had started a roundup, that the cemetery was being surrounded and someone would start picking people out to be taken away. Then I heard cries. The runners were shouting something to one another.

The other people in the cemetery too, those standing near the gate or in the line to the shop, now began to call attention to the runners.

"What's going on?" one old person asked.

"Maybe they're bringing a message," another replied.

They raised their hands to shield their eyes from the sun.

There were about a dozen people running and they were all very angry, which you could hear from their yelling. Maybe they're crazy, I thought, they reminded me of people running amuck I once read about. It is said that on the Malaysian islands people get infected with this ailment, even U.S. soldiers. They run and run and have a gap in their memories. They are very dangerous. My God, my God, can't our nation even avoid this kind of danger?

Suddenly, the runners started dodging about, some charging off to the right, others to the left, they waved their arms and occasionally jumped high into the air out of the rye as if their lives were at stake. They were panting, but you couldn't understand what they were shouting.

We instinctively withdrew to the gates of the cemetery to seek protection. And yet no one was showing any signs of cowardice—it was a sunny day and it seemed as if disasters were impossible.

Then, luckily, everything, or at least half of the problem, was cleared up: large pigs rushed out of the rye. They stopped for a moment, stared stupidly in the direction of the people in the cemetery, then awoke from their torpor, almost immediately scaled the ditch, and galloped off along the cemetery wall.

The men followed, puffing and panting.

The riddle had a perfectly simple solution!

One of the pursuers, an old man who could no longer run, sank down near to us in the grass. He was given some Pepsi-Cola and he drank avidly, so that the brown frothy liquid ran down his beard. In the end he managed to say:

"Well . . . Linda opened the pigsty door . . . I can't run anymore . . . damn it . . . let them run, I'm not going to. Damn it, I'm not going to."

"Do the pigs belong to the sovkhoz?" a woman asked.

"What d'you mean 'sovkhoz'? They belong to the *kolkhoz*, don't they?" said the old man angrily. He tried to get up, but couldn't. Someone tried to help him, but the old man refused:

"Stop. Let me rest a bit. Stop, will you!"

Gradually, people lost interest in him.

The brass band started up again in the cemetery.

The rye field was deserted and yellow.

Had madness entered the people again?

Mother crept back to the car, leaning on her stick.

There were many of us and I had to take you on my lap.

The driver turned the ignition.

Afterwards, we were again driving through fields, in a strange car, among strangers.

The grain was growing lush, the rain was on its way, the grain at risk as always.

The cemetery was left behind, including all the flesh, blood, skin, and bones.

The grain was bright, swayed, billowed. Yes, just like the sea, only white.

The grain was bright, the sky dark.

The sky is darker than the earth, I've known that since I was a child. In winter the sky is darker than the snow. In summer the sky is darker than the grain.

I said to You:

"Look."

"What?" You asked. "Where?"

"There, there, quick, look."

You looked but no doubt saw nothing.

I pointed with my finger. You looked.

Then You turned to me.

"It was just as if there were little eyes out there in the rye, little ones, black ones. Am I right?"

"You're right, my dear."

The rye ended, now there were potato fields, then came the beets, then potatoes again.

There were trends in those years, ones that did not of course leave me untouched either, though I tried to let them affect me as little as possible. There were various trends and a number of them really did affect me directly. I noticed phenomena around me that were hard to define, but they got mixed in with things I had loved for years. I had, for example, been involved for years with the fate of the world. I now felt a slight nausea when the thought struck me that I was responsible for everything. That kind of metamorphosis was calling forth reality, everyday life that was of course as opaque as always, like a Mayan veil covering everything, myself included. I was walking as if in a thick fog, though the sky was clear. Later on, I read in the papers that the world and mankind had begun to decline and the end was near. Lethargy started to appear everywhere. So we felt we all had something in common. In its own way, it was a pity that we weren't being honest with one another, weren't sharing our impressions. On the other hand, it was good that we didn't understand why we were happy. Now, my dear, I know. We no longer needed to develop or evolve in any way. We were doomed to die and we were no longer linked to life by any kind of responsibility. We could be as free as the pigs who ran in the fields. Those were beautiful years, beautiful autumn days.

AFTERWORD

Setting the Scene

Mati Unt (1944-2005) was born in Estonia and lived there all his life. He spent his early years in the village of Linnamäe near the university town of Tartu. His life, like that of so many Estonians, was rooted in the countryside and nature, something evident in all of his works.

Unt made his breakthrough as an author early in life, publishing his first prose in the early 1960s while still at school, and later while studying literature and journalism at Tartu University. Since that decade Unt was heavily involved with the theater, where he adapted, staged, and wrote numerous plays.

In order to appreciate a novel written by an author from a relatively unknown country, some explanation is needed for the benefit of readers unfamiliar with the historical, cultural, geographical, and political features that constitute the background to the book. Here are some remarks on Estonia, Mati Unt's literary generation, his work in the theater, his other works, and the novel itself.

1) Estonia

Estonia is a small country on the shores of the Baltic Sea. It faces Finland to the north across the Gulf of Finland, and has a land border with Russia to the east and Latvia to the south. Although about the size of the Netherlands, it has around one tenth of the population, i.e., around 1.4 million inhabitants.

Estonia has suffered colonial rule since the Middle Ages. Parts of what is now Estonia have been ruled at various times by Swedes, Danes, Poles, and Russians, with Baltic German aristocracy acting as a class of superintendents between the prevailing power and the indigenous peasant masses. For much of this time, Estonia was part of the Russian Empire. In the mid-nineteenth century it underwent a process of national awakening, parallel to that in nearby countries such as Finland and Poland. This led the Estonians to rapidly develop and expand their own culture.

The Estonian language closely resembles Finnish, and is spoken by about two-thirds of the present population of the country, the other language being Russian, which is spoken mainly by immigrants who arrived during Soviet times. As Estonian is a Finno-Ugric language, it has no affinities with Scandinavian, Slavic, and Baltic languages. Most loan words come, however, from Low German, because Tallinn (then known as *Reval*) is one of the cities that once belonged to the trading cartel known as the Hanseatic League.

By the time that Estonia became independent in 1918, it was running all its national affairs in the Estonian language, unlike other postcolonial countries such as Ireland and India, which have kept and fostered the language of the former metropolitan nation.

Secular Estonian literature had been growing since the mid-nineteenth century and by the time of independence there was already a small sprinkling of modern literature, plus a large stock of folk poetry that had been handed down orally and was committed to paper from about the 1850s onwards. Between 1920 and 1940, many works of literature were produced in the Estonian language.

This period of national and cultural independence came to an abrupt end in 1940 when Estonia was annexed by Soviet Russia, invaded one year later by Nazi Germany, then again by Soviet Russia in 1944. From that time onwards until independence was regained in 1991, Estonia remained a marginalized republic, unwillingly incorporated into the Soviet Union. Much of its intelligentsia and middle class had already fled in 1944 to the United States, Canada, and Australia via Sweden and Germany, where they were initially housed in displaced persons' camps. This diaspora did not end until the early 1990s when a few children of the original exiles chose to come back.

During the first decade of Soviet occupation—the mid-1940s to mid-1950s—a last-ditch resistance effort was put up by the Forest Brethren (*metsavennad*) who hid in bunkers in the forest and assassinated various Communist officials and KGB agents. They were hoping for help from the West that never came, and were completely eradicated by the early 1960s. In this novel, therefore, the forest takes on a further connotation over and above that of being a place for the innocent picking of mushrooms. Descriptions of abandoned buildings and silent strangers approaching thus allude to the Forest Brethren.

Estonia is largely rural, flat in the north, hilly in the south. To the west of Tallinn, the capital, are some impressive chalk cliffs resembling the White Cliffs of Dover in miniature. Off the western coast lie several islands, the largest of which being Saaremaa (*Ösel*, in Swedish and German) and Hiiumaa (*Dagö* in those languages).

To the east, forming a boundary with Russia, is Lake Peipus (or Peipsi). In the northeast lies a bleak area where oil shale was mined for Soviet industry, devastating the environment. And yet in some other parts of the country, rare habitats have been preserved with flora and fauna that can be found nowhere else in Europe.

The main concentration of population is in Tallinn. The remaining urban dwellers live in smaller towns with populations of several tens of thousands. While Estonia was part of the Soviet Union, a large number of gray concrete apartment blocks were built, especially in large towns such as Tallinn itself, the university town of Tartu (*Dorpat*, historically), and the seaside health and recreation resort of Pärnu (*Pärnau*) on the west coast.

Tallinn itself has an impressive medieval Old Town at its center. Parts of the city wall with its towers have been preserved to this day. But this tourist attraction is surrounded by high-rise housing districts including Mustamäe, Õismäe, and the predominantly Russian-speaking Lasnamäe, the last of which features prominently in the novel.

Lasnamäe was intended for Russian immigrants who were encouraged to move to Estonia to work in heavy industry. They were allowed to jump the housing queue, much to the chagrin of the indigenous population. The demographic reason for encouraging Russians to move to Estonia was to reduce the proportion of ethnic Estonians living in the republic, and was ultimately meant to lead to a total assimilation of the Estonian people in a mono-ethnic Soviet Union. Russification was also attempted during the Czarist Empire, most seriously around the turn of the twentieth century. But such attempts have never met with success and now in the twenty-first century, Estonia has joined NATO and the European Union as a sovereign state.

Street names in Estonia take on an unusual significance. German and Russian occupying powers have changed them on several occasions to suit the order of the day. One street in Tallinn mentioned in *Things in the Night*, originally named after a Russian merchant back in Czarist times, was subsequently given the names of a Baltic German councilor and a Russian scientist, only to have the German councilor's name restored after the fall of the Soviet Union. Such changes are widespread and reflect the anxiety of the colonial power to maintain political correctness.

On the outskirts of Tallinn, there remain large patches of forest and scrub, plus agricultural land still recovering from the economic and social devastation of enforced collectivisation during the Soviet era. The town has often encroached on the countryside in a haphazard and unplanned manner, creating urban moonscapes, especially in the suburb of Lasnamäe, as is evident from the novel. The Russian film *Stalker* by Andrei Tarkovsky was also filmed in one of these borderline areas of Tallinn.

The antithesis of Lasnamäe is the garden suburb of Nõmme where the Russian-born *nomenklatura* of the Estonian Communist Party enjoyed rubbing shoulders with the impoverished bourgeoisie left over from independence who were, for some reason, still allowed to live in private houses and villas throughout the Soviet occupation.

Psychologically, the Soviet rule of Estonia was felt by indigenous Estonians as an encroachment from the East. While Russia is part-European, part-Asian, many of the troops used to police this northwestern zone of the Soviet Union were taken from its more Asiatic areas so that they would feel less loyalty to the Baltic peoples should there be an insurrection against Soviet rule. One absurd aspect of the Soviet occupation of the Baltic countries was the fact that Balts were prohibited from visiting the shoreline, which had been taken over by the military. Also near some of the towns there were military zones surrounded by barbed wire, which ordinary citizens were forbidden from entering. The housing shortage caused by the large number of immigrants also had a detrimental effect on everyday life. Many people had to live in collective flats where they shared kitchen and toilet facilities with neighbors. Even those who got divorced often could not move away from their former spouses for years.

The Soviet economy, with its central planning, inefficiency, and corruption makes itself felt under the surface of this novel, written during the very last years of Soviet rule, when there were food shortages and a run on consumer goods, while the Soviet Union teetered on the brink of bankruptcy and disintegration.

2) Mati Unt's Literary Generation

Mati Unt belonged to the Sixties Generation, which denotes a number of Estonian writers born in the 1940s and who emerged as writers and intellectuals some twenty years later. During the years leading up to the Prague Spring, Estonian intellectuals had high hopes of a Dubcek-style "socialism with a human face." Their hopes were soon dashed. Nevertheless, Estonia always managed to evade the full brunt of Soviet repression and censorship.

Many of the Estonian Sixties Generation are well-known cultural figures today. Jaan Kaplinski, poet and essayist, is perhaps the most famous internationally; several collections of his poetry appeared during the 1990s in English. Marju Lauristin, daughter of Communist revolutionaries, is nowadays Professor of Journalism at the University of Tartu. Arvo Valton, who spent his teens as a deportee in Siberia, is a well-received writer of absurdist and surrealist short stories. The poet and playwright Paul-Eerik Rummo was Minister of Culture for a short while. During the Brezhnev era, such people used to listen secretly to Western radio stations and, latterly, watch Finnish television. So they were certainly well-informed about what was happening in the West.

In the 1960s and 1970s, when Stalinism had waned, various key works of international literature were made available to the citizens of the Estonian Soviet Socialist Republic in Estonian translation by such authors as Whitman, Faulkner, Salinger, Scott Fitzgerald, Wilder, Malamud, Baldwin, Capote, Updike, Oates, Bellow, Golding, Bergman (film scripts), Kafka, Borges, Butor, and Camus. This was thanks to an unusual initiative, an addition to one of the cultural monthlies, where many shorter works of international literature managed to appear. In 1964, Jean-Paul Sartre and Simon de Beauvoir made a brief visit to Estonia, and even works frowned upon by the central Soviet authorities, such as Aleksandr Solzhenitsyn's *One Day in the Life of Ivan Denisovich* and Mikhail Bulgakov's *The Master and Margarita*, were also published in the Estonian language. The Soviet authorities presumably thought that the translation of controversial works into a language spoken by no more than one million people could do little or no harm to the predominantly Russian-speaking Soviet Union.

Literary parallels can be drawn with the situation in various other parts of the Soviet Bloc. In her helpful monograph "Nowa twarz postmodernizmu" (The New Face of Postmodernism), the Polish academic Halina Janaszek-Ivanicková shows how Eastern and Central Europe had their own tradition of modernism, latterly postmodernism, which arose parallel to that of America and Western Europe. The precursors were such major Polish writers as Witkiewicz, Gombrowicz, and Schulz in the 1930s; later came others such as Mrocek, Kundera, Konwicki, and Havel. The concerns of the early modernists were part personal, part societal, while a whole range of later writers used grotesque images and absurd scenes as an antidote to totalitarian thinking. Unt, despite not belonging to a Slavic nation, somehow fits into this Central European trend represented mainly by Czechs, Slovaks, Poles, and the various peoples of what was then Yugoslavia.

3) The Author and the Theater

For much of his working life, Mati Unt was connected with the theater, staging plays regularly from 1981, when he became stage director and scriptwriter for the Youth Theater in Tallinn, to his death in 2005.

It is often thought that the Soviet Union was entirely cut off from Western theatrical trends, but this is not entirely true. During the 1960s thaw, new ideas in the theater seeped in through the Iron Curtain and from the more liberal satellite states to the Soviet Union itself. Names such as Artaud, Grotowski, and Peter Brook became familiar to Estonians.

Over the past decades, Mati Unt staged many plays of international renown by dramatists such as Sophocles, Corneille, Shakespeare, Goethe, Schiller, Strindberg, Ibsen, Chekhov, Gombrowicz, Genet, Weiss, Havel, and Beckett, plus adaptations of Euripides and Bulgakov, many of these at the Vanemuine Theater in Tartu. One of the most recent plays he staged was Harold Pinter's *The Caretaker*, in the provincial town of Rakvere, and Unt was working in the last months of his life on a dramatization of Emily Brontë's *Wuthering Heights*.

Mati Unt also wrote several plays of his own. As early as 1967, Unt was experimenting with the introduction of Brechtian techniques to Ancient Greek material in his play *Phaethon, Son of the Sun*. In 1975, he published a play consisting of short scenes on the subject of parting and farewell called *Good-Bye Baby*, the title being in English in the original. Farewells are taken by everyone from Ulysses and Holofernes, through Parsifal, down to Che Guevara and Salvador Allende. The following year, Unt produced what he termed "puppet theater for adults" in his play *Gulliver and Gulliver*, which included songs with lyrics by the Estonian poet Juhan Viiding (1948-1995) and was a kind of Swiftian musical with songs in styles such as boogie-woogie and "sexy-disco soul."

Unt's most complex play is *Dress Rehearsal* (1977), where in Pirandellian fashion he examines the life of a Soviet revolutionary with actors on a film set performing in and discussing what is in fact a rather hackneyed adaptation. The real revolutionary, now an old man, stands around the set giving monosyllabic advice, and seems rather indifferent to the myth his life is being turned into.

4) The Author as Novelist

The style and leitmotifs of Mati Unt's fiction changed little since he first began publishing. Unt's prose is rooted in the mythology of everyday life, personal relationships, sexuality, and especially that of modern urban living, although the national trauma of occupation by a foreign power always lurks under the surface. To this he adds the deadpan humor of the eternal observer, someone who never quite succeeds in getting fully involved with others, and yet is always present among them.

Unt was always interested in popular science; the most unexpected associations and references appear in his works. He was also keen on examining paranormal, esoteric, and pathological phenomena such as vampires, werewolves, cannibals, sex criminals, and those driven by obsessions and *idées fixes*.

Mati Unt's early novels clearly show the direction the author was moving in. His first novel, *Farewell, Yellow Cat* appeared in his school annual in 1963. Here the protagonist is in an ideological battle with his aunt, who owns a house—something that was rather politically incorrect in the Soviet days. Anything harking back to "bourgeois times" had to be painted in a negative light. But by mentioning them at all, Unt was taking a stand.

Then came his novella *The Debt* (1964), which caused a literary storm. Under the edicts of Socialist Realism, Soviet literature was supposed to provide models for how people should conduct their lives. Instead, Unt chose a protagonist who was having sex while still at school and who gets a girl pregnant, something that was shocking to the hypocritically puritan Soviet society.

In 1970 Unt produced a Kafkaesque murder mystery parody called *Murder At The Hotel*. Two years later he wrote a love triangle novella, *An Empty Beach*, where a young married writer has to contend with the advances made to his wife by a violinist; and which, he claims, contains elements of self-mockery. Under the same cover was *Mattias and Kristiina*, which is again about a young couple struggling against society, and who end up in a kind of Tristan-and-Isolde tragedy.

This was followed in 1975 by the novella *And If We Are Not Dead, Then We Are Alive Right Now*. This deals with werewolves and contains numerous references to literature on the same subject, a stylistic trait that remains constant in the rest of Unt's oeuvre.

Unt's most famous novel, *Autumn Ball* (1979), was translated into English back in the Soviet era and tells the story of six people who are destined to meet at an event at the end of the book. All these people live in blocks of flats in the Tallinn high-rise suburb of Mustamäe: a poet, an architect who is a technocrat and futurist, a misanthropic barber, and a TV-addicted woman and her young son. Here, Unt's coolly objective yet tongue-in-cheek style and interest in popular science came into their own.

Unt's novels, stories, and a few plays were collected in two volumes, totaling some 650 pages, in 1985.

The following year, he published a volume containing a collage of novellas and other short texts entitled *They Speak and Keep Silent*. The texts include a semi-theatrical conversation between a woman and a taxi-driver; a short play about the nineteenth-century poet Lydia Koidula (see below) and the twentieth-century folk tale author Aino Kallas; diary entries by a woman whose husband disappears without trace; and a postmodernist text that discusses the translation of a poem by Dante Gabriel Rossetti.

In 1990, the same year as *Things in the Night*, Unt published a second novel, *Diary of a Blood Donor*. This is the usual Untian mixture of fact and fiction and takes one of the most sacred names in Estonian literature in vain for the second time. Lydia Koidula (1843-1886) is regarded as the first Estonian woman poet of significance, also the first poet to express an Estonian longing for independence and freedom. But Unt rather blasphemously weaves this national icon and her Latvian doctor-husband into a postmodern tale of vampires and a mysterious trip to Leningrad.

Since 1990, Unt published only one major work of fiction, a documentary novel about Bertolt Brecht's meeting with the Estonian-born Hella Wuolijoki, who later became a Communist and broadcaster in neighboring Finland, entitled *Brecht Appears at Night*. The night is clearly something with which Unt has affinities.

In true Untian style, the author mixes episodes from the history of Estonia and Finland into a tale set around WWII, including historical documents and a rather playful description of the very bourgeois and somewhat fastidious and autocratic theater genius who would like to feel at home with workers, but is too busy with his alienation effect, wife, and mistresses.

5) Things in the Night

Things in the Night, Unt's second-longest novel, appeared as *Öös on asju* in 1990, and deals with electricity in all its forms: a source of urban heating and lighting, but also a dangerous and untamed force. Unt also introduces further leitmotifs from popular science and everyday life: pigs, cacti, holography, urban cannibalism, and the ever-present blocks of high-rise flats, almost identical to those found throughout the former Soviet Union.

Ihab Hassan's table of contrasts between modernism and postmodernism does give the impression that we are dealing here with a postmodern rather than a modernist work. The suggestions of game-playing, anarchic behavior, absence, schizophrenia, irony, and so on, fit in well with the tenor of *Things in the Night*. Nevertheless, there is, as in other postmodernist works from the former Soviet Bloc, a touch of light moralism in the novel. The Estonian critic Kalev Kesküla sums up the work up as follows:

> The novel consists of the author's confessions, novel fragments, snatches of plays, comments on how to write a novel, poems, minutes of interrogations, letters, and quite a few quotes from popular classics. There are amusing adventures and pointless ratiocinations. From time to time, the writer-protagonist personifies the compulsive

scribbler who is unable to curb his urge to write when attempting to describe electricity, who tells yarns about accidents and shops. The characters in the novel have strayed into a world where other people's words, clichéd behavior and serious scientific literature are jumbled up together. In its artistic radicalism, the novel is very modernist, while very postmodern in its zest for irony. The ideas that bear the novel along appear to be a fear of people and an underlying misanthropy, themes familiar from Unt's earlier works. Here again we have the criminals, farmers who set their dogs on those wandering through the night, arctic hysteria, and cannibalism.

I once compared one of the main characters, Tissen, with Raskolnikov from *Crime and Punishment*: both are caught in a net of other people's words and commit their misdemeanors on the strength of the ideas of others.

The heuristic discovery of the book is the figure of Lennart Meri who, after Tissen has deprived the world of electricity, becomes its salvation, using both political and other means.

Mati Unt was born on January first, and this is incorporated into the novel when the main crisis and its dénouement occur on that day and those following.

The name of the protagonist's girlfriend, Susie, has an association for Estonian readers that is absent in English. There are two words in Estonian for "wolf": *hunt* and *susi*. In dialect, the former word is often pronounced without the "h," so Mati Unt's own surname also means "wolf."

During the course of the novel, Unt shifts quite often, sometimes within the same paragraph, from the past tense of the narrative to the present tense, which represents the overheated thoughts racing through the minds of the main characters.

The few Estonian figures of note mentioned in the novel are listed at the end of this afterword. These are mostly figures from cultural life, well-known at home, unknown abroad. While internationally renowned scientists and others can easily be looked up on the Internet, this is much harder with regard to Estonian figures, since most of the information is available only in the Estonian language. One figure who should be introduced right away is Lennart Meri.

6) Lennart Meri

Meri is quintessentially Estonian and quite as unusual in real life as he is in the novel, where he acts as a kind of savior-cum-shaman with international connections, and ultimately rescues Estonia when there is a large-scale power failure in the northwestern part of the Soviet Union, which included Estonia.

Lennart Meri (born 1929) is the son of the diplomat Georg Meri, who represented an independent Estonia in the 1930s in Paris and Berlin. Lennart therefore spent several years attending schools in both these capitals and soaking up the French and German languages.

After this privileged childhood, things changed abruptly for Lennart Meri during the first year of Soviet occupation in early 1941, when his father became *persona non grata* and the whole family was deported to Siberia—along with some 12,000 other Estonians—where it remained until 1946. When the family returned home, Georg Meri was no longer allowed to play any role whatsoever in what were now Soviet politics and diplomacy. Instead, he channeled his efforts into translating thirty-two (!)

of Shakespeare's thirty-seven plays into Estonian and became a founding member of the International Shakespeare Society. This cultural interest in faraway places, their literatures and cultures rubbed off on his son, Lennart. On graduating from Tartu University, Lennart Meri initially worked for radio and film. Later he became an explorer, documentary writer, and filmmaker, traveling to many of the more remote parts of the Soviet Union, filming and conducting interviews with representatives of the indigenous peoples of the Carpathians, Kamchatka, Altai, and the Komi region. He wrote speculative ethnographical books on the origins of the Estonian people, and his translation of Solzhenitsyn's *One Day in the Life of Ivan Denisovich* appeared in 1963.

By the time that Mati Unt was writing *Things in the Night* in the late 1980s, Lennart Meri was already traveling outside the Soviet Union to places like the United States, Canada, and Australia, fostering personal contacts and compiling documents in the hope that Estonian independence could be restored—so the shaman of the novel is, in part, true to life. By 1990, Meri had become the Foreign Minister of an Estonia in limbo between being a Soviet republic and becoming fully independent. Estonian independence was declared in 1991, and the following year Lennart Meri became President of Estonia, an office he held until 2001.

Lennart Meri's surname means "sea," and in the text there are one or two untranslatable puns made on this name concerning seascapes opening up, and so forth.

7) The Author as "Blogger"

Many things about Mati Unt's writing remained unchanged over the four decades he was active as an author. In one of a series of articles written to mark Unt's sixtieth birthday—January 1,

2004—Marju Lauristin, who remembered him from his early days as a writer, wrote an appreciation entitled "Mati Unt's *Blogosphere*." In it she examines Unt's last literary guise—that of a columnist in the cultural press, where he wrote short, weekly pieces that almost resemble "blog" entries. The following "blog" by Unt is from October 2003. It has an atmosphere that the reader will recognize from reading *Things in the Night* itself: a measure of egocentric pessimism and pseudo-moralism; the feeling of being a loner, keeping aloof from his fellow human beings; the unexpected focus on trivial, if exact, detail; and the abrupt change of topic to literary matters. All this is very *Untian*; self-mockery cannot be ruled out.

A year ago somewhere in Räpina—or was it Antsla?—I was walking along the main street in the middle of the day, eying the shop windows and guessing the secrets that lay hidden behind them. It was autumn, as always. A Sunday.

On one street corner—where Käo and Konna Streets crossed, I think—a few teenagers were hanging around. Eighteen-year-olds. About a dozen of them. As they tend to do. Most of the time. The boys were teasing the girls who were crying out loudly for help. There was a lot of joking and laughter. Somebody was drinking beer, another cider, a third kvass. In other words, a slum environment, people of proletarian origin . . . With nothing to do on a Sunday. But as soon as they saw me they began to yell my name, demanding: Mati! Mati! Where're you off to? Come and join us!

Where did they know me from? I hadn't appeared on TV or on the front pages of the dailies for ages; stage directors tend to be anonymous people. And I'm not vain either. Really I'm not. I got a little scared. I broke into a run and hid behind a tree round the corner. It took five minutes for me to dare to emerge. The teenagers had found something else to amuse them, so I hunched up my shoulders and disappeared into the house I had been making for. I should have been rather proud of my fame. But the fact that kids in the slum had recognized a reclusive stage director was pretty absurd. This was no proof of culture. I would even say that it demonstrated an absence of culture.

In Russian times we Estonians were, well, a literate people, you could say. Books by Thackeray, Smollett, Herzen—you could find them in every home. Also books about life in Ancient China. This wasn't quite natural. And we know now that even at the start of national independence, a favorite author among Estonians was in fact the popular Latvian Communist writer about fisherfolk, Vilis Lacis. Under the shiny surface lay a lot of dirt. But people did look at paintings and listen to music. People read the cultural weeklies. And knew what was going on in the world, insofar as they were allowed to. People always listened to the Voice of America and Radio Free Europe. And even the Russian language service of the BBC!

Now I get the feeling that despite all the new textbooks available, the new teachers, and the schools that have received their *Eurorefurbishment*, learning and culture are on the decline. There is a danger that we just don't notice what is really going on. One day, all this will have gone—and that'll be it. All that will remain is the noise of teenagers on the corner where Käo and Konna Streets cross.

Well, maybe it's natural that art is only a fabrication, a contrived phenomenon that will have to make way for another, for instance, football; maybe it's also natural that soulless noise will replace the sonnet; maybe it's also natural that spirituality will vanish altogether from the face of the Earth. OK, let it vanish, there's no point in yelling about it like an angry old man. What's gone is gone.

But for the time being, we ought still to battle against chaos, as I, a dyed-in-the-wool follower of Camus, tend to think. School is, of course, the front line! And theater too can still try to put up a fight—can try to avoid sinking into the mire, try instead to swim over to beautiful shores, where all may be different.

When Mati Unt died in August 2005, it was front-page news in the Estonian press. He lies buried in the writer's corner of the Metsakalmistu cemetery in Tallinn, where he rubs shoulders in death with many of the key figures of nineteenth- and twentieth-century Estonian literature. Their graves are grouped together, rather like Poets' Corner in Westminster Abbey, but in a more modest, truly Estonian way. The vaults of the abbey are here replaced by the branches of trees.

Eric Dickens
October 2005

Alphabetical List of Estonian Cultural Figures
Mentioned in the Novel

Eduard Ahrens (1803-63). Linguist. One of the first to describe and systematize Estonian grammar within the context of Finno-Ugrian languages.

Ain Kaalep (born 1926). Poet, editor, critic. Has translated literature from Spanish, French, and Ancient Greek. Fought in the Estonian brigade in Finland against the Soviet Union in World War Two and was subsequently kept in prison for a year by the KGB on his return to Estonia. Interested in the structural and technical sides of poetry.

Jaan Kaplinski (born 1941). Poet, essayist. Son of a Polish-Jewish lecturer at Tartu University, Kaplinski has become perhaps the best-known Estonian poet internationally. Three collections of his poems were published in English translation with Harvill (London) during the 1990s.

Aleksander Kurtna (1935-83). Translator. The son of the steward to a manor house in Räpina and a Russian language teacher, he studied and worked from 1936-42 at the Vatican in Rome. Spent the years 1945-54 in prisons and labor camps in Russia. On returning to his homeland, Kurtna became a prodigious translator from Polish, Italian, French, and Romanian. The well-known Estonian author Jaan Kross has written a play *Brother Enrico and His Bishop* based in part on Kurtna's life.

Juhan Liiv (1864-1913). Poet and short story writer. Born on the grounds of Alatskivi Castle, a replica of Balmoral in Scotland, built by a German eccentric. Liiv gradually began to show signs of severe mental illness and his work is suffused with this. Regarded nonetheless as a major poet.

Yuri Lotman (1922-93). Semioticist and expert on Russian literature. Of Russian-Jewish background, Lotman came to Estonia in 1950 to escape the anti-Semitism in his native Leningrad. From then until his death he worked at Tartu University. Was a leading member of the Moscow-Tartu School of Semiotics.

Lennart Meri (born 1929). See afterword.

Voldemar Panso (1920-77). Estonia's best-known stage producer. A long association with the Tallinn Drama Theater made him a colleague of Unt's at various times.

Lembit Sarapuu (born 1930). Naïvist painter. Lyrical landscapes and portraits.

Mart Susi (born 1965). Educationalist. Founder in 1989 of the Estonian Humanities University and associated with the Lutheran Church.

Vanemuine Theater: Housed in a Jugendstil building designed by the Finnish architect Lindgren from 1906 until 1944, when it was bombed by the Soviet Air Force. A new theater was built in 1968.

SELECTED DALKEY ARCHIVE PAPERBACKS

PETROS ABATZOGLOU, *What Does Mrs. Freeman Want?*
PIERRE ALBERT-BIROT, *Grabinoulor.*
YUZ ALESHKOVSKY, *Kangaroo.*
SVETLANA ALEXIEVICH, *Voices from Chernobyl.*
FELIPE ALFAU, *Chromos.*
    Locos.
IVAN ÂNGELO, *The Celebration.*
    The Tower of Glass.
DAVID ANTIN, *Talking.*
DJUNA BARNES, *Ladies Almanack.*
    Ryder.
JOHN BARTH, *LETTERS.*
    Sabbatical.
DONALD BARTHELME, *Paradise.*
SVETISLAV BASARA, *Chinese Letter.*
ANDREI BITOV, *Pushkin House.*
LOUIS PAUL BOON, *Chapel Road.*
ROGER BOYLAN, *Killoyle.*
IGNÁCIO DE LOYOLA BRANDÃO, *Zero.*
CHRISTINE BROOKE-ROSE, *Amalgamemnon.*
BRIGID BROPHY, *In Transit.*
MEREDITH BROSNAN, *Mr. Dynamite.*
GERALD L. BRUNS,
    Modern Poetry and the Idea of Language.
GABRIELLE BURTON, *Heartbreak Hotel.*
MICHEL BUTOR, *Degrees.*
    Mobile.
    Portrait of the Artist as a Young Ape.
G. CABRERA INFANTE, *Infante's Inferno.*
    Three Trapped Tigers.
JULIETA CAMPOS, *The Fear of Losing Eurydice.*
ANNE CARSON, *Eros the Bittersweet.*
CAMILO JOSÉ CELA, *The Family of Pascual Duarte.*
    The Hive.
LOUIS-FERDINAND CÉLINE, *Castle to Castle.*
    London Bridge.
    North.
    Rigadoon.
HUGO CHARTERIS, *The Tide Is Right.*
JEROME CHARYN, *The Tar Baby.*
MARC CHOLODENKO, *Mordechai Schamz.*
EMILY HOLMES COLEMAN, *The Shutter of Snow.*
ROBERT COOVER, *A Night at the Movies.*
STANLEY CRAWFORD, *Some Instructions to My Wife.*
ROBERT CREELEY, *Collected Prose.*
RENÉ CREVEL, *Putting My Foot in It.*
RALPH CUSACK, *Cadenza.*
SUSAN DAITCH, *L.C.*
    Storytown.
NIGEL DENNIS, *Cards of Identity.*
PETER DIMOCK,
    A Short Rhetoric for Leaving the Family.
ARIEL DORFMAN, *Konfidenz.*
COLEMAN DOWELL, *The Houses of Children.*
    Island People.
    Too Much Flesh and Jabez.
RIKKI DUCORNET, *The Complete Butcher's Tales.*
    The Fountains of Neptune.
    The Jade Cabinet.
    Phosphor in Dreamland.
    The Stain.
    The Word "Desire."
WILLIAM EASTLAKE, *The Bamboo Bed.*
    Castle Keep.
    Lyric of the Circle Heart.
JEAN ECHENOZ, *Chopin's Move.*
STANLEY ELKIN, *A Bad Man.*
    Boswell: A Modern Comedy.
    Criers and Kibitzers, Kibitzers and Criers.
    The Dick Gibson Show.
    The Franchiser.
    George Mills.
    The Living End.
    The MacGuffin.
    The Magic Kingdom.
    Mrs. Ted Bliss.
    The Rabbi of Lud.
    Van Gogh's Room at Arles.
ANNIE ERNAUX, *Cleaned Out.*
LAUREN FAIRBANKS, *Muzzle Thyself.*
    Sister Carrie.
LESLIE A. FIEDLER,
    Love and Death in the American Novel.
GUSTAVE FLAUBERT, *Bouvard and Pécuchet.*
FORD MADOX FORD, *The March of Literature.*
CARLOS FUENTES, *Christopher Unborn.*
    Terra Nostra.
    Where the Air Is Clear.
JANICE GALLOWAY, *Foreign Parts.*
    The Trick Is to Keep Breathing.
WILLIAM H. GASS, *The Tunnel.*
    Willie Masters' Lonesome Wife.
ETIENNE GILSON, *The Arts of the Beautiful.*
    Forms and Substances in the Arts.
C. S. GISCOMBE, *Giscome Road.*
    Here.
DOUGLAS GLOVER, *Bad News of the Heart.*
    The Enamoured Knight.
KAREN ELIZABETH GORDON, *The Red Shoes.*
GEORGI GOSPODINOV, *Natural Novel.*
PATRICK GRAINVILLE, *The Cave of Heaven.*
HENRY GREEN, *Blindness.*
    Concluding.
    Doting.
    Nothing.
JIŘÍ GRUŠA, *The Questionnaire.*
JOHN HAWKES, *Whistlejacket.*
AIDAN HIGGINS, *A Bestiary.*
    Flotsam and Jetsam.
    Langrishe, Go Down.
    Scenes from a Receding Past.
    Windy Arbours.
ALDOUS HUXLEY, *Antic Hay.*
    Crome Yellow.
    Point Counter Point.
    Those Barren Leaves.
    Time Must Have a Stop.
MIKHAIL IOSSEL AND JEFF PARKER, EDS., *Amerika:*
    Contemporary Russians View
    the United States.
GERT JONKE, *Geometric Regional Novel.*
JACQUES JOUET, *Mountain R.*
HUGH KENNER, *The Counterfeiters.*
    Flaubert, Joyce and Beckett:
    The Stoic Comedians.
DANILO KIŠ, *Garden, Ashes.*
    A Tomb for Boris Davidovich.
NOBUO KOJIMA, *Embracing Family.*
TADEUSZ KONWICKI, *A Minor Apocalypse.*
    The Polish Complex.
MENIS KOUMANDAREAS, *Koula.*
ELAINE KRAF, *The Princess of 72nd Street.*
JIM KRUSOE, *Iceland.*
EWA KURYLUK, *Century 21.*
VIOLETTE LEDUC, *La Bâtarde.*
DEBORAH LEVY, *Billy and Girl.*
    Pillow Talk in Europe and Other Places.
JOSÉ LEZAMA LIMA, *Paradiso.*
OSMAN LINS, *Avalovara.*
    The Queen of the Prisons of Greece.
ALF MAC LOCHLAINN, *The Corpus in the Library.*
    Out of Focus.
RON LOEWINSOHN, *Magnetic Field(s).*
D. KEITH MANO, *Take Five.*
BEN MARCUS, *The Age of Wire and String.*
WALLACE MARKFIELD, *Teitlebaum's Window.*
    To an Early Grave.
DAVID MARKSON, *Reader's Block.*
    Springer's Progress.
    Wittgenstein's Mistress.

FOR A FULL LIST OF PUBLICATIONS, VISIT:

www.dalkeyarchive.com

SELECTED DALKEY ARCHIVE PAPERBACKS

CAROLE MASO, *AVA.*

LADISLAV MATEJKA AND KRYSTYNA POMORSKA, EDS.,
Readings in Russian Poetics: Formalist and Structuralist Views.

HARRY MATHEWS,
The Case of the Persevering Maltese: Collected Essays.
Cigarettes.
The Conversions.
The Human Country: New and Collected Stories.
The Journalist.
My Life in CIA.
Singular Pleasures.
The Sinking of the Odradek Stadium.
Tlooth.
20 Lines a Day.

ROBERT L. MCLAUGHLIN, ED.,
Innovations: An Anthology of Modern & Contemporary Fiction.

STEVEN MILLHAUSER, *The Barnum Museum.*
In the Penny Arcade.

RALPH J. MILLS, JR., *Essays on Poetry.*

OLIVE MOORE, *Spleen.*

NICHOLAS MOSLEY, *Accident.*
Assassins.
Catastrophe Practice.
Children of Darkness and Light.
The Hesperides Tree.
Hopeful Monsters.
Imago Bird.
Impossible Object.
Inventing God.
Judith.
Look at the Dark.
Natalie Natalia.
Serpent.
The Uses of Slime Mould: Essays of Four Decades.

WARREN F. MOTTE, JR.,
Fables of the Novel: French Fiction since 1990.
Oulipo: A Primer of Potential Literature.

YVES NAVARRE, *Our Share of Time.*

DOROTHY NELSON, *Tar and Feathers.*

WILFRIDO D. NOLLEDO, *But for the Lovers.*

FLANN O'BRIEN, *At Swim-Two-Birds.*
At War.
The Best of Myles.
The Dalkey Archive.
Further Cuttings.
The Hard Life.
The Poor Mouth.
The Third Policeman.

CLAUDE OLLIER, *The Mise-en-Scène.*

PATRIK OUŘEDNÍK, *Europeana.*

FERNANDO DEL PASO, *Palinuro of Mexico.*

ROBERT PINGET, *The Inquisitory.*
Mahu or The Material.
Trio.

RAYMOND QUENEAU, *The Last Days.*
Odile.
Pierrot Mon Ami.
Saint Glinglin.

ANN QUIN, *Berg.*
Passages.
Three.
Tripticks.

ISHMAEL REED, *The Free-Lance Pallbearers.*
The Last Days of Louisiana Red.
Reckless Eyeballing.
The Terrible Threes.
The Terrible Twos.
Yellow Back Radio Broke-Down.

JULIÁN RÍOS, *Larva: A Midsummer Night's Babel.*
Poundemonium.

AUGUSTO ROA BASTOS, *I the Supreme.*

JACQUES ROUBAUD, *The Great Fire of London.*

Hortense in Exile.
Hortense Is Abducted.
The Plurality of Worlds of Lewis.
The Princess Hoppy.
Some Thing Black.

LEON S. ROUDIEZ, *French Fiction Revisited.*

VEDRANA RUDAN, *Night.*

LYDIE SALVAYRE, *The Company of Ghosts.*
The Lecture.

LUIS RAFAEL SÁNCHEZ, *Macho Camacho's Beat.*

SEVERO SARDUY, *Cobra & Maitreya.*

NATHALIE SARRAUTE, *Do You Hear Them?*
Martereau.
The Planetarium.

ARNO SCHMIDT, *Collected Stories.*
Nobodaddy's Children.

CHRISTINE SCHUTT, *Nightwork.*

GAIL SCOTT, *My Paris.*

JUNE AKERS SEESE,
Is This What Other Women Feel Too?
What Waiting Really Means.

AURELIE SHEEHAN, *Jack Kerouac Is Pregnant.*

VIKTOR SHKLOVSKY, *Knight's Move.*
A Sentimental Journey: Memoirs 1917-1922.
Theory of Prose.
Third Factory.
Zoo, or Letters Not about Love.

JOSEF ŠKVORECKÝ,
The Engineer of Human Souls.

CLAUDE SIMON, *The Invitation.*

GILBERT SORRENTINO, *Aberration of Starlight.*
Blue Pastoral.
Crystal Vision.
Imaginative Qualities of Actual Things.
Mulligan Stew.
Pack of Lies.
The Sky Changes.
Something Said.
Splendide-Hôtel.
Steelwork.
Under the Shadow.

W. M. SPACKMAN, *The Complete Fiction.*

GERTRUDE STEIN, *Lucy Church Amiably.*
The Making of Americans.
A Novel of Thank You.

PIOTR SZEWC, *Annihilation.*

STEFAN THEMERSON, *Hobson's Island.*
Tom Harris.

JEAN-PHILIPPE TOUSSAINT, *Television.*

ESTHER TUSQUETS, *Stranded.*

DUBRAVKA UGRESIC, *Lend Me Your Character.*
Thank You for Not Reading.

MATI UNT, *Things in the Night.*

LUISA VALENZUELA, *He Who Searches.*

BORIS VIAN, *Heartsnatcher.*

PAUL WEST, *Words for a Deaf Daughter & Gala.*

CURTIS WHITE, *America's Magic Mountain.*
The Idea of Home.
Memories of My Father Watching TV.
Monstrous Possibility: An Invitation to Literary Politics.
Requiem.

DIANE WILLIAMS, *Excitability: Selected Stories.*
Romancer Erector.

DOUGLAS WOOLF, *Wall to Wall.*
Ya! & John-Juan.

PHILIP WYLIE, *Generation of Vipers.*

MARGUERITE YOUNG, *Angel in the Forest.*
Miss MacIntosh, My Darling.

REYOUNG, *Unbabbling.*

ZORAN ŽIVKOVIĆ, *Hidden Camera.*

LOUIS ZUKOFSKY, *Collected Fiction.*

SCOTT ZWIREN, *God Head.*

FOR A FULL LIST OF PUBLICATIONS, VISIT:
www.dalkeyarchive.com